In the Spotlight

A Rockstar Romance

J.L. Ostle

Enjoy the lickable Dom
JOstle xxx

IN THE SPOTLIGHT

(A Rockstar Romance)
Copyright 2016 J.L. Ostle
All rights reserved

No part of this publication may be reproduced, distributed, or transmitted in any form or by any means, including but not limited to; photocopying, recording or other electronic or mechanical methods, without the prior written permission of the author, except in the case of brief quotations embodied in critical reviews and certain other noncommercial uses permitted by copyright law. This is a work of fiction. Any resemblance to peoples either living or deceased is purely coincidental. Names, places, and characters are figments of the authors imagination, or, if real, used fictitiously. The author recognizes the trademarks and copyrights of all registered products and works mentioned within this work.
All rights reserved.
Edited by Nouvelle Author Services
Proofread by Jen Wildner
Formatted by Leigh Stone
Cover by Kathryn Jacoby

Dedication

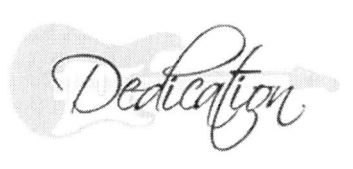

I always dedicate my books to my little boy, I love you Jake with all my heart.

I also want to dedicate this book to my brain twin, my best friend Elmarie Pieterse. You have been by my side every step of the way since we met after you read my second book. I don't know what I would have done without you. You have been a lending ear as I bounced my ideas off you, helping me make this book better. I loved teasing you on where I wanted the characters to go. Thank you for being there for me. You mean so much to me, I am glad I have met you.

Book whores for life ;)

Chapter 1

Sky

I take in a deep breath and look out the window of the cab I'm sitting in. I can't believe I'm here. I pay the driver and hop out. He helps me grab my suitcases from the trunk and wishes me a good day.

Today *is* a good day.

I'm finally away from my controlling parents and moving in with my sister. I shake my head, getting rid of all the nasty words they spewed at me as I was leaving. They basically disowned Lake, their eldest daughter. Since I was the only child left, they put all their expectations and demands on me. I felt all the pressure to be the good daughter. The one with a future they can dictate and manipulate.

Control.

I push the memories away, not wanting to ruin this moment. Rolling my suitcases up the marble path to a two story house, I look around and see children laughing as they ride their bikes; people talking, waving at each other as they walk past. I feel like I walked into Pleasantville.

I love it though. It's different from my norm and that is exactly what I need.

I take in another deep breath as I knock on the white door and wait. My heart is beating frantically. I haven't seen my sister in over four years. Not since she left, telling our parents to basically go fuck themselves. Her words, not mine. She found love and moved in with her boyfriend, Leon. She knew how to get out of their clutches. She found the loop hole.

The day she left, I felt like my whole world crashed down around me. She was the one thing that kept me going. She made the horrible days bearable. She begged for me to come with her but I was underage, so I couldn't. I was stuck with them.

I remember holding her, not wanting to let go. Tears sliding down my cheeks as Dad pulled me away. Telling his oldest daughter that she was a waste of space. Nothing but a disappointment. She had screamed for me to stay strong, that she would stay in touch. That we would be together again. I knew it broke her heart to leave me. But I understood why she did it. Growing up in that place was our personal hell.

I wanted to leave so many times. I wanted to run away and never look back. They knew I couldn't. If I left, I wouldn't be able to touch my trust fund. The trust fund that my grandmother left me. They found a way to dig their claws in and never let go. Until now.

I packed my things and left without looking back. I know it will catch up with me, but now, *now* I am free. Lake kept her promises and we stayed in touch over Facebook. She kept me updated on her life and her relationship with Leon, which is still going strong. He's in a band that she helps manage. They aren't anything big, but my sister has high hopes for them. She sent me their songs from time to time, knowing I love music, and I'm sure I know every word at this point. I think they will make it big.

As soon as I told her I was leaving, she offered me the spare

In the Spotlight

room in her home. She lives with Leon and the guitarist of the band, Dominic. She mentioned him a few times, but she normally gushes over her man more than anyone else. She is head over heels and I couldn't be happier. She deserves to be happy. We talked for months, planning and preparing for this day, and now it's finally here.

The door slams open and noise from the inside filters out. The person standing there is my gorgeous older sister, Lake. She still looks mostly the same from when I last saw her, but there are subtle changes that make her even more beautiful. Her hair is longer, and she looks curvier. I saw pictures on her Facebook page, but seeing her in person is so surreal. I run to her and wrap my arms around her. I can't help the tears that fall down my cheeks.

I missed her so much.

My rock.

She holds me just as tightly before taking my hand to step back and look me up and down. I do the same. Where I have raven black hair and white, pale skin, she has dark brown hair with bronzed skin, obviously spending loads of her time in the sun. We both have blue eyes, hers a clear, ocean blue, mine dark, like the evening sky. That's how we were named. You would never think we are related. She is the confident, gorgeous one. The one that guys turn their heads for. I am more the shy, quiet type. I keep to myself.

"I can't believe you are finally here." She smiles brightly at me.

"Neither can I!" I return excitedly. We both laugh.

"Come on in. Let me show you your new home." She grabs a suitcase and guides me into the house.

We walk down a cappuccino colored hallway to a huge living room. The first thing I notice is the fifty-inch TV hanging on the wall, a sound system and a few game consoles. There are three dark brown couches with cream cushions surrounding a glass coffee table. There are paintings hanging on the walls. It feels very homey.

"Want something to drink?" Lake asks and I nod. We leave my things and head to the kitchen. She grabs a bottle of water from the fridge and hands it to me. I look around as I open my bottle and take a sip. I feel so overwhelmed for some reason. I grew up in a huge house with the top of the line furniture and appliances but it looked more like a show room. A museum. Something to show off to my parent's friends. This place... it's actually a home. Like I've seen in the movies. The black granite counters, the oak cupboards. I can even see magnets on the fridge.

I follow Lake to a door that leads to a dining room with a beautiful carved table and chairs. She sits down and I follow suit. She takes my hand in hers and I see sorrow and guilt in her eyes.

"I hate that I left you there with them. You know if I could have taken you away I would have. I even formed plans of kidnapping you," she chuckles. I place my free hand on top of hers that is covering mine.

"I know. I'm not angry with you for leaving. I understand, trust me. That place was awful. You found love and were able to leave without them punishing you. Hurting you any more than they did," I try and comfort her.

"I still feel bad. I'm just happy you are here. We won't let them take you away. This is your home now." I don't comment, but nod. I would love to never go back. I would love to find my happily ever after, too. "Right, let me show you your room." She stands.

We grab my suitcases and walk up the stairs that are near the dining room. As we move down the hallway of the huge second floor,

In the *Spotlight*

she points out her and Leon's room. Dominic's room is further down and directly opposite of my new room. We walk inside and my mouth hangs open. It's painted purple, my favorite color. Even the bedding and curtains are purple. I remember growing up telling Lake that, one day, I was going to have a purple room. There is a bookshelf and desk on one side of the room. I see two doors and open each one. One leads to my own bathroom and the other a closet. It's perfect. I run to Lake and give her a hug.

"This is amazing. Thank you so much. It's perfect. My dream room." I beam up at her. I feel like it's Christmas day.

"I knew you would like it. As soon as you said you were coming, I ran to the hardware store and painted. I'm going to go make dinner and let you unpack okay? If you need me, you know where I will be." She hugs me.

"You can cook?" We always had someone to cook for us so I'm surprised that she can. But a lot can happen in three years.

"Yup. I always wanted to learn so I got some books and taught myself. If I say so myself, my cooking isn't bad." She winks at me before leaving.

I stand in the middle of my new room and look around. I feel like I'm dreaming. This is too good to be true. I see my huge bed and do what I have always wanted to do, knowing I wouldn't get in trouble for being unlady like. I jump up and down on my bed, ruffling the sheets. I jump one last time and land, lying on my back, laughing and squealing to myself.

If I am dreaming, I never want to wake up.

🎸—★—🎸

I unpack my things and decide to go help with dinner. I may not be able to cook but I can help set the table or cut something. I close my door and can't help but look at the one opposite me. I wonder where the guys are. I hope they like me. As I near the kitchen, I can hear giggling and walk in to see a tall guy with his arms around my sister, nuzzling her neck. I feel my cheeks flush. I recognize Leon from the pictures that I've seen. Feeling like I am walking in on something, I try and walk back out before they notice me, but as I'm not at all stealthy, I bump into the door frame, banging my elbow.

Ouch.

At the noise, they both turn. I can't believe I have only been here for an hour and already I feel like I'm in the way. I should've yelled or shouted that I was coming in the kitchen. Maybe I should have waited till she called me for dinner. I look at the ground, my hair blocking my face.

"I am so sorry. I didn't mean to interrupt. I'll be in my room. Just tell me when I need to come down," I say quickly and turn around. I don't take two steps before Lake grabs my arm and turns me around. I feel like such an idiot that a tear escapes.

Lake swipes it away, holding onto my cheeks in her palms. "Don't you dare apologize; this is your home too. You come and go anytime you please, you don't need permission to leave your room; you do what you want now, okay?" She wraps her arms around me, but I still feel bad for interrupting them.

"I interrupted you and your boyfriend." She pulls back and gives me a serious look.

"You weren't interrupting anything. This is just how we are; very touchy-touchy when we're around each other. It doesn't mean you have to leave the room. Now come meet my lover," she says wickedly, linking her arm with mine.

In the Spotlight

We take the few short steps to a guy that towers over both of us and could definitely pass as a model. He has light brown hair that is spiked up, giving him that Edward look from *Twilight*. I never watched the movies but I saw the posters. He has dark brown eyes and tanned skin. I can't help but look down his body and it appears he works out by how his clothes cling to him. No wonder my sister is in love with him.

He's gorgeous.

He watches me and I see confusion in his eyes as they wander to Lake and back to me. Her hair is down, framing her beautiful face; my hair hides mine. Lake wears clothes that fit her figure; I wear clothes that make me look like a librarian.

We are total opposites.

I never felt comfortable in wearing clothes that showed off my breasts or stomach. I don't even feel comfortable wearing skirts that show off too much leg. Mom always taught me that if any guy is going to want the real me, I don't need to show off my body. That people who show too much attract men who will use them and walk away.

"Baby, this is my little sister Sky. Sky this is Leon." Her smile is so huge that it lights up her entire face. I see the adoration that shines in his eyes when he looks at her and can't help but feel jealous. Not of Leon, but of what they have. I hope one day someone will look at me like I'm their world.

"Nice to meet you." I put my hand out. Before I know what is happening his arms are around me giving me a hug. When he lets go I can't help but look at the floor. The only person who ever gave me any sort of affection is my sister yet this guy hugs me like I'm family.

"No formalities needed. You're going to be my little sister one day so, remember, if you need anything, you come to me. Need to kick someone's ass, you come to me. Okay?" I look at him and he gives me a warm smile and a wink. I can't help but giggle at him.

"You got it." What else can I say? But with the look on Lake's face, she is thrilled that we made a good first impression.

◦—★—◦

We ate dinner and talked. I still can't believe that my sister cooked this. I told her over and over how amazing it was and she beamed with my compliments. She made lasagna with homemade garlic bread and I never tasted anything like it. After having some ice cream, the day started taking its toll. My stomach also feels like it's about to explode.

I kiss my sister goodnight and give a small wave to Leon. I walk to my room and can't help but notice that I still haven't met Dominic. I hate that I never brought it up. At least Leon likes me. Well, I hope he does.

He seems to.

I quickly grab a shower and change into a tank and shorts before I take out the Kindle that I hid from my parents over the years. The only literature I was allowed to read was what they permitted; anything else would delude my brain. Lake bought me this before she left and downloaded some books. Trust me, the books she recommended definitely had some hot scenes that made me blush. I tuck myself in but realize I don't have anything to drink.

I walk back to the bathroom to see if I can find anything to use as a cup, but no such luck. I sometimes wake up dehydrated, so I learned to always have a glass of water near me so I don't need to leave the warm comfort of my bed. I walk down the stairs and head to the kitchen, opening the fridge to see it stocked full of bottled

In the *Spotlight*

water. I take one and am about to head back up the stairs when I hear my name being said.

I know that it's wrong to eavesdrop. I know I should just go back upstairs and tuck myself in, finish the book I'm reading, but I can't help myself. What if Leon doesn't want me here? Or what if I did something wrong? I need to know so I can make it right. I tip toe closer so I can hear them clearer.

"I missed her so much, three years away from my baby sister; I can't believe she is actually here. She was strong enough to leave the comfort of her life, the only life she knows. I just hate how much she hides herself. She has turned into such a beautiful woman and I bet they made sure she covered that up; they really dug their nails into her. I hate them for it. I hate..."

"How submissive she is?" Leon finishes her sentence. I flinch.

"The way she kept apologizing, hiding behind her hair, looking at the ground constantly. They've really done a number on her. She listened more than talked during dinner; spoke when spoken to." I swallow and look down. I hate that I just looked down, it's a bad habit.

"She's here now. She'll come out of her shell with the help of her loving, big sister. She has you. Now she has me. I have to admit I was shocked when I saw her. You can see her innocence a mile away. That look in her eyes, you can tell all this is new to her. We need to make sure we keep her safe. There are some dicks out there that would take advantage of that. I love you Lake, I'll protect her for you. The line of business we are in; the bands, the future tours, they will eat her up if we don't keep an eye on her. *But* we need her to spread her wings. We can't smother her."

"I know. We will. Talking about dicks, why didn't he show up?

I told him my sister was coming and he couldn't take ten minutes out of his life to meet her?" Her voice rises.

"You know what he's like. Was probably screwing some girl and forgot. I'll have words with him."

"The one thing I'm glad about is that he wouldn't go near her. If I didn't know his number one rule, I would threaten his dick and balls. My sister deserves happiness from everything she's been through and no womanizer is going to take her light."

"Light? Is that what kids are calling it these days?" I hear him chuckle followed by a thump, which I think is her hitting him. "Ow."

"You know what I mean. I want her to be happy, find love; if she doesn't..." I feel tears in my eyes, and I know she is probably getting upset.

"She will."

"I can't lose her Leon. I can't let them take her away. I can't let them control her anymore. It would kill me. I know what they want from her. She won't be happy."

"They aren't going to take her. They don't know where you live. Plus, they would have to get through me."

"I love you. Thank you for being there. For Sky."

"I love you, too. I will always be there, for both of you. You are my world; I won't let anyone upset my girl." With that I walk away, wiping the tears away.

I walk back to my room and lay down. I'm new to being independent. Well more independent than what I was before. I *will* find my way. I don't feel up to reading anymore, so I stare at the ceiling till sleep finally takes over.

Chapter 2

I wake up from a peaceful sleep, stretching my arms and looking around my new room. I still can't believe I'm here. Looking at the alarm on the side table, I see it's just before ten. I can't remember the last time I stayed in bed this late. I stand up to play some music when I see a note near my door.

> *Didn't want to wake you.*
> *Going to get some bacon and eggs.*
> *Remember, help yourself to anything.*
> *Love you.*
> *Lake x x*

I smile and lay the note on my desk, taking notice that I drank all of my water last night. I poke my head out the door and, sure enough, the place is silent. *I'll just go grab a bottle of water and get ready for the day.* I wonder what Lake has planned. But bacon and eggs right now sounds so good. Mom never allowed fried foods in the house so I'm looking forward to breakfast.

I head down to the kitchen and grab a water. Uncapping it, I drop the stupid lid under the counter. Typical. I get on my hands and knees, trying to reach it, and can see it's pretty far back. I finally get my fingers around it when I hear a cough behind me. I freeze, dropping the lid back on the floor.

Oh no.

I don't make a move. I think maybe, if I don't move, the floor could open up and swallow me whole. Why can't I have the magical ability to be invisible? Or why can't it be my sister that's behind me right now? But, from the masculine sound of the cough, I know it's a man. I look down at my tank and shorts and feel my entire body heat up.

Why didn't I get ready? Oh yeah, cause I'm an idiot.

"You going to stay down there all day? Not that I'm complaining, I do have a good view from where I'm standing." The voice sends shivers down my spine even though the comment was quite crude. Is he staring at my ass?

I know I need to stand up. I know the longer I stay here, the more it will look like I'm insane. I gather all my strength and stand, my back to him. I don't want to turn. I'm too embarrassed. Footsteps come towards me and he leans in so close that I can feel his heat radiate off him. He softly strokes a hand down my arm, causing goose bumps in its wake. He opens up my palm and places my cap in it. He picked up the lid.

No man has ever touched me. I haven't even seen who this guy is, what he looks like, but my body is screaming for him. I feel him stand in close so that my back is to his front. My breathing is coming in fast and I gasp when I feel his erection press against me. Oh my God.

He is turned on by me.

His erection is touching me.

"You smell so good," he whispers in my ear. I am sure I just whimpered. All common sense has left me. I'm letting a complete

In the Spotlight

stranger, whose face I haven't seen, touch me, make my body feel things it never has before. "Tell me your name." I feel his stubble stroke against my cheek.

Oh God.

"Sky," I whisper and his body tenses up.

"Sky? As in..."

"My baby sister, you ass. Get your filthy paws away from her," Lake interrupts. I feel like someone threw cold water over us.

"Sorry, how was I supposed to know?" I hear him ask behind me as he moves away. For some reason, I hate that he is no longer near me. That I can no longer feel his heat.

"Why else would there be a girl in her pjs in our kitchen at this time of day?" Lake scolds him.

"Wishful thinking? I'm sorry okay? Sorry, Sky." With that I finally turn around to see my sister giving evil looks to the most beautiful man I have ever seen.

This guy was just behind me? This God? This perfect specimen of mankind? He is leaning against the wall with his arms crossed. His massive arms. With how tight his gray shirt is, the rest of his body looks toned and muscular. His jeans hang perfectly on his hips. When I finally look up, even his face is perfect. Bright green eyes; long, thick brown hair. The kind you want to push your fingers through. I can't help but stare at his lips; hating that I wonder what it would be like for them to touch mine.

I have never had a chance to kiss a boy, have never felt like I wanted to, but now I needed to. He looks too good to be true. What would have happened if my sister didn't come back? Would he have kissed me? Why am I even thinking about this? This isn't me. I don't care about boys.

But he isn't a boy. He is a man.

"It's okay. I'm sorry for looking," I sweep my hand up and down my body, "indecent." I notice that his eyes follow my hand movement, stopping at my legs. It feels like he is undressing me with his eyes alone. Now I *do* feel uncomfortable. No one has really seen my body this close to naked.

I wrap my arms around myself.

"Sky?" I turn to Lake and I know she can tell I feel uncomfortable. "Go get dressed and come down in twenty, breakfast will be ready then." I give her a quick hug, whispering a thank you in her ear before running up the stairs. All the way to the top I can still feel his eyes on me.

☆

Dominic

Fuck me sideways.

That's Lake's sister?

Wow.

I thought maybe she was a groupie that snuck in last night. Seeing her on all fours, her perfect, tight ass in the air; I felt my dick harden in seconds. Feeling her body tremble against mine, how responsive she was. Touching her flawless, white skin. I didn't have to see her face, from what I could see, her body was perfect. Her strawberry scent surrounded me.

Hearing her say her name caused my once hard erection to quickly disappear; especially when Lake walked in. Walked in on me hitting on her baby sister. Lake is hot. Her body is smoking. Perfect ass and tits. I would have tried to bang that if it wasn't for Leon. They were head over heels and shit. I wouldn't do that to the guy. He has been there for me since we were kids. Plus, Lake does see through

In the Spotlight

my bullshit.

Once Sky turned around, I was a goner. She reminded me of a hotter version of Snow White. Raven black hair flowing down her back. Dark blue eyes that I'm sure I saw a hint of purple in. Pale, white, soft skin.

Fuck.

Why couldn't she be a groupie?

She's going to be living under the same roof as me? Living across the hall from me? I need to control my dick and not touch her. Yeah, easier said than done.

Fuck my life.

I wouldn't do that to Lake. I wouldn't spoil our friendship. Even though she gives me crap, we are a family. She's helped our band get out there; working on our social media, booking gigs. She bought the house that we live in using an inheritance she received from her grandparents. I was also given more than enough to live comfortably for a while when my parent's passed away so, for now, none of us have to work. We get to do the thing we love. Music will always be my number one priority. I don't need a girl I don't even know messing up the life we have gotten comfortable in.

There are plenty of chicks out there, plenty who are willing to open their legs for the lead guitarist of an upcoming band. Sky is family. I need to make myself believe that.

Then stop looking at her ass while she walks up the stairs, dick.

I walk to the living room and lay down on the couch. I'm exhausted from partying all night. I need to get the dark haired girl out of my mind. I hang around gorgeous women all the time. I think the reason I find her appealing is maybe because I was told not to go near her. Maybe I see her as a challenge. Just thinking that makes me sound shallow and, worse of all, a huge ass.

"I need words with you." Lake stands in front of me with her hand on her hip. Great. She's going to go all mother hen on me.

"I won't touch her okay?" Well, I hope I don't.

"I know you. I've known you for years. I know what you're like and I love you; you are a great friend, we are family, but when it comes to women..." she pauses, "you're a dog." Wait, what?

"Hey, hold on just a minute." I sit up. How dare she say that?

"Come on. You don't see a girl more than once, they come walking in and out of here like it's a hotel. You're a womanizer. I love you, but it's true. You are a great person but you think with your dick." What the hell?

"It's true man. Not saying it's a bad thing. You tell them where they stand but you don't hang around one girl longer than a night. I get it, we're young, but you go through women like toilet paper." Leon steps up, wrapping his arms around Lake's stomach. I watch her snuggle into him. I want to vomit.

"Thanks man, thanks for having my back." He shrugs.

"I just want to explain to you that Sky is different. She is sweet and innocent; I don't want her hurt. She believes in love and happily ever after's. I don't want you tarnishing that. She's a good girl, not one of *your* girls."

"Right, okay. I won't touch her. I promise." She looks me straight in the eye to make sure I'm telling the truth before nodding in acceptance.

I watch her and Leon walk back towards the kitchen but she stops in the doorway. "By the way, she's a virgin. She's innocent." She walks away.

In the *Spotlight*

Fuck.

She's a virgin? How can that be? She's gorgeous. What guy wouldn't take one look and want to sleep with her? Maybe she's waiting for that special someone. Waiting for the perfect guy and the perfect time. It is my number one rule. I don't do virgins.

Ever.

Virgins get attached. Girls always remember the first person they sleep with. I will not let any girl go through that. I don't want their first time to be a one-night stand. I may be an insensitive jerk when it comes to the opposite sex, but I do have morals. Knowing that Sky is one hundred percent a virgin, I know I can't touch her.

I grab my phone from my pocket and flip through my contacts. I got a few options from last night and now I'm taking my pick. I need a good fuck. My dick is still semi hard and I need a release. I send a text and lay back down, waiting. I know she will come- in more ways than one.

They always do.

I smell something good when I finally take my lazy ass off the couch and follow the aroma. Lake is plating up some bacon and eggs and my stomach automatically rumbles. I go to the fridge and grab a carton of OJ and pour out four glasses and Lake gives me a warm smile in thanks. I knew she wouldn't stay mad at me for long.

I'm looking through my Facebook when Lake yells out to Sky to come down. Has she stayed up there all this time? I look through my newsfeed to stop myself from looking at her when I feel her close by. It doesn't help.

I glance over at her and I'm shocked at what I see.

The girl that was wearing tight shorts and a tank is now

wearing a white blouse with a long black skirt. I mean the skirt literally goes to her feet. She looks like an old school teacher; her hair is even up in a tight bun on top of her head. If I saw her looking like this first, I wouldn't believe what's hiding underneath. It's like meeting two completely different people.

She sits opposite me and I try to look distracted, but I keep thinking that I had to have been dreaming this morning. I know I didn't since I keep feeling Lake's eyes on me. She has nothing to worry about. I don't do virgins and I don't do girls who hide behind themselves. I like the girl next door types but this girl, she is hiding. I know that if you're hiding, you don't want to be found.

Chapter 3

Sky

I went for a more casual look since I still feel embarrassed that Dominic saw me the way he did. I kept to my room since I didn't want to let them see me so worked up. Acting like a child. Being pathetic over something they don't think twice about. But I let a complete stranger, a stranger who my sister thinks is a player, touch me. I didn't even stop him. I still can't describe the feelings that I felt. My body heated up. I had butterflies swarming around in my stomach. The weird thing is, I liked it. I know I shouldn't.

But I did.

We are sitting around the table eating our breakfast and I have to stifle a moan. I've never tasted anything like this, ever. Growing up, we ate salads because Mom always said that girls like us can't afford to get fat. Men want *desirable* women. If she ever thought we gained a single pound, we would starve. Now as I take each bite, I wouldn't care if I blew up like a balloon. How can people not just eat this three times a day? It's amazing.

"You like it?" Lake asks as she gives me a knowing smile. All I can do is nod my head vigorously and she chuckles as we continue eating. She knows what it's like growing up on mainly lettuce.

I feel eyes on me every now and then but I don't dare look up. I'm almost finished when there is a knock on the door and Leon stands to answer. I hear voices coming from the other room and one that stands out is a woman's. I turn my head towards the door and see a very beautiful blonde wearing a dress that looks more like lingerie. I can't help but eye her up and down. Long legs, gorgeous figure. My eyes land on her huge chest that looks like it's about to pop out of the top.

How can she walk around like that in public?

"Dom, you ready?" she purrs, and that's when it sinks in.

She's here for him.

Ready for what? I look at Dominic and see him giving her a once over and his eyes have gotten darker. Is that lust? Looking again at the goddess and down at myself, I feel stupid that I thought he could ever see me as attractive. I could never compare to a girl like that. Is this the type he goes for? I've read in books where men go for confident, sexy women; I guess it's true in real life. Why am I even comparing myself to her?

"Yeah. Let's go," he responds while standing.

I must be a glutton for punishment as I watch as he saunters towards her, fisting her hair before placing his lips on hers, her body arching towards him. Embarrassed that I'm watching something so intimate, I turn away. Why do I keep landing myself in other people's intimate moments? I hear them walk off with her giggling.

"It's not even lunch time and he's having a booty call?" my sister asks in disdain. I watch her grab the empty plates and head towards the kitchen. The food that I just enjoyed moments ago starts to rumble unpleasantly around my stomach.

"You okay? You look a little pale. Well paler than normal." Leon brings me out of my thoughts. I look up at him and he is giving me a warm smile that I return I can see why Lake likes him. He's nice.

"Yeah, I'm sorry. I've never seen girls dressed like that. Mom

In the *Spotlight*

always said intimacy is for behind closed doors, yet the two of them looked like they were about to devour each other." I look down, playing with the hem of the table cloth.

"Your sister has talked a little about how she grew up. How you both grew up. I'm sorry your life was like that. All those rules. I can't imagine growing up like that," he says as he leans back in his chair.

"It was the only thing I knew. As long as I had my sister by my side I was happy. She protected me. I remember when I was twelve and she got me a disc-man. She found some CD's and we would listen to different kinds of music. We've both loved music ever since. I love how each song, each melody, can be different. Mean different things. I wanted so many different options of music growing up, I wanted rock, pop, jazz, anything but I knew I couldn't," I sigh. "After she left, I felt like my parents knew I was it. They had to force me to do better. Be better. Be the person *they* wanted me to be. But all they did was make me feel more trapped. When I got the chance to leave, I did. I want to experience life before I can't anymore." I feel tears prickle behind my eyes.

"What do you mean before you can't?" he asks.

"Sky? You want to take a tour to the mall? We can get some new clothes?" Lake interrupts us. With the sadness I see in her eyes, I know she heard me.

"Sounds great. Let me go get my shoes." I smile at Leon before I head up the stairs.

I am in my own world, thinking of my past, when I hear grunting down the hall. My defences go on alert. I know Dominic came up here with that girl, but is she hurting him? What if he's hurt? I hear the noises again. Should I yell for help? Should I get my sister? I open his door a little to make sure he's okay, but what I see will haunt me forever.

Dominic is standing near the edge of the bed and the woman he left with is on her knees. His jeans are around his ankles; his shirt is off. I look at his broad chest and shoulders; his toned stomach. My eyes trail down even more to the fine hairs that lead further down. It's what she is doing that makes my whole body heat up. Her mouth is around his erection, her hands on his sack, and his head is thrown back in passion.

Oh my God.

She is giving him a blow job.

I need to leave. I take a step back to do so but, like he can sense that I'm there, his eyes open and land directly on mine. I feel like I'm in a trance as our gazes stay locked together. The girl groans and Dominic squeezes his eyes shut as he growls. It's a very animalistic sound. With the connection finally broken, I run away, going to my room and grabbing my shoes before running back down the stairs.

My heart is beating a million times a second and I am sure I look like a tomato. I go to the fridge and grab a bottle of water, chugging down most of it. Why did I have to be so nosey? Why couldn't I have just gone straight to my room? They do say ignorance is bliss.

You thought he was hurt. You were trying to be there for him, my head tries to console me.

I lean against the counter, trying to get my head on straight. What if he tells Lake that I perved in on them? I groan into my hands as I feel the embarrassment come back. Hopefully he's just as embarrassed as I am.

He didn't look embarrassed. He kept his eyes on yours.

"You ready?" I jump at hearing Lake's voice.

In the *Spotlight*

"Sorry, you scared me. Yeah I'm ready," I respond quickly, bending down to put on my shoes.

"You okay?"

"Yeah. Just excited to spend some time with you." Plus, I just walked in on my new roommate getting a blow job.

─── ★ ───

"Come on, you have to get it; it looks amazing on you." I'm standing in front of a mirror wearing a blue, strapless dress that stops just above my knee.

I have never worn anything so revealing. I look at myself and am shocked at what I'm seeing. The material clings to me, and I hate how skinny I look compared to Lake, who is wearing a red dress that shows off curves in places I don't have. I look like a pole compared to her.

"I like it, but I think it would look better on you. I look too skinny in it." I go back into the dressing room and put my blouse and skirt back on.

"Hey, you look beautiful. You have a great ass. Mom starved us, so after a few more of my meals you're going to fill out a bit more, trust me. Remember, I've been there. I was stick thin when I left home. Now? Now I love my body. If anyone doesn't like it, tough shit. As long as I'm happy, that's all that matters. You will love your body, and soon you will want to show it off," she says in the next dressing room. I can't remember what her body was like before she left, it was that long ago. I never paid attention but Mom made her eat like a rabbit too, so maybe she's right. Well on the filling out part, not the showing it off part.

"I'm going to buy these cardigans though," I say, changing the subject. The cardigans I have chosen are red, black, and blue.

They're a very thin material and are long enough to cover my ass.

"They did look cute on you. Get the jeans too. They made your ass look amazing. I wish I had your ass," she sighs. I pull open the curtain and Lake is standing there with piles of clothes over her arm.

"What's wrong with your ass?" I look at her body. She is perfect.

"I wish it was bigger. The weight I gained went to all the right places except there. You've always had a great ass." I scoff at the idea. I can't believe we are in the middle of a store talking about our asses.

We go to check out and Lake offers to treat me to the clothes. After, we go to a nearby diner and order cheeseburgers and shakes. I can't help but moan when I take my first bite. If anything, I'm not going to forget these amazing tastes. I feel like I've died and gone to heaven.

"So, what do you think you're going to do while you're here? You can do nothing and have the life of luxury, if you want. I'm just curious." I pause as I think about the question. What am I going to do with my life? I grew up with expectations: Marry a man that my parents think will benefit the family name, pop out babies, look after my husband and children. But I'm twenty-one, I'm still young. I don't want my life to end yet.

"I never really thought about it. I don't really have any passions to follow except reading."

"I didn't mean to rush you, I just wanted to know. I want you to do something you love, and if you want to read books all day, every day, then do it. Just do what makes you happy. I love that I manage Leon's band; I can't imagine doing anything else." I can see that she is telling the truth by the way her face lights up talking about

In the Spotlight

Leon and the band.

"It will come to me; I just need to think about it." I continue eating the rest of my delicious burger.

"You can be a book reviewer. Start a blog. If you need any help, just come to me," she offers.

"You know I will."

⸺ ★ ⸺

The rest of the day we bounce from shop to shop. I have never seen so many clothes in my life. It was a thrill making my own decisions on what I wanted to wear. My clothes have always been picked out for me to be sure I fit the image of what the perfect daughter should look like. We have bags of clothes that I'm sure will last me for years. I notice Lake's leg bouncing as we drive back home and my curiosity spikes, knowing she does this when she is excited about something.

We park and Leon comes out the door straight away, grabbing our bags and walking off without saying a word. That was weird. Lake loops her arm through mine and practically skips us to the door. I can hear music on the other side and when the door opens I am surrounded by strangers who yell out 'Welcome'. I almost jump from fright.

I look at my sister who's bouncing with excitement. She threw me a party? I see a welcome sign and balloons and people drinking from red cups. Lake walks me towards the crowd and starts introducing me to everyone. There are so many people, I know I am going to have trouble remembering their names.

I'm talking to a girl with short pink hair when I can't help but look up at Dominic who is talking with some guys, a different girl on his arm. This one is a red head. Like the one I saw this morning, she is stunning. She is wearing tight jeans and a shirt that is high enough to show her flat stomach. So he doesn't hang with the same woman twice?

As if he can feel me staring, he looks up and gives me a nod and continues back to his conversation. He didn't look at me like I just watched him get a blowjob six hours ago. No disgust or cocky smirk. Hopefully he's willing to forget it ever happened. If that is the case, I will thank my lucky stars. Some other girls come up to me, introducing themselves. Lake told them that I'm a huge fan of reading so we are discussing the books we've read. One even calls herself a book whore, which I blush at.

I am enthralled in our conversation, openly talking about a recent book that I read, when I see a girl out of the corner of my eye walk through the door like she owns the place. She has long blonde hair with pink tips, flawless makeup, and a leather skirt to go with her leather jacket. She screams bad girl. The kind of girl my parents warned me about. I can still hear my mom's voice drilling in my head that anyone that wears leather is bad news. Boy or girl.

I watch her walk through the crowd, men watching her, girls whispering and pointing. Who is she? She looks familiar but I can't put my finger on it. It isn't until she stops by Dominic that it clicks. She's the lead singer of the band. My sister showed me some pictures, mostly of Leon, but I remember her showing a picture of a man with his head turned and a girl posing to the camera.

"That's Sherry, the lead singer of their band. She's a badass. If she doesn't get her own way though she can be a real bitch," the girl with pink hair, Charlotte, whispers.

"My sister showed me a picture of her once, it just took a second to sink in." We continue watching her talk to Dominic and

In the Spotlight

some of the guys.

"Yeah, she thinks because she's the lead singer she's the boss of the band. I'm a huge fan, I go to every gig, but she is so full of herself. They only put up with her shit because they need her."

Sherry turns her head and glares at me and I realize we are openly staring at her. I start to feel out of my element, so I look around the crowd, trying to find my sister. I'm still searching when I feel someone poke my shoulder. I turn and see Sherry; the look she is giving me isn't welcoming.

"Excuse me, I don't know who invited you, but can you please leave?" What? It's more of a demand than a question.

"Umm... the thing is... this is ummm," I stutter over myself. I look around the crowd again trying to find Lake.

"Umm, umm, umm," she mimics me. "This is a private party. So if you can find the door, we won't make this any more of a scene." She takes a few steps away before turning back around. "Oh, and I don't know what look you are going for, but the teacher-geek look won't get you laid. F.Y.I." What is F.Y.I? How can she just come up to me and kick me out?

"I'm not leaving. I..." I try and talk with more confidence than I have but I'm sure my voice is all shaky.

"Listen love. I know the people who live here. What I say goes. Now LEAVE!" She yells at me. I can feel the tears start falling fast.

All the memories of my parents yelling at me, telling me I'm not good enough. I need to do better. All of my insecurities are coming to the surface and I can feel everyone's eyes on me.

"Listen you up tight bitch..."

"Shut up Charlotte. I don't appreciate you bringing in riff raff. I know you want to show off your friends to the band but don't bring in any stray dogs," she seethes at her. Did she just call me a dog? "What the hell is going on here?" Dominic walks towards us and Sherry loops her arm through his, batting her eyelashes up at him.

"I was telling this girl that she can't just crash this party. I was politely telling her to leave before she refused to go. You can tell she's an attention seeker. Look at her; look how she's dressed." She looks at me in disgust. I look down at my outfit and hers and I thought I looked more casual. This is how I dress. How I was taught to dress.

"Sherry, for fucks sake. This is *her* party. She moved in last night. When Lake hears about...

"What the FUCK?" I hear Lake shout across the room. She's walking towards us, looking majorly pissed off. I have never been more grateful for her presence. I run to her, wrapping my arms around her as I let the tears fall. I know I'm being pathetic, but I have never had someone, a stranger, tell me how pathetic I look. "It's okay. I will sort this," she tries to soothe me.

"I just want to go to my room." I try and wipe the tears away but they won't stop coming.

"No, this is your party. YOU." She points at Sherry. "This is *my* sister. This is *her* house. How dare you? I had to hear from someone that you tried to kick her out? Who the fuck do you think you are? You can't come to *my* home and kick people out. *Especially* my baby sister. You have gone too far." I've never seen Lake look so angry. I'm pretty sure I see a vein on her head pulse.

"My bad, okay? How was I supposed to know this was your sister? I was expecting a mini version of you. Not... *this*." She swipes her hand up and down at me.

In the Spotlight

"I don't give two shits. You don't kick out my guests. This is *my* house. Now I want you to leave. You ruined my sister's party, now leave," she says firmly, pointing to the door.

"What? No! You aren't kicking me out. I'm the most wanted person here. You can't have a party without me. Dom, come on." She points at him for backup. I can see the frustration on his face. I also notice his eye roll.

"Don't ask him. This is my house. Mine. Now get the fuck out or I swear to God I will kick your ass out." Sherry glares at me. I look at the ground.

"Fine. Whatever. Trust me Lake, you will pay for this." I feel her eyes on me before I hear her walk away, then the door slams shut.

"I am so sorry about her. She thinks she is the queen of everything. She is a complete bitch." Lake hugs me. I hear people talking again amongst themselves but I feel too embarrassed to stay any longer.

"I want to go to my room. Thank you for the party, but I want to get away. Is that okay?"

"I understand. I'm sorry again. Go lay down, I'll be up in a bit." I give her a hug before I walk away.

"Sky, wait." I stop and Charlotte comes running to me. "I'm sorry about her. I'm giving your sister my number and Facebook name. I loved having another book lover to talk to. Call me whenever you want to meet up. We can swap some book boyfriends." She gives me a smile.

"I'm sorry for not staying longer, but I would love that. Thank you." I give her a quick hug before heading to my room.

I walk up the stairs and feel eyes on me. I look down to see

Dominic standing at the bottom. He mouths sorry, and I just nod. I turn around and walk away. Sherry is in the band which means I am going to see more of her. I'm not looking forward to it. The plus side though is that I made a new friend.

Chapter 4

I've been here for a few days and luckily haven't had another run in with Sherry. I overheard my sister planning a rehearsal with the band for an upcoming gig which means I am going to see her at some point soon. I know my sister most likely had words with her, seeing as how protective she is of me. She thinks what happened is her fault but I don't blame her. I know that I won't be able to look Sherry in the eye again, though.

It's two a.m. and I'm having trouble sleeping. I had a bad dream that my parents found me and took me away, taking me from Lake. I can still picture them dragging me from my new home kicking and screaming; Lake trying to get to me but never can. I quickly grab a robe that I recently purchased, so that I don't have another embarrassing encounter in my PJ's, and decide to head down to watch TV.

I tip toe down the hall so I don't wake anyone and head to the kitchen first, to make myself a cup of tea, before heading to the couch and switching on the TV. I flip through the channels, making sure the volume is down low, and decide on The Vampire Diaries, a show that I have kind of gotten hooked on.

I'm watching Damon trying to find Elena and sipping on my cup of tea when I feel like someone is watching me. I'm sitting in the dark, in the middle of the night, watching a supernatural show but I can't get rid of that feeling so I turn my head and almost scream when I see a person standing in the doorway. Dominic?

"You scared me. What are you doing hiding in the dark?" I press my hand against my chest, trying to calm my nerves.

"Sorry. I was seeing what crap you were watching." He sits down on the end of the couch I'm sitting on, asking, "Couldn't sleep either?" He glances over at me and I sit up, tucking my legs under me.

"Bad dream. You?" I take another sip of my tea that has now gone luke warm.

"I have trouble sleeping at night. My body is used to being awake during the night and asleep during the day. Being in a band messes with your body clock. So what has you so enthralled?" he asks, facing the TV. I turn in time to see Damon snap some guys neck.

"The Vampire Diaries. I think I'm obsessed with the show. I can't get enough." I chuckle. I turn and he is staring at me. I mean *really* staring at me.

"Hmm." That's all he says. I turn and face the TV again, trying to block out that he is sitting a few inches away from me. "Can I ask you a question?" he asks.

"Sure." I pause the show so he has my full attention.

"I don't want to pry, and you can tell me to keep my nose out, but why do you act like you've been on a different planet? I watch you at times and see you experience things, normal things, for the very first time. You're what? Twenty-one? Were you brought up in the woods?" He chuckles and I give a poor attempt of one back. Lake never told him about our parents, I guess. Or how we grew up.

"Umm, it's going to sound stupid, but our parents were kind of strict. They wanted us to eat healthy, do things that would benefit us

In the *Spotlight*

or them. I've been brought up to be exactly how they wanted me to be. So yes, most things right now I am experiencing for the first time." I look down, playing with the tie on my robe.

I feel his thumb and index finger on my chin, guiding my head back up. He lets go and pushes hair behind my ear, stroking my cheek, causing my skin to heat up. I am so glad it's dark and he can't see what he is doing to me.

"I didn't mean to pry," he says softly.

"It's okay," I barely manage to get out.

We sit there in silence, just enjoying each other's company. We don't need to say anything. After a few more minutes, he takes the remote, pressing play on my show before standing.

"Goodnight Sky."

"Goodnight Dominic."

I wake up to banging on my door. I didn't get back to bed till five. I'm exhausted. I grab my pillow and put it over my head so I can ignore the sound and go back to sleep, but whoever is on the other side is persistent and they open my door and jump on my bed, causing me to groan.

"Get up sleepy head. Today you're finally going to watch the band rehearse. I want to show you how good they are. Plus, you can't stay in your room all day, every day. Come on." Lake pulls my blanket off me and the cold automatically causes me to shiver.

"You hate me. It's too early to get up," I grumble into my pillow.

"It's one in the afternoon. Now get up or I will drag you out just as you are. Don't think I won't." I groan out loud and finally sit up to see Lake smirking at me. I throw my pillow at her, causing her to laugh before leaving my room.

Great, I'm going to watch the band rehearse, which means I am going to be near Sherry. Why couldn't my sister give me a warning so I could have forced myself to sleep more instead of watching three hours of Damon? I head to my shower and let the heat wake me up.

With a towel wrapped around me, I look through my closet, wanting to wear something that Sherry won't put her nose up at. I know it's pathetic. I never let anyone bug me about what I wore, not even the kids that went to my school. But the kids at my school knew who my parents were, so they were probably too scared to say anything negative about me.

I decide on a pair of black jeans, a white T-shirt, and a blue cardigan. I look in the mirror and decide I like it. It's student-y. I put on my black flats and head downstairs to see Leon planting loads of kisses on Lakes cheeks. I cough to let them know I'm here.

"Sorry, this is his good luck charm for a good rehearsal." Lake scrunches up her face as he lays more kisses on her. I can't help but laugh at them.

"Okay, think I'm lucky enough. Let's go kick ass." Leon walks outside and we follow.

I was expecting to get in a car, but I follow them around the house to a door instead. We walk inside and I see stairs that I realize go down to a basement. I look more closely and I'm shocked at what I see. There is a mini recording studio in the corner and a stage on the other side.

"I know right." Lake takes in my shocked look and laughs. "I didn't want to tell you so I could see your face right now. It's amazing right? There's a full sound system, it's even sound proof so no one can complain about how loud we are down here.

I watch Lake and Leon start moving things around, plugging in

In the Spotlight

instruments. I sit on a chair and watch; I don't want to break anything. I hear the door open and Dominic walks in with a guy behind him. The guy has shaggy blonde hair and large muscles. What is it with this band? Did all the guys have to be so godly? The guy with blonde hair sees me and smiles, walking towards me.

"You must be Sky. I'm Chris the bassist. I heard you're the new roommate." He puts out his hand for me to shake.

"Hi, nice to meet you. I think my sister showed me a picture of you once but your hair was shorter back then." God could I sound any lamer?

He runs his fingers through his hair and chuckles. "Yeah, I grew it out once I realized that girls like having something to hold on to," he says, winking at me. My face turns bright red, instantly understanding what he is insinuating.

"Oi, Chris leave my sister alone or I will cut your strings." Lake has scissors in her hands, cutting thin air and Chris puts his hands up, backing away. I have to admit; they are quite amusing to watch.

"You're just jealous because I wasn't hitting on you," Chris states, sauntering up to her.

"You wish."

"Do you want me to kick your ass?" Leon runs to Chris, tucking him under his arm in a head lock and starts rubbing his hair.

"You're going to pay for that," Chris whines.

"Just you try it." I see them stand apart and run at each other, wrestling to the floor. Lake stands there rolling her eyes and steps over them to a sound system. I just watch the guys roll on the floor. I can't help but laugh at them.

"I thought this was a closed rehearsal," a snide voice says from the doorway and sure enough, Sherry is standing there in tight leather pants and a black top, that looks more like a bra, with a leather jacket. She really does scream rock star.

"Stop it, Sherry. She's my sister so where I go, she goes. Get used to it." My sister walks towards me and wraps an arm around my shoulders.

"Whatever, just keep the groupies out of my way." She saunters to the made up stage near the microphone.

"Just ignore her. She's a jealous cow. Sit on the couch and enjoy the show." With that she walks off back to the sound system. "Right guys, take your spots. Let's do this." Leon and Chris stop their boxing match and climb up on the stage.

Chris takes a bass guitar, Leon sits behind some drums, spinning the sticks around his fingers. Wow, now that's awesome. Dominic steps up with a black guitar that looks really expensive. When he wraps the strap around his neck, he looks even more godly, if that's even possible. Sherry takes off her jacket and yeah, that top definitely looks like a bra. Her chest is right in your face. But with them all up there, they look like they're made for this.

"Let's do this." Leon taps his drum sticks and my eyes can't stay off Dominic as I watch his fingers pluck the strings.

His eyes concentrate on his instrument and after a few seconds Sherry's, voice flows through the room. It has that feminine yet husky quality. It suits the tune of the music. They are so in sync with one another. They play song after song and I even recognize a few and can't help but move my lips along to the words.

I look back to Dominic and he is smiling at me, watching as I sing quietly to a song that they are playing. I stop moving my lips, feeling embarrassed once again. Their music is really good and they even play a couple of covers. After a few more songs, they stop, the

In the Spotlight

guys high fiving each other.

"What did you think?" Lake asks, beaming.

"It was amazing. Their music is so raw, it's so good." I say in a rush.

"You really liked it." My body shivers as I hear his words surround me.

I turn around, smiling at him. "It was amazing. You are so good. You play awesome." God, could I sound any more stupid? But he gives me a huge smile that I swear causes something to stir in me.

"I'm glad you enjoyed it." He walks away to Chris and my eyes follow him, forgetting my sister is beside me. I catch Sherry glaring at me before a confident smirk covers her face and she walks towards Dominic, wraps her arm around his neck in a hug, and whispers something in his ear. I don't know why it bothers me. They look good together. She was all over him at the party. She openly shows him affection.

They must be together in some way.

Friends with benefits maybe?

Chapter 5

I joined Lake to the bands gig to cheer them on. It's the first time I've been to an actual bar. Lake told me I should try an alcoholic drink but I don't feel confident enough yet. I'm legal, but I know alcohol can change your personality; I experienced that first hand from my mom. I watched the girls and guys around me, some acting like idiots while others acted like they were behind closed doors; making out or going way past second base.

If this is what alcohol can do to you, I don't think I will ever be ready. The crowd screams at the band; yelling out for more. Women even throw their underwear at them. Chris laps up the attention. Dominic never seems fazed by it all but, I suppose if he's with Sherry, he can't really lead anyone on. She wore something that looked like paint but, according to my sister, sex sells. Even though she eye rolled at the comment.

Sherry loves the attention, the fame. After the show she proceeds to drink until she's wasted. You think sober Sherry is nasty. A drunk Sherry is one mean girl. She insulted me in any way she could, always making sure I was alone. Following me to the bathroom, to the bar to get a coke. She made fun of my appearance. On how pathetic I looked following my older sister like a lost puppy. I was glad when we left. I want to support the band, support what Lake loves doing, but Sherry is making it hard for me to be around them.

In the *Spotlight*

Tonight, Lake is taking me to a karaoke bar. She says that I need a fun night out. Leon tagged along, and Dominic and Chris are going to join us later, saying they had something to do first. Sherry wasn't invited, thank God. I don't think I could enjoy myself if she would have been here. I never told Lake what she did; I didn't want to be a pain by going to her with my problems.

We grab a table near the front and someone is already on stage singing and I recognize that it's a song by ABBA instantly. My mom loves ABBA. I look around, noticing how different it is from the bar the band played their gig at.

Lake is making sure I join in on their conversation and we talk about the good points of our childhood. I have never enjoyed myself so much. I go to the bathroom and when I return to our table my sister has a huge grin on her face. I know she did something. I know her too well when it comes to her facial expressions.

"What did you do?" I look at her with a pointed look. She flutters her eyelashes at me, trying to look innocent.

"Me?" She points to herself. "I didn't do anything." Then I hear my name being called and I look back at Lake, who is now cheering, and I groan into my hands.

"What did you do?"

"I may have put your name in to sing." Oh god, she didn't?

"I can't believe you. You know I'm not that good. How could you?" I may be whining like a little girl but I get nervous when I get on a stage in front of everyone.

"You are an amazing singer. You know they always made you lead in the school plays, you always had the solos in the choirs. You *are* good." I hear my name being called again. Dammit. "Now go up.

Go on, shoo." She waves her hands at me. I'm going to kill her.

"You suck." I stick my tongue out at her.

"I know." She winks back at me.

I head up to the stage and there is a large screen where words to the song come up and a microphone stand. I love singing, don't get me wrong, but it's always the beginning that makes me want to throw my guts up.

"What're you singing?" asks a guy who looks like he's in his forties with blonde hair that's starting to recede already. Lake didn't pick my song? Thank God for that.

"Umm, Michelle Branch *All You Wanted*." He nods at me before handing me the mic. I stand awkwardly in the middle of the stage, looking around, trying not to throw up.

Most of the people are engrossed in their own conversations, not caring that I'm up here, And I start to relax. I didn't want all eyes up on me. I see the song title appear on the screen and take a deep breath; I know this song like the back of my hand. The intro starts and I close my eyes as I let the words fall from my lips.

I get lost in the music, the words. Singing was always an escape for me. Letting me feel more alive. I keep on singing with my eyes closed and when I get to the chorus, I belt out the words with all my heart. My body hums and I feel like I'm a different person.

I finally open my eyes and everyone is staring at me but I don't care. I keep on singing and when I get to the second chorus, people in the crowd start whistling and cheering. I can't help but smile through the words. My sister cheers the loudest. I sway my body to the rhythm and I close my eyes again as the next chorus comes on.

When I open my eyes again, I see Dominic and Chris have joined the table, looking up at me in surprise. Chris is sitting down

In the Spotlight

but Dominic continues to stand, his eyes on me; I don't look away. I feel like he is looking into my soul. Looking at the me I want to be. I continue singing with everything I have, letting the words stream out of me. I sing the last line and before I can take my next breath I am getting a standing ovation.

"That's my sister!" Lake screams out. I laugh as I step off the stage to people telling me how amazing I was or shaking my hand as I walk toward our table.

"I knew you still had it in you. That was awesome!" Lake squeals, grabbing me in a hug. I look down at the ground feeling shy. The adrenaline that I had when I was singing is gone.

"It was okay," I mumble, shrugging it off.

"That was better than okay. You have some voice. You show so much passion, so much emotion. It's beyond words. You rocked girl." Chris is shaking his head at me. I look at Dominic and he is staring at me still. This time I look away.

"You were amazing." His words affect me more than the others, for some reason. I don't know why.

─── ★ ───

Dominic

Chris wanted to fuck some girl that's been messaging him. Well, more like sending him pictures of her pussy and tits. What guy could say no to that? The catch was, I had to hang out with her friend. What are good friends for if they don't help a friend in need? From seeing the odd picture Chris was willing to share, his girl was hot. The friend on the other hand, was gorgeous but, oh my God, she couldn't shut up.

She wouldn't stop talking about her ex. I mean *everything* that we brought up ended back to the guy that wanted his cake and to eat it too. After thirty minutes of hearing her go on and on, I was ready to leave.

Chris left, looking happy with himself. I, on the other hand, couldn't wait to down a beer ASAP. Maybe even two. Walking into the karaoke bar, I head straight to the bar and order three shots. I pass one to Chris and down one before picking up the other, heading to the table Leon messaged they were at.

"Come on man, it wasn't that bad," Chris says, putting his hand on my shoulder.

"Trust me, it *was* that bad. While you were fucking that girl, I was hearing what Tina's ex was missing out on. I swear, if I heard that she is better off without him one more time, I was going to leave your ass there." I really would have.

"Least I got some." He smirks at me.

"Yeah at least you did..."

"Holy shit, is that Sky?" Chris interrupts me.

I look at the stage and, sure enough, there she is, singing so beautifully. Her eyes are closed but I can see so much emotion on her face, in her body language. Fuck, she is amazing. Her voice is soft but powerful; I can't take my eyes off her. I follow Chris to Leon and Lake and they can't keep their eyes off her either. Lake has a huge smile on her face. I'm not surprised, that girl can sing.

I see Chris sit down in the corner of my eye but I can't move. It is like I'm frozen to the spot. When her eyes open and land on mine, I swear, I have never seen someone so beautiful. It's like I'm seeing that girl that was in the kitchen on her hands and knees. She looks more content, confident. More self-assured, like she's where she is meant to be. Her eyes don't move from mine and her voice surrounds me like a cocoon.

In the Spotlight

When she finishes, I want to scream at her to sing some more. I want her soothing voice to continue. People stand and cheer; I wouldn't expect anything less. She was perfect. Who would have thought that this shy girl had the voice of an angel? A voice that can get anyone down on their knees. I watch her as she comes to the table and Lake goes on about how good she was, but Sky is back to that reserved girl from before. I want the girl who was on stage back.

Hearing Chris tell her how good she was, I feel like I need to say something, but there are no words that can describe what I thought, what I felt. I tell her she was amazing but I want to say more. So much more. She turns to smile at me and I just know that she is going to turn my world upside down. I don't know if that's a good thing yet.

★

Sky

I'm sitting on the couch reading my Kindle while the guys watch some basketball game on TV. Luckily Sherry isn't here; it's the only reason I'm not hiding in my room. I'm engrossed in my book when I'm startled by Lake running into the room, out of breath. She looks excited but she is trying to control her breathing.

"Oh my God, spit it out sister," Chris says before throwing popcorn at her.

"You will never guess what I just lined up for you. You are going to die when you hear this!" she squeals.

"Baby, calm down and tell us. You know I hate suspense." Leon stands up and wraps his arms around her waist, kissing her head.

"I got us in on Mitch's Roll Call night!" All the guys jump off the couch, shouting what's and how's. I can see the excitement on each of their faces. "I've been trying to get us in for the last year.

Well, one of the bands split up, something to do with the lead singer sleeping with the guitarist's girl. Anyway, they had to give up their spot and now Mitch has asked *you* to take it." Despite her explanation, I'm still confused on what's going on.

"Sorry to interrupt, but what's going on?" I speak up and they all turn to me laughing, slapping each other on the backs.

"Sky, this is an amazing deal. Mitch's Roll Call is where bands get a shot to play one song, it has to be a cover, and if you are good enough, they ask you to play regularly. Not only is it a regular, well-paid gig, but talent scouts and producers show up. This could be a start in the right direction," Lake says in one breath.

"Oh my God, that's amazing! What song are you going to do?"

"Fuck, we need *one* good song. It has to be good enough. It has to match our sound." Dominic grabs his tablet and starts looking through it.

"We need to practice, practice, practice. Call Sherry. Tell her to come now. We need get this figured out. Wait, when is it?" Chris asks while getting his phone out.

"Umm, in two days," Lake says sheepishly, looking down at the ground.

"What!?" the guys exclaim at once.

"We can do this. Come on guys, this could be our one chance for ages. We can do this." Leon walks back to Lake and squeezes her.

"Yeah we can. Let's do this." They all start to leave the room in excitement.

"Sky you coming?" Lake asks me. I really don't want to see Sherry again.

"You go, I'm really into this book and need to know how it ends," I lie.

In the Spotlight

"If you need me, you know where I am." She comes to me, giving me a hug and a squeal and runs out. Leaving me alone. I hate being on my own.

An hour has gone by and my curiosity gets the better of me; I want to know what song they picked. If Sherry is busy on stage, she won't be able to go near me. Plus, Lake is always a few feet away so she can't corner me. With one last breath of encouragement, I stand and leave the house, going around to the door to the basement.

As soon as I open the door, familiar music flows up. I take a few steps down and realize it's a faster version of *Poison* by Alice Cooper. I like what they've done with it. I stay where I am and just listen. I hear them go at it a few more times. I hear Sherry start complaining about the key of the song and with that, I leave.

I grab Lake's laptop that she told me I can use at any time and head to my room. I switch it on and wait for it to load up. When it's ready, I go on YouTube and put in *Poison,* finding a link by Groove Coverage. I click on it and it's like the version the band is playing; faster and more upbeat. I play it over and over. It's so addictive and catchy that I start singing the words, dancing around my room.

★

It's the night of Roll Call and we just arrived. Lake made sure I got a free ticket to join them. I decided to wear jeans, a black tank, and a black cardigan, hoping to fit in. At the last gig, most people wore black, so it must be the look. The guys go in the back and Lake and I stay out front, listening to the other bands that got spots. Some are really good and it's making me nervous for Leon and the band. The guys on stage are very easy on the eye; Lake's words not mine. They *are* good looking, I guess, but when you're in a band I suppose that's almost as important as the music.

Lake tells me that Risen Knights will be going on after three more bands. I start getting nervous for them. I want them to do well. They worked so hard. They have been stuck down in the basement for hours on end, only coming up to eat and use the bathroom. I want them to get a permanent spot. I want someone who can take them to the top. They've earned it.

Lake and I are laughing and talking when she gets a text on her phone. The blood drains from her face and she hops up, telling me she needs to head to the back, before quickly running. Something happened, I can feel it. I hope Lake can fix it, whatever it is. She is a determined woman. If something can be fixed, she can fix it. I'm sitting on my own, listening to the current band, Dixon's World, when Lake finally comes back looking pissed off.

"What happened?"

"Sherry is fucked off her face. She isn't even here. She went to a party knowing the band wasn't going on till after eleven, now she's too drunk to even get her ass here on time. This was their shot. I could feel it. I could *feel* something good was going to happen." I feel so bad for her. For Dominic, Chris and Leon. I can't believe Sherry did this.

No, actually I could.

"I'm so sorry." She is nodding her head, blankly looking around when suddenly she jerks her head towards me. That look makes me nervous. Why is she looking at me like that?

"You could fill in," she states/begs. Wait what? She can't be serious.

"What? You can't be serious," I speak out my thoughts. "I can't go up on stage. You know how nervous I get. I'm not good enough anyway. I can't, I'm sorry," I ramble out, shaking my head

In the Spotlight

vigorously.

"You are amazing! I wouldn't ask you if I didn't think you could do this. I've heard you sing the song they chose. Please." She is now pleading to me.

I'm getting a major case of butterflies and I haven't even agreed to anything yet. This is different from karaoke night. As soon as I stand up on this stage, everyone's eyes will be on me. I look at the stage and back to my sister and she looks like the one who is going to pass out. She has done so much for me. She let me move in with her. Rent free. She hasn't pushed me to do anything. I can do this for her. It's just one song right? I can do this.

"Okay. I will do this for you, but if I'm not good enough, I'm sorry." I need her to know if they don't get their permanent spot that I warned her.

"If they don't like us, it's fine. At least we tried. You can do this." I nod and she shrieks. "Okay, come with me.".

I hope I'm good enough.

Chapter 6

We walk through a door that leads us to the back of the bar and I see a few rooms but we keep walking till we see Leon pacing back and forth, pulling his hair. I can see that he is stressed out and once he sees us, he walks towards us in a panic.

"Baby, what are we going to do? I can't believe this shit. We worked so hard to get here and she's fucked it up for us. I could strangle her." He pulls his hair again, staring at the ceiling.

"I've sorted something out. Go get the guys and get ready. Do what you've rehearsed. We got this." She stands on her toes and kisses his lips softly.

"Is Sherry here? Did she show up?" I look at Lake; she looks calm while I feel ready to combust.

"Just go, you're going to be brill." He looks at her for a moment then nods and walks away. Wow, he must really trust her to not to ask anything more.

"Why didn't you tell him I was going to sing?" I think I'm ready to start pulling *my* hair out. I don't know if I can do this. I'm watching people walk around with instruments, preparing themselves for their slot, and I feel like I am so out of my element.

"I don't want them to second guess my decision. I know you are going to be amazing. I wouldn't ask you to do this if I didn't think you could help them win. How many times over the years have I told you that you could sing? That your voice is going to take you places?

In the Spotlight

You can do this." She holds my hands looking intently into my eyes.

"I thought that was just you being a big sister. Supporting me, telling me what I wanted to hear."

"I would never lie to you. I've always believed in you. You can dance, you can sing; you have so much passion inside you, you just need to let it out. You have talent and now it's time to shine."

"Okay. Okay," I say over and over. "I can do this." I think.

"I know you can. Now though, we need to sort out your clothes. You can't show up on stage looking like a nun. Come with me." She grabs my hand and pulls me into one of the rooms that is luckily empty. "Take off your top and cardigan and wear this." She strips off her black top that has one sleeve and shows off her stomach. I look at her standing in her bra and quickly take off the top half of my clothes and pull her top on. I look down at my midriff and already feel too exposed. Why couldn't she have worn something that covers me more?

"Now unclip your hair." I do as she says and she comes in closer and pushes her hands in my hair, waving it out. "Right, I think you're good. Proper rock and roll. Come on, we're going on any minute," she says as she pulls me back out of the room. We start walking in the direction I presume the stage is at and see two guys standing nearby; they wave when they see us.

"Where's Sherry?" one of the guys asks.

"Don't ask. This is my little sister Sky. Sky this is Reese and Joey; she is taking Sherry's spot. Sky, they are professional dancers; they were supposed to be dancing with Sherry. Since we are going to wing this, I need you to just go with the flow. Sky, you'll go up first and when the song comes to the middle, you two come and start trying to pull her away, but in a sexy dance type of thing."

"Like an expressive dance? Contemporary dance?" I ask.

"If that's what it is, then yeah. Just go with the music. You three have experience with this sort of thing so I believe you will do it justice. We need that something extra and I think this is it." We all nod.

Just don't fall, my head mocks me.

"So you can dance?" Joey asks me. He is very attractive with floppy blonde hair and big, brown eyes.

"Yeah. I've been dancing since I was four. My mom thought it would help me be more graceful." I shrug. I hated dancing when I was a kid but, growing up, it was the chance to get away from my house, away from my parents. Lake went to every competition, play, show, you name it.

"That's good. That Sherry may sing but she has two left feet. She wanted us to be all over her. Picking her up like a queen. It was ridiculous." I can imagine.

"Right, come on let's get to the stage." Lake claps her hands. We walk a few more feet and I see Leon walking to his drums, Dominic and Chris waiting on stage. Oh God, this is it. "You can do this Sky." Lake places a head piece on my head with a little microphone near my mouth.

Lake gives me a quick hug and pushes me a little closer towards the stage. I take in a deep breath and try and block out all the noise from the crowds. I notice Dominic looking at Leon, saying something to him. I remember they don't know what's going on. Well, I hope I do them proud.

Just please God, don't let me make a fool of myself.

I take in another deep breath and let the first words fall from my lips, starting a slow walk across the stage. I keep my eyes on

In the Spotlight

Dominic the whole time. I feel like I need something to focus on and I chose him. He looks at me with his eyes wide open in surprise. No one is playing yet but I continue singing, then after a moment, I hear the drums go, and soon Chris and Dominic follow. Playing along with my voice.

I walk closer to Dominic and his eyes stay on mine. I stop and sing to him, swaying my hips; at the moment in the song when the line says '*black lace on sweat*' I pick my top up, showing a little flesh. When the song slows down, I start to walk closer to him again. I feel the music flow through me, the energy from the crowd. I let it sink into me. I let the music guide me. I stand close to Dominic, my chest rising up and down with adrenalin. I lean my mouth towards his but then I'm pulled away by Joey and Reese lifting me, gliding me backwards.

I continue singing as Reese twirls me out and then back in, but Joey stands in front of him, blocking the path, wrapping one of my legs around his waist as he spins me away. He lifts my arms up and I keep my own in the air as he slides his hands down my body before he comes back up. Reese places his hand in mine and spins me around so I'm facing him. I grab the back of his hair singing towards his mouth. Arms wrap around my waist, making me arch my back.

Joey and Reese are on either side of me so I slowly slide down them and come back up. Reese puts his arms around my waist holding the bottom of my back as he dips me. I kick my legs in the air and do a slow flip backwards landing back on my feet. Joey grabs my hand and spins me into him before spinning me back out for the final time. I let go of his hand and start to walk slowly towards Dominic again and his eyes are trained on me. I circle around and when I'm behind him, I lean my back against his. With the line '*I want to hold you*', I glide down a little, quickly turning so my front is now to his back. I pull his hair so his neck is exposed and sing into his ear. I let go and he turns his head so he is looking at me. I lean my mouth near his and I sing the last lines.

The music stops and my breathing is coming out fast. I don't move and neither does Dominic. I'm still flush against him. His head is still turned. My mouth is so close to his. I still feel the adrenaline of doing what I just did flow through me. All I have to do is lean in closer and my lips would be on his.

My first kiss.

I'm pulled away suddenly by Lake who is screaming at me with excitement. It's then that I look into the crowd and notice they are also screaming, chanting out '*more, more, more*' over and over. I shake my head in disbelief. I've been here all night and they haven't shown this much enthusiasm with any of the other bands. Leon and Chris come to stand with us and we all entwine our fingers together. I feel an electric pull shoot up me, spreading across my entire body. Dominic holds my hand and I face him. Again his eyes are on mine. Lake raises my hand in the air and I do the same with the hand that's holding Dominic's. The crowd goes wild. I laugh.

They actually enjoyed it.

They liked me.

"Told you they would love you!" Lake beams at me. She lets go of my hand and hugs Leon who spins her around. I notice Dominic doesn't release me. I don't want him to.

🎸—★—🎸

A few more bands had to go up after but some people were disappointed that we weren't going to do another song. I'm glad we're done. I was lucky this time that I knew the song they had

In the *Spotlight*

practiced. People here were treating us like celebrities. Telling us how amazing we were and wanting pictures. Mostly girls were coming over and trying to get with the guys. Chris was loving the attention, having a girl in his lap and another under his arm. Leon of course declined each one, saying he's with his girlfriend. Lake, though, would give each girl a look that said 'back off.' Dominic declined each one also which made me feel happy for some reason.

We are still talking about Lake persuading me to sing and how Joey and Reese and I danced so well with no proper instruction. I told them that I followed their lead and just went with the music. Now, looking back, I have to admit the dance moves were probably too sexual. I had my legs around them, let them touch me in intimate ways, but at the time it felt right with the song. The crowd seemed to like it.

If your parents could see you now. They would gut you alive.

"Sky?" I look behind me to see Reese standing there smiling at me.

"Yeah?" I ask, giving him a warm smile in return.

"I was just wondering if you wanted to go for a drink sometime?" I look at him in shock. Is he asking me out? I look around the table and they are all watching us. Lake has a huge smile on her face. Leon and Chris are just watching in interest, but Dominic is looking at his phone. Why would I think he would care?

"Umm, Reese that is so sweet of you but I'm still trying to find my feet here. Maybe when I'm more settled?" I don't think I'm ready for a relationship. I've never had one. I don't want one yet.

Unless the guy who sleeps across the hall asks? That voice in my head chimes in.

"Sure, here's my number just in case you change your mind.

You were great out there. You were like a different person. You were made for the stage. Hope to see you again." He leans forward and kisses the corner of my mouth. I don't know why, but I close my eyes and enjoy that small contact. I hear him walk away and when I open my eyes again, they land on Dominic. He stares at me intensely before I watch him stand up and head to the bar.

"You should have let him take you out. It could have been fun," Lake says, picking up a piece of paper that Reese must have left. I snatch it off her and put it in my pocket.

"I just moved here. Baby steps okay?"

"Okay. But he's nice and you two looked hot up there. Damn I am amazing. I knew I made the right decision." She rubs her nails against her top, well mine, and pretends to admire her nails. How can even my boring clothes look so amazing on her?

"Yeah, too bad Sherry is our singer, that bitch has gone power mad," Leon joins in. I knew this was a one-time thing but I am a little gutted that I couldn't do it again. Just hearing Leon say that Sherry is the lead singer and not me, makes me feel sad knowing I won't be able to do it again. I did have fun up there. After I let myself go.

"Don't even bring her up. I still want to slap that bitch. If it wasn't for my quick wit and Sky's voice and hot dance moves, the band wouldn't have gotten the praise it needed. You heard that crowd, they loved you and she could have ruined it," Lake says angrily.

Leon and Lake start talking about band stuff and Chris is kissing, well more like sucking, some girls face off. I look towards the bar and see Dominic talking to a girl. Another blonde. I don't know what it is, but I don't like seeing him talking so closely to another girl. I hate that now I'm starting to feel like a third wheel. I

In the *Spotlight*

was having a good time and now I just want to go home and go to bed. I'm about to speak my thoughts when an attractive man in an expensive suit walks up to our table.

"Hi, I watched your band perform tonight. I have to admit, it was awesome. I love your sound. I love what you did and putting that extra bit with the dancing gave it even more of an appeal," Mr. Suit says.

"Yo, Dominic, come over here!" Leon shouts out. I hate that he brings the blonde over with him. I see his hand is on her ass and blush, knowing I shouldn't have been looking.

"Who's this?" Dominic asks.

"I'm Robert Daniels. I was just telling the rest of your band that I enjoyed tonight's show. I come here now and again and I'm glad that I showed up tonight."

"Sorry, but what is it that you want?" Chris speaks up.

"I'm with Delta Record Company. I have seen a couple of your shows but tonight was so raw and different. We're interested in you. If you're interested in us representing you, come to our office nine a.m. Monday and we can talk contracts and strategies. Here is my card, my number and the studios address are both on it. I hope to see you there." He shakes each of our hands and walks away. I pick up the card that is laying on the table with my mouth hanging open.

They did it.

They're going to be famous.

"Fuck yeah! We did it! We fucking finally did it!" Chris stands on his seat. "I'm going to be a rock star!"

🎸—★—🎸

Dominic

Fuck me. I can't believe it. I take the card that Sky is holding and look at it. Shit it's actually happening. Music is my life, my whole world. I know there are hundreds of bands trying to make it big; I never actually thought we would have stood out from the rest.

You were spotted because of the girl with creamy white skin, black hair and deep, dark blue eyes, my head mocks me.

It's true; this guy was here and if Sky didn't stand in we might not have had this chance. Her voice was sexy and smooth, her body flexible and moving so effortlessly. No one would be able to take their eyes off her. I knew I couldn't. I watched her from beginning to end. Fuck, I was so tempted to kiss her. Her body flush against mine. I even got hard when she pulled my hair.

Fuck, I'm getting hard again just thinking about it.

"Dude, we're going to have a record deal. We're going to have albums, tours. This is a fucking dream come true!" Chris jumps off his seat and stands near one of the girls that is flocking him, planting a hard kiss on her. She looks more than happy to accommodate. Who wouldn't? She knows he's going to be big one day.

We all are.

"What about Sherry?" Leon asks. My body that was just on cloud nine falls fast. Fuck, fuck, fuck. *She* is the lead singer. She's been with us from the making of the band. She is a bossy little bitch, but we can't kick her out. I look at Sky and she is looking at her hands. I don't want her to leave either. She was perfect.

Is perfect.

"I was only here to fill in. I'm not taking Sherry's spot," Sky speaks up.

"Sky, you were amazing up there. Sherry..." Lake starts, but Sky interrupts.

"Is the lead singer. I'm not stealing her spot. She earned this,

In the Spotlight

not me. I did one song. She has done so many. This is hers not mine." She stands. "I'm going home. With all that excitement I feel drained. I need my bed." I notice she won't look at me.

"I'll come with you." Lake whispers something in Leon's ear and they both wave before they leave.

"Fuck man, what are you going to do?" Chris looks at me. I notice the girls that were hanging around him are gone too.

"What do you mean, what am I going to do?" I scoff at him.

"Come on man, Sherry may think she's the leader of this band, but it's you. You were the one to start it. It's your choice. We'll go with whatever you say," Leon states, taking a sip from his bottle of beer. I rub my face with my palm.

"Sky said she didn't want to take Sherry's spot. Sherry has been here from day one, so we keep her. I know she has become a total bitch, demanding and a grade A ass but we have to do what's right for the band." Even though I know what is right is the girl who is sleeping across the hall from me.

"Even if Sky rocked it? She was hot out there. The crowd could feel it. I saw how everyone's eyes were mesmerized by her. Even you Dom." Chris wags his eyebrows up and down.

"Fuck off man, I was shocked okay? Come on. Hearing her voice, watching her come out onto the stage, watching her dance. Who could blame me?"

"Well, Lake will kick your ass if you try to touch her. Just warning you." Leon downs the rest of his beer.

"Yeah, got the memo a hundred times. I haven't tried to touch her yet so it's all good. Plus, it was her that came to me on that stage," I say defensively.

"True, but I noticed something that Lake wouldn't like."

"What?"

"How you said yet. You said you haven't touched her *yet*."

Fuck.

Chapter 7

Sky

Lake finally dropped the topic of me becoming their lead singer. Even though Sherry is a bitch, I wouldn't take that from her. She knows all their songs. Knows the band, knows what's what, where I have no clue. I wouldn't know how to set up the equipment, I wouldn't even know if I could remember every single song they have ever written. It's too much pressure and I have made my decision anyway.

That's why you keep thinking about it? I just want to bang my head against the wall.

Dominic invited Sherry over the following day to tell her about Robert. You think she would have been happy that they're finally getting a deal, but no. What she focused on was me singing in her spot.

"What the fuck, you let her sing? You let her sing in my fucking spot? That whore?" She points to me.

"Watch what you're fucking talking about. The only whore in this house is you. At least she doesn't spread her legs to any willing dick that will enter her!" Lake screams back.

"Will everyone calm the fuck down? You fucked up Sherry. You were drunk off your face. Sky was nice enough to step up and sing. Because she did, Robert has shown an interest. That's the point of all this. We are going to get signed. So shut the fuck up and sit down," Dominic seethes at her. "You okay Sky?" He looks at me with concern and I nod, what else could I do?

"She's trying to steal my spot! I want her kicked out of this fucking house. She is trying to 'single white female' me. She wants my fucking life." Her eyes never leave mine and I'm fearing for my life right now. If Lake wasn't blocking the door I would leave.

"Fucking hell, you're such a drama queen. She doesn't want your life. She even said she doesn't want your spot. It was a one off okay? Get the fuck over it. I'm sick of this. This is supposed to be an amazing moment in my life and you're fucking ruining it with your dramatics." Chris lies on the couch, pressing his hand to his forehead.

"Why can't she live somewhere else though? I don't feel comfortable with her living here." She walks to Dominic trying to act all wounded and upset.

"For the last time, this is MY FUCKING HOUSE! It's not Dominic's. It is mine. No, let me correct that. It is mine and Sky's. If she *ever* wants to kick your ass out, she can. You know why? Because this is her house too. Don't like it? Tough shit." Leon has to walk to Lake and put his arms around her waist, probably to stop her from attacking Sherry.

"What the hell? I'm an important member of this band. You should be nice to me, or else."

"Or else what? You'll leave? Go ahead. I am *begging* you. Once you do, I will plead with my sister to take your spot. So don't you dare threaten me. My sister is too nice to take it from you, but if you ever fuck up, I swear I will make her lead singer. She is so much better than you anyway." That comment truly pisses Sherry off.

"I will gut that bitch before she ever takes my spot. This is *my*

In the Spotlight

band."

"No it's not. It's Dominic's. Stop thinking everything is yours. It's not."

"Will everyone calm the fuck down? I'm starting to get a fucking headache with you two bitching at each other. Sky isn't moving out. No buts," Dominic says when Sherry tries to interrupt. "This is Lake's house and it's up to her who stays. Second of all, Sky did say she didn't want your spot so stop thinking that she does. Lake, please don't wind her up about the lead singer role. We are meeting Robert tomorrow, so let's have a goodnight sleep and start the next chapter of our lives," he finishes but stops before walking out the door. "By the way Sherry, stop being a spiteful bitch when it comes to Sky, it's not a good look on you." He winks at me and leaves.

I walk past Sherry to go upstairs but I can feel her eyes on me. I just want tomorrow to come so she can be happy that she got what she wanted. I just want her to see I'm not in the way. I'm a nice person, and could be a good friend if she let me. I get ready for bed and hope sleep can take me away.

🎸 ★ 🎸

I'm standing in front of a huge building with glass windows and doors. A huge sign on top of the door says Delta Records. I didn't want to come this morning but Lake wanted me to be here when the band celebrates their huge deal. They're going to continue using Lake as their manager, as they should. She was the one who has been there for them since day one and booked the gig that even got them noticed.

I knew Sherry wasn't impressed I was tagging along but she didn't say anything. She's probably too busy thinking about becoming a famous rock star. But who wouldn't? Their lives are about to change forever.

I walk in last with Lake and can't help but look around. The walls are pure white while the floors are a shiny black marble. I notice posters of bands and singers in frames hanging on the walls. Gold and platinum albums everywhere.

We walk to reception and I hear Dominic say who they are and we are instructed to go up the far elevator to the top floor. Waiting in the confined space with so many of us, I can feel the excitement radiating from each member.

The doors open and we walk towards another reception desk and a woman who looks like she is in her thirties smiles at us. She is very attractive with her sleek blonde hair tied up and wearing an immaculate grey pants suit.

Another blonde.

"Hi can I help you?" she asks warmly. I see Dominic smile at her. I think it's more than a smile. I'm not surprised; in the short time I have known him, I have seen him charm more blondes than any other. I see her name plate, Carly Renucci, PA.

"We are here to see Robert Daniels. He's expecting us." He leans his arms on the desk and the woman gives him a sultry smile.

"Yes of course. Take a seat and he will see you in a moment." She licks her lips and I quickly turn away and take a seat.

"You okay?" Lake sits next to me, putting her arm around my shoulder.

"Yeah, I'm fine. This is it for you guys. I'm so proud of you. You've made so much of your life in such a short time. I hope I can be like you one day."

"You did help get us here. You'll find your path. I can feel it in

In the Spotlight

my bones." I can't help but laugh at her.

"I love you," I giggle at her.

"Love you too," she replies, pulling me towards her.

"Mr. Daniels is ready to see you now." I look up at Carly and she is opening the main door to which I presume is the office.

"You coming?" Lake asks me.

"Nah, I'll be fine here. You go do your thing." I try and give her a warm smile but I'm sure she knows it's forced.

"You sure..."

"She said she's fine so come on." Sherry stands and walks through the door with the guys following. Dominic looks at me, looking hesitant, but Chris pushes him forward. Lake gives me one quick smile and follows. I sit there and wait.

I don't know why, but I feel a little out of it. I can't explain it, but I feel like they are taking this huge step forward and I am getting left behind, which is stupid. I'm not in the band. I sang one song. But why does it feel like I'm the one who is missing out?

―★―

Dominic

Fuck this is awesome.

I enter the office and see Robert sitting behind a huge, black, glass desk. I guess these people like glass. This place is head to toe with it. Robert is on the phone and signals us all to take a seat. This is it. This is where my life will change. This is day one of the rest of my life. Music is my life and I'm going to let the world know who we are.

"Sorry to keep you." He hangs up and walks around his desk and sits in front of us. "So you thought over what we talked about the other night? We want to sign you. We've been looking for that special something; something raw but powerful. I think that's you. I hope you will let us help you further your career." Fuck this is it.

"Yeah, we're ready. We were born ready to do this. We work hard and we know we can go all the way." I look at Chris and shake my head. God he sounds cheesy.

"I'm sure you will," Robert chuckles at him. "Okay but first off, where is the singer from that night? Shouldn't she be here?" Fuck, fuck, fuck. He wants Sky?

"That girl was just covering for me. I'm the lead singer of the band. I'm Sherry." She licks her lips and sits forward, showing off her legs and tits.

"Could she be any more obvious?" Lake whispers to Leon, but I can hear her.

"I'm sorry, but I liked the other girl. No offense Sherry," he says her name mildly. "When I saw her up on that stage, she was mesmerizing. I couldn't take my eyes off her. Judging by the other people there, and their reactions, the music world will love her. I want her as lead singer. I'm sorry to be blunt, but either she's in or I can't move this forward." With that I feel my heart plummet to the ground. He wants Sky. He wants fucking *Sky*. I don't blame him. Even though I hate how he mentioned that he couldn't keep his eyes off her, she said she wouldn't take the spot.

Shit. Mother fucker. We were so close.

"I can have a word with her. She's right outside." Lake stands but Sherry stands too, looking pissed off.

"What the hell? *I'm* the lead singer. This is *my* band. If you don't accept me, we all walk. Right guys?" She turns and looks at each of us but none of us says a word. This is fucked up but I think about her missing rehearsals, bossing us around. Telling us that we

In the Spotlight

aren't playing our instruments right when she misses a line of a song. She's only been coming to our house more since Sky moved in.

"I'm sorry, but it is how it is." Robert stands and goes to sit back down in his chair.

Fuck.

"You three aren't taking this deal. I fucking forbid it. You wouldn't be anything without me. You guys only got this far because I'm the front lady. I made us who we are. Now let's go," she yells at us. I feel like screaming at her. Who the hell does she think she is?

Forbid us?

Wouldn't be anything without her?

We worked fucking hard on the songs and music.

"You are a two faced mother fucker. You only want to be in this band because you love the attention. You are a pain in the ass. This isn't your band. Fuck. I can't believe this shit. I would have been happy to leave if you weren't a stuck up bitch. You think we aren't good enough huh? Well this guy, who is willing to make us famous and rich, thinks we are. You know what the funny thing is?" Chris walks to her and I can see her biting her lip in frustration. "He doesn't think *you* are good enough to be a part of it. He wants Sky. That's what you're upset about. Because she is better than you and you can't handle it." I'm shocked when I hear a slap. She slapped him.

"Fuck you! No way in hell she is better than me. And YOU are not taking this deal."

"You haven't even heard her sing. She is worth one hundred of you. I *am* taking this deal. I have only put up with your shit because we thought we needed you. We thought you were a part of the team but you only think of yourself. I'm staying. You guys in?" He turns to us.

"I'm in." Leon stands up.

"Me too. Sherry you are one nasty bitch. I know you wouldn't think twice about throwing this band to the gutter if you got an offer that didn't include us." Lake stands and Sherry balls her hands into fists.

"Dominic? You're really going to say yes to this? After everything we have been through?" I look at her and at the guys who have been like family to me. When I really think about it, Sherry has changed into someone I don't even like anymore. I hate what I'm about to do but I need to stand by my band, even if it doesn't include her anymore.

"I'm sorry, Sherry, but I go where they go. You've changed and I don't think it's good for the band. You don't work as hard as you used to. You are either late or not showing up at all. We've worked hard on this. We can't pass it up. I'm sorry."

"You're sorry? YOU'RE SORRY?" she yells at me. "I *am* the fucking band. You will fail. I know you will. Especially with that prude sitting outside. I knew she would fuck this up for me. Well fuck that. She isn't going to get away with it." She walks out the door and Lake quickly follows.

"Nigel, call security," Robert says to someone and we all quickly run out to stop her from doing anything stupid.

Chapter 8

Sky

I'm flipping through a magazine when the office door slams open. I look up and see Sherry breathing hard, her face bright red. She is glaring at me as she runs towards me. I quickly stand and try to run, but she grabs my hair, pulling me towards her. I feel pain shoot through me.

No not this again. Not the hair.

"I knew you were bad news," she seethes in my ear before banging my head against the wall. The impact is so hard I feel lightheaded. "Like hell I'm going to let you take my spot. It's mine. Not yours." She bangs my head again and I scream out in pain. I feel liquid slide down my forehead to my eyes.

"Leave her the fuck alone!" I hear Dominic roar somewhere from behind but I can't see him. "I swear to God Sherry, let her go!"

"Fuck off!" I hear Lake yell. I'm being pulled back by my roots, causing me to groan in agony.

"Get the fuck off me slut. She is going to pay for this." I turn my head, my vision a little blurry, and see Lake is trying to pull Sherry off me but she holds onto me in a tight grip. Dominic holds her at the waist, trying to pull her away from me.

"Fuck, Sherry, stop!" I hear Chris shout. Sherry finally let's go and I fall to the floor, pressing my hand against my head. I pull my hand away and see some blood.

"I'm so sorry, Sky. I'm here." Lake grabs my face and I see a few tears slide down her face. Oh my God, is it that bad?

"Gentlemen, please escort this lady out. If you ever come back here, I will call the police." I hear a voice say that I'm sure belongs to Robert.

"Fuck this studio. Once I'm a huge rock star, you're all are going to pay. You haven't heard the last of me. That I can promise you." I hear some scuffles and then it's quiet again.

"Is she okay?" I see Leon crouch down next to Lake looking me over.

"I should have gotten here sooner. Look what that bitch did." Lake hugs me.

"Sky?" Dominic asks as he crouches down next to me. "Can I have a look?" He is so close to me; I can feel his breath on my skin and my body involuntarily shivers. All I can do is nod. He takes my face in his hands and turns it side to side, checking me over. "Do you have a first aid kit?" he asks out loud to anyone nearby.

"Yeah, come use my private bathroom." Dominic stands and I feel two pair of arms pick me up from the floor. I feel a little dizzy by the impact.

"Come on, let's go clean you up."

"Dominic, maybe I..." Lake tries to interrupt him.

"I got this. Just give me two minutes." We stand there for a moment; I'm still looking at the ground but Lake must have given him permission since we start walking again but my legs feel a little wobbly. "Here, let me." Before I know what that meant, he has me picked up bridal style. I quickly wrap my arms around his neck to get my balance. My heart beats erratically for some reason. I hope he doesn't notice. He walks into a huge office but I don't have a

In the Spotlight

chance to look around properly.

He takes me to a bathroom that has a shower, toilet and sink. Dominic sits me down on the toilet seat and starts looking through drawers and cabinets until he finds a first aid kit. He opens it up and gets on his knees as he looks at my forehead. I can't help but look into his eyes. He looks down into mine and it feels like time has stopped. The first thought that enters my head is his lips against mine. He looks away first and starts taking things out.

"This may sting," he warns before putting some liquid onto a cloth and pressing it against my head. I wince from the sting; hell, that hurts. "I'm sorry she touched you. She's so unpredictable and obviously threatened by you." He keeps on dabbing at my head and I see some blood on the cloth. He takes out a wipe and cleans the wound then takes out a bandage and places it on my head.

"Why would she be threatened by me? Have you seen me?" I try and joke but he looks back into my eyes and I'm sure this time I stopped breathing. His eyes are so intensely on mine; I feel like I'm stuck on the spot.

Frozen.

"I have," he says so softly I barely hear the words.

We stay looking at each other, not moving. I've never wanted to be kissed so badly before. I want his lips against mine. Just thinking it, I lick my lips and I see his eyes go to my mouth. I gasp lightly. He looks back up and then it happens. His lips land on mine. It's so soft and gentle. He starts to open his mouth and I follow.

This is my first kiss.

I'm actually kissing a boy.

A man.

I follow his lead and when I feel his tongue glide against my bottom lip, a whimper leaves my mouth. I hear him growl in the back of his throat and start to feel an ache between my legs. I rub my thighs together to ease it but it seems to intensify it instead. His tongue enters my mouth and I feel like I'm flying. Lost in sensation. I don't know why, but I put my fingers through his hair like I wanted when I first met him, and pull him closer to me. The kiss turns more urgent.

I never want this to stop.

He pulls away from me, breathing hard. I'm wondering why he pulled back when I hear knocking on the door. I didn't even hear it. I press my fingers against my swollen lips, not believing I finally got my first kiss. I just want him to kiss me again but he is shaking his head and standing.

"I'm sorry, I can't do this. I shouldn't have kissed you." He is still breathing fast, pulling his hair. His words hurt. He regrets kissing me. I have to take in a deep breath to make sure I don't let the tears that are gathering behind my eyes fall.

He looks at me one last time and opens the door. Lake and Leon are standing there looking worried. I'm sure I look a mess. I stand up, feeling more steady than what I did before, but my head is now killing me. I look in the mirror and can see a bruise forming under the bandage.

Crap.

"Is she okay?" Lake runs to me, squeezing me, and all I want is to cry and tell her what just happened but I know I can't. I don't want her to be angry at him. It's not his fault he feels nothing towards me.

"She's going to be fine; it's a bad cut but not deep. It's very badly bruised but she'll be fine," Dominic says and walks away. I accidentally let a tear fall and quickly swipe it away.

In the Spotlight

"Does it hurt that bad?" Lake strokes the bandage on my forehead.

"A little, definitely need some painkillers." She helps me up and Leon is on my other side.

We walk back into the office and Robert is leaning against a huge, black, glass desk; Chris and Dominic are talking quietly, sitting down. Lake sits me down next to her. I look at the ground, not wanting to see anyone. I just want to go back home.

"I'm sorry you had to go through that, Sky. You okay?" Chris asks me with concern as Dominic looks anywhere but at me.

"Yeah, I'm fine, just a headache."

"Here, I got you these." Robert walks towards me and kneels down, giving me some tablets and water. I take them, wanting anything to ease this pain.

"Thank you," I whisper.

He smiles at me and I notice he doesn't stand back up. I look at him, really look at him, and notice he is actually quite attractive for someone much older than I. He must be in his early thirties. He has some stubble on his strong jaw. His light brown hair is short on the sides but long on top. His light brown eyes seem so warm. I notice that we are still looking at each other when someone coughs, causing me to feel even more embarrassed, and he finally stands. I look around and see Lake is trying not to smile but I feel eyes on me again and turn to see Dominic glaring at Robert. Why is he looking at him like that?

"Back to business," Robert clears his throat and once again he has a serious tone. "Even after all that, I'm still interested in you as a band but as long as we have Sky as the lead singer."

"Wait, what?" I interrupt and look up.

"Yeah, he wants you as the lead singer. He was telling Sherry that he wouldn't take the band if you're not in it, that's why she went all psycho on you. They want *you*, Sky," Lake beams at me. Maybe it was my head being bashed in but I can't understand how he wants me. I just sang one song. I have no experience in performing.

"You can't have me. I don't even act or look like a rock star. You have to reconsider, I don't think I can do it," I mumble out quickly. I can't do this. They can't rely on me. Lead singer is the front person. The person everyone looks at. God, I would pass out before I even got a word out of my mouth if I was on stage in front of thousands.

"Sky, they want you, which means they think you are amazing. You can do this. You wanted to find your path; this could be it. You'll be working alongside me. I'll be there every step of the way." Lake is holding my hand but I can't seem to digest all this.

"I know it's a lot to take in, but you are a brilliant singer. You have such a good girl appeal. The fans will love you. The good girl with the sex appeal. This will be big for you and your friends." Just hearing him say the word *sex* makes my face turn red. "Think it over. If you agree, then we can set up another meeting and we can talk about the contract," Robert goes on.

I sit there and listen to him go on and on about what will follow next, but the words that repeat in my head is that they won't sign the band if I'm not in it. I look over to Lake and she gives me a bright smile. She is excited for this. I think about the guys bouncing off the walls as we were on our way here; they wanted me to celebrate with them. They wanted something to celebrate. How can I take their dream away from them? Maybe this could be my dream.

"I'll do it," I blurt out, and Robert stops talking.

"What?"

In the *Spotlight*

"You will?"

"Fuck yeah!" They all say at once.

"Yeah, I'll do it. You'll have to be patient with me, but yes I will join your band." Before I have a chance to finish my sentence, Leon and Chris are picking me up onto their shoulders, cheering. I laugh at them as Lake starts doing a crazy dance next to them.

"You won't regret this. We'll take it slow. I can't believe it. We're going to be big, baby." Chris hugs me and I wince, still sore. He apologizes but still laughs in excitement.

"You sure you want to do this?" Dominic looks at me. I can't look him in the eye. I still feel hurt that he regrets that one special moment that I will treasure always.

"Yeah I do," I say softly.

"Welcome on board. Now let us talk about the contract. I brought a lawyer for you to talk it out with so you know what you're signing and they are here as a witness," he continues on. I can't believe I'm the lead singer of a band. But not just any band.

I am now a member of Risen Knights.

Chapter 9

We went through the contract with the lawyer that was provided for us and I knew I shouldn't have signed. Deep down I knew that this couldn't last, but I wanted a piece of happiness, and maybe this could be it. I signed on the dotted line and that was it. My new life is about to start.

We have two weeks till we need to start recording, which means I have two weeks to learn all the songs and for the bruising to heal. I knew some, but others I needed to remember. Lake was nice enough to give me videos she filmed when Sherry was in the band. I still feel bad that I took her spot but then I remember what she did to me. My head still has some light bruising, but it's going down.

I have been stuck either in my room or in the basement with the band helping me. They even rearranged some of the music to suit my voice. I hardly even sleep, wanting to make sure I know this stuff by heart. I don't want to let anyone down.

Dominic has been nice to me but distant at the same time. I'm letting him have his space. I have no idea when it comes to men but, I do know if they are putting distance between you, it's best to just follow. I just hope we can get past this.

🎸★🎸

It's the first day of recording and I'm nervous as hell. We walk back in the glass building and are lead to a recording room that looks three times the size of the one in the basement. Instruments are in a

In the Spotlight

room with a microphone in the middle. This seems even more real now that we are here.

"This is sweet," Chris almost shrieks and heads to the bass guitar. I watch Leon go to the drums, patting it like it's an animal. I walk cautiously to my mic.

"Hi guys. Welcome to day one of the rest of your lives." Robert joins us, rubbing his hands together. "We're going to record as a band then you just by yourselves to make sure we have the perfect sound. So let's get this show on the road." He walks out of the room and enters behind the glass window where a few men already are waiting. I assume they're the ones that record the songs. "You ready?" I hear Roberts voice boom through the room.

"Ready."

"Hell yeah."

"Let's do this," they all say and I just nod.

Robert points to us to start and I feel those butterflies in my stomach again big time. I close my eyes and take in a few deep breaths. Leon starts the drums and after a second, Dominic and Chris join in, then I start. I let the music guide me. Letting it take over. I don't think, I just do. After the song, I finally open my eyes and the guys are high fiving each other.

"That rocked," Chris says excitedly.

"Guys, that was awesome. We're going to go through it a couple of more times, but keep doing what you're doing?" Roberts voice flows in the room again. I stand, waiting to start again, when he talks directly to me. "You okay, Sky?" I look up and he is smiling at me. It's such a nice smile.

"Yeah, I'm good. Just a little nervous," I chuckle.

"Don't be, your voice is amazing. Just keep going, if you need a break, just say." I nod. "Okay guys, from the top." With that we start again. We sing it three more times till we are ready for the next song.

It's three weeks later and twelve songs have been recorded to perfection. Robert even wanted *Poison*, the song I sang at Mitch's, to be on the album. We all did our best and now we're waiting to hear the final product. We are in the dining room eating breakfast when Lake's phone rings and I watch her go to answer it. The guys are talking amongst themselves but I'm in my own world. I had another nightmare last night. This one was different. It felt so real. I was dragged away from the band as well as my sister. I'm just happy it wasn't real. But why do I feel like it's all going to get snatched away from me?

"Guys turn on the radio!" Lake screams before entering the room again. Leon stands and turns on the radio and we listen for just a second before I hear us.

Us playing.

We are good.

"Holy shit," Leon says as he turns up the volume. It's *Poison*. It's so surreal hearing us play. Hearing my voice. We are quiet until the song ends then the DJ's voice comes on.

"That was *Poison* by a new, upcoming band, Risen Knights. I can't wait to see what they come up with next." Leon turns the volume back down and I hear Lake scream as she bounces up and down.

"Fuck, we were good. That was awesome. Holy fuck." I am still sitting there looking at the radio. This is it. Our first song is out there.

"Robert just called to say he was able to put the songs on some

In the Spotlight

radio shows early. He wants to meet us in a few hours to discuss what's next." Lake looks like she is ready to burst.

We all get up and start to get ready. I take a quick shower and get dressed. When I come back down, I see the guys also showered and changed their clothes. We talk about the song until it's time to go. Heading back to the place we've hardly left is starting to feel normal. The people here know who we are and wave and say hello as we head to the elevator.

The blonde, Carly, Robert's PA, is waiting for us and guides us in but I notice she checks out Dominic up and down. I feel myself blush just by how she is looking at him. Robert is standing near the windows when we enter and he is all smiles like normal.

"Hi guy's, thanks for coming. Please, take a seat." We all do. "Okay as you heard, the first song, which is going to be your first single, is out virally. Now we need to get you guys out there physically. Let people know who you are. So the next step is a music video."

"Holy shit," Chris says and I think that's becoming his motto as he keeps saying it.

"I've booked out a set and we start filming in a couple of days. I have a great idea on how I want to lead this. Sky and Dominic, you two looked hot together on the stage when I first saw you, so I think we should keep the fans wanting to know more. Are they, aren't they? That type of thing. So I suggest we start with a bar, Sky with friends having fun until she lands eyes on you," he points to Dominic, "we take it to a date shot then end it with you tying her up. BDSM type of thing since women are all over that Fifty Shades franchise. It will suit the music and has that sex appeal that people want these days.

"We get flashes of you being a normal couple but flashes back into the BDSM thing. What do you guys think?" I'm sure my eyes are bugging out. BDSM is like whips and stuff. I know the words in the song are whips and chains, but to film something like that? Filming me for thousands, even millions to see? Me, half naked?

"I don't think I can do that. You know what I'm like. I'm shy, quiet; how am I supposed to be able to do that?" I think I'm hyperventilating.

"You can do this. It's all going to be professional. Tasteful. It will be only a few minutes at a time, but I really do think this video will do great things getting your name out there. Sex sells in this industry." Robert kneels down in front of me, his hand on mine. "Trust me." I hardly know him, but I know he knows what he's doing. He is the professional.

"Sky, no one is going to judge or look at this distastefully. You can do this. I think this will help you get out of your shell a bit more." Lake puts her arm around me, pulling my head towards her so I'm lying on her shoulder. I know I'm being stupid but it's out of my comfort zone.

"You can do this," Dominic speaks up and, I don't know if it's his voice that gives me strength or that he has faith that I can actually do this, but I agree.

"Okay, I'll try," I whisper. I know this job is going to have harder moments than others but all this is still new to me.

"You will be great." Robert strokes my hand and stands back up. "I've booked a photo shoot as well for next week and after that we will talk about tours. In this line of business, we need to keep going, keep moving, so I'm going to let you guys be the opening act to a more known band, Absolute Addiction. They're getting ready for

In the Spotlight

their tour which you will be joining them on, and when we start to get more of a fan base, we will go bigger and start your own tours, but one step at a time." God this is so much to take in. One step at a time. I'm just going to think of one thing at a time. First thing being this music video.

After the meeting, we all head to a diner to have something to eat. I'm still so full of nerves that I don't think I can eat even if I wanted to. We order burgers and fries and the first thing we start talking about is the music video. Just hearing them go on and on about it makes it sound scarier.

"You okay?" Lake asks me and I just nod. "Come with me." She stands and tells the guys we're going to the bathroom. I follow her and once we are inside, Lake hugs me; she knew I needed it. "Talk to me. Is it the video? I know you weren't happy about it." She looks at me with concern.

"I don't think I can do it. I can do everything he said but it's the... it's the..." I can't even say it.

"The BDSM bit?" I nod. "It's not real. Dominic isn't going to whip you. You know he wouldn't hurt you." Yeah physically, but I don't say that.

"I know that but it's the half-naked thing. I know Robert is going to want me to be in less clothing than I'm used to. I'm going to have to stand there wearing probably just my underwear in front of loads of people. Dominic and Chris are going to see me like that. Leon loves you so I know he wouldn't look, but it's everyone else. How am I supposed to sing if I'm peeing myself in fright?"

"Oh honey. I keep telling you this. You are gorgeous and since you've been living here you've gained weight in all the right places. Your boobs have gotten bigger, you're curvier and your ass is still amazing. If anyone looks, it's because of how hot you are. But they are going to be professional. Just think of how many women they see half naked. They aren't going to make you feel uncomfortable, they're going to try and make you feel anything but. You are going to rock this video and people all over the world are going to see how brilliant you are. They are going to love the song, the video, and you are going to get the praise you deserve. And I will be there every step of the way." She hugs me again and hearing her say all this does help.

I need to grow up and stop with the insecurities. My sister believes in me. She wouldn't make me do this if she thought I wasn't good enough. She is protective of me; she wants what is best for me. I need to stop acting like a baby. I need to pull up my big girl panties and grow up. I'm in the big world now and I need to start acting like it.

"Thank you, Lake. I don't know what I would do without you." I return her hug.

"You'll never have to. I will always be here." I hope so, I really do.

Chapter 10

It's the day of the music video and I've been giving myself a pep talk. *You can do this.* Hundreds of women do this. I watched all kinds of music videos for the last couple of days and women wear hardly anything. Some even go topless, but I will never do that. It's going to be tasteful. Lake has promised she's going to be there just a few feet away so, if I need her, she is there.

A car picked us up from the house and has taken us to a closed up set. I feel like I'm dreaming all this. It was only six weeks ago I showed up at my sister's door and now I am the new lead singer of a band. A band that is going to be famous.

The first person I notice when we pull up is Carly. She sways her hips as she walks towards the car and smiles brightly when she sees Dominic. I'm starting to hate how she looks at him. I hate how he smiles at her in return. They are always touching, laughing. I think at times I feel a little jealous. Why can't he be that comfortable around me? The only time we talk is about band stuff, the music; never anything else. I've been living with him for six weeks and we act like strangers. The first actual interaction we are really going to have since that kiss is going to be on the music video.

Oh what fun, I think sarcastically.

Carly leads us through a building and it's huge. I see at least a hundred people working away with cameras and equipment. I notice one side is built up to look like a night club and there are people wearing going out clothes. Another set is made up to look like a restaurant, another of a beach, and the one that sticks out the most is the BDSM room. There are whips, chains and belts hanging on the wall. I notice a cross in the middle of the room. I swallow harshly, looking at it.

Don't look at it, just keep it out of your head till you have to, my head tries to console me.

I can do this.

I'm a big girl, *I can do this.*

"Welcome," Robert greets as he walks towards us.

He gives me a hug and puts his arm around my shoulder and starts to lead me around the building. I look behind me and notice Dominic is glaring at Roberts arm. Carly is next to him, still talking, but he isn't paying attention. Like he feels me looking at him, he looks up and I see something in his eyes, but it's soon gone before I can figure out what it was.

"This is where the magic happens." Can this guy be any cheesier? I try not to giggle as I think to myself that he has been in this business for far too long. "The dressing rooms are over on the far side." He points at some trailers. "Your make-up artist and stylist are ready. We're starting at the club. You, Sky, will start the song. Look like you're having fun with your friends. Then start looking around the club and when you see Dominic, you keep his stare. Remember though to keep singing until the director says cut. Just like you would do at the movies." I nod. He goes on about the other scenes and luckily the last one we will be doing is the BDSM one so I don't have to think about it till the end. "Any questions?"

"Yeah, I have one," I speak up. We all stop as Robert looks at me with a raised eyebrow, waiting for me to ask away. "Well, with

In the Spotlight

the club scene you're saying I'm with friends. I know they are actors, but I want my sister to be there too," I mumble out.

"What?" Lake asks.

"I want you to be a part of this. It's only a small bit but I think I'll feel more comfortable if she's there. It's my first video and all, and the first scene..." I look at the ground as I talk.

"Consider it done. Would you like anything else?" I look up and he is looking intensely into my eyes and it does something to me that I can't explain. I feel like he is trying to look inside my soul. I just shake my head as I can no longer speak. "Good," he whispers, not taking his eyes away from mine.

"Holy fuck, I'm going to be in a music video," Lake says and Leon is spinning her around. I look back at Robert and he smiles down at me. I can't help but smile in return. "You are the best sister ever." Lake runs to me, squeezing me so hard I can hardly breath.

"I love you. I know you're the manager but I want you to be seen too." I see a few tears slide down her face.

"I love you." She hugs me again.

"I love you, too."

"Okay, now that we've done all this mushy shit, let's do this." Chris claps his hands together and we burst out laughing.

"Right, Sky and Lake go to trailer one and get in your outfits, then head to trailer two for hair and make-up. You guys go to trailer four for your clothes and then trailer six for hair and make-up." Robert directs us.

"Make up? Hell no, I'm not wearing makeup." Chris folds his arms.

"Make-up is required so you look flawless on camera and not too shiny with the lights. All musicians and actors do it," Robert explains.

"Why aren't we going in trailer three and five?" Chris adds in sullenly.

"They are for the directors and crew members. Come on, let's get started. We're probably going to be here till late, so let's get going, shall we?" We all nod and start heading to the trailers.

"I can't believe we are on an actual set. I still can't believe I'm going to be in a fucking music video." Lake is jumping up and down like a school girl.

"God, you swear too much, I think those guys have rubbed off on you," I chuckle at her.

"Well one definitely has." She waggles her eyebrows at me.

"You're so gross." I push her shoulder and she laughs.

🎸—★—🎸

I come out of the trailers wearing a very short, tight, black dress. I can't help but keep pulling down the hem. The shoes, I have to admit, look amazing. Black suede that comes to my ankles and make my legs look even longer than what they actually are. My hair has been cut, giving it more volume. I like how the fringe sways over my eyes a little. The tips are now blue; the hairdresser said that black hair like mine would make the blue stand out. I love it. The dress, on the other hand, makes me feel uncomfortable. I'm sure if I bent over, people would be able to see my ass, it's that short.

"Sky, you look amazing. Could hardly recognize you." Robert walks towards me with his jacket now off, smiling at me as he checks me out. "This is definitely a good choice. Now come with me, they're waiting for you." Robert guides me to the club set and I see people everywhere talking, looking all glammed up.

"Okay, you sit here with your sister. These two girls are also

In the *Spotlight*

going to pretend to be your friends." I hate how he said pretend. My mother use to always go on that the kids at school didn't really like me. That they were only pretending so they could one day use me for their purposes. All the way through school I was always paranoid when someone was nice to me. Here, no one knows who I am or where I'm from. Who my parents are. I'm finally away from their clutches and yet, I feel like they are still here. Telling me to be what *they* want me to be.

"You okay?" Lake asks me. I nod. She is wearing a dark purple dress that cuts low down to her chest. She looks awesome. Her hair looks wild and messy but in a good way.

"Yeah, just nervous," I lie. I hate that I did. I don't like thinking about the people who brought us up. I doubt Lake would want me to bring them up.

"You're going to be great. Just remember, let the music guide you. Sing for *you*." I hug her.

Someone calls out a few instructions and the lights go down. The place has different colored lights flashing around. People who were just mingling before either start dancing or talking. I look around and feel like I'm in a different universe. I hear my name being called, saying that I need to start singing in a moment. They count down. I quickly look at Lake as she squeezes my hand for good luck.

I hear the intro of the song then I sing. I can hear my voice in the background but I sing along with it. The two girls, the actresses, move their lips as they pretend to talk, and laugh. Lake is going with the flow and doing the same. I keep my mind focused on the song. I pick up the glass of water that's supposed to look like an alcoholic beverage. I turn so I'm facing the dancefloor, looking around. The crowd opens up and I see Dominic. He is sitting on the other side of the room.

His eyes focus on me. Chris and Leon are pretending to laugh and talk to each other as Dominic ignores them and keeps his focus on where I am. I continue singing but I feel my body start to heat up. I keep my eyes solely on him. He sits forward, spreading his legs open and leaning down, leaning his arms on them. His eyes never move away as I sing a few more lines.

I watch him stand and slowly start to walk closer to me while people dance around him. He walks so gracefully, like no one else is there. He stops half way and smirks at me and I feel something drip between my thighs because of it. What the hell is happening to my body? I tighten my thighs but it makes it worse so I open them, maybe too widely, and Dominic's eyes go hooded.

"Cut. That was brilliant. So hot. Ok, we are going to take that again. We want a few different angles. Let's start from the top!" someone shouts and I assume it's the producer. I turn myself back around again, wondering how I'm supposed to keep doing this if he keeps looking at me like he could eat me?

It's pretend. He's acting. Exactly what he's supposed to be doing. I know my head is right, but why do I have to get my hopes up that he may actually like me?

🎸★🎸

We've been here for hours and done repeats over and over. I'm tired but when they say the last scene is next, my heart goes spiralling out of control. All the way throughout making this video, Dominic has made me feel things that I can't explain. I get some kind of ache between my thighs and stomach. I even feel like I'm leaking at times. I feel this moisture in my hardly there panties. I need to

In the *Spotlight*

speak to Lake about it but I'm too embarrassed.

I'm in the trailer getting my hair and make-up done, wearing black lace underwear. Luckily they gave me a robe to wear and assured me that I can put it back on as soon as the scene is finished. I'm going to be practically naked and it's going to be in front of hundreds of people.

"All done sweets, go rock them. I can't wait to see the video when it's done. It looks like it's going to be awesome," my stylist says. I give her a quick hug and head out. She has been so nice to me and very patient. She couldn't believe that I've never dyed my hair before. If I did, my parents would have probably cut it all off.

Literally.

Carly is waiting for me and I notice she eyes me up and down before turning and indicating for me to follow her. I am a few steps behind her as we walk and then we are on the set that I have been dreading. The cross stands out, looking so much bigger now that I'm standing in front of it. I raise my hand and stroke along it, waiting for it to bite my hand or something.

"Right, we are all tired and want to go home so let's see if we can do this in one take. Since it's the last scene, I got all cameras around to film at different angles. So Sky, when you're ready love," the director, Austin, says to me. I take in a deep breath and close my eyes as I take the robe off. I feel someone come close and take it away.

Breath.

Just breath.

God, just hurry up so I can go home and die in peace.

"Dominic, you ready?" Austin asks. My eyes are still closed but there's no reply. Then instructions are being yelled out and the music comes back on.

I start to sing again, keeping my eyes closed just for another moment. I suddenly feel hands on my throat and open my eyes to see Dominic standing there, his body close to mine. He isn't choking me to where I can't sing, just firmly holding me. I feel his stubble press against my throat. I'm surprised I haven't forgotten the words or what I'm doing.

He pulls his shirt over his head in one sweeping movement and I'm staring at a body that I'm sure I will never forget. He has lines and bumps all over. His body is perfect. He walks closer to me again and entwines my fingers with his, raising them up in the air. Next thing I know; I'm being strapped to the cross.

When my wrists are strapped in, he stands again in front of me, looking into my eyes. He strokes my cheek and I can't help but close my eyes. I soon open them when I feel his hard erection press against my stomach and I try not to moan. Is he trying to make me slip up on purpose? I see him walk away and come back with a whip. He stretches it in the air, showing off his muscular biceps and brings it back down, whipping thin air.

He walks closer to me and wraps his hand around my throat again. I don't know why, but a part of me kind of likes it. I feel so messed up for thinking it. He grinds himself against me and I try and pull my wrists to touch him but I can't. He moves away from me and brings up the whip in the air and, on the last word of the song, he lashes it down. It never touches me but, in that moment, I accidentally arch my body towards it.

I don't even know why I did.

Dominic

In the Spotlight

I watch Sky as her eyes close and mine roam her near naked body. Seeing her in just her black lace bra and panties causes my dick to stir. God, she is beautiful. I want to touch every inch of her; to lick, bite and kiss her perfect, creamy white skin.

I watch her as she starts to sing, hearing her beautiful voice flow through me, pulling me towards her. I stand in front of her and place my hand gently around her throat, feeling her pulse beat erratically. She opens her eyes, her deep blue's drawing me in, making me want to claim her right here and now, not caring that there are cameras on us.

I take a small step back and pull my shirt over my head and when my eyes land back on hers, I see her taking me in, but I don't care; seeing her desire turns me on. I walk towards her slowly and entwine my fingers with hers, seeing her soft small hands in my tanned big ones, raising them up, making her body stretch as I strap her to the cross. I look down at her and see her breasts being pushed up, I can see her hard nipples poke through.

God how I wish I could see them, taste them.

I stand straight in front of her, meeting her eyes once again, seeing the trust in them. I want to scream at her to never trust me, my thoughts are impure. I just want to pull her panties aside and ram my hard dick into her but, knowing she is a virgin, I could never do that to her.

I stroke her cheek and when she closes her eyes and leans into my touch, I almost cave; something in my head screams at me but it's so faint I can't hear it. Her eyes widen when she feels my erection press against her and I quickly step back and walk to the wall of items, picking up a whip and trying to control my dick.

I stretch my arms out, trying anything but to think about how good she smells, and whip thin air to get rid of my pent up frustration. How can this girl get me so fucking hard that I can't think straight? There are loads of people watching and a part of me doesn't care. I storm towards her and grab her throat once again, looking into her eyes. I can feel her heat against me and I grind myself against her, feeling her body shake at my touch.

I growl in the back of my throat. How can I have this much restraint, seeing her strapped up, her body begging to be touched, to be tasted? I take in a deep breath and walk back and on cue, when she sings the last word, I lash the whip near her and almost come right there and then when I watch her body arch towards the leather.

Chapter 11

Sky

It's been a week since the music video and I've mostly stayed in my room. Robert assured us that we can take a break since we worked so hard on our album and making the video. After the last scene was over, Dominic unlocked me from the cross and I couldn't look him in the eye. I was embarrassed.

He saw me nearly naked and I'm sure he caught me arch myself towards the whip. I bet he thinks I'm a freak. I can't even explain what was going through my head at the time. I try and reassure myself that I was just in the moment but I don't fully believe that.

God I'm so messed up.

Seeing Dominic shirtless is something I won't be forgetting any time soon. I've been avoiding him; trust me, it's hard to do when you're living under the same roof. Lake keeps coming into my room, making sure that I'm okay, but I keep telling her I'm fine and just wanting to enjoy being on my own until my life turns crazy. Well, even more crazy than it is already.

I am laying on my bed flicking through music videos on YouTube; I'm now sure that my favorite music generations are the eighties and nineties. I am a huge fan of power ballads. I love how the songs make me feel so many emotions. It moves me in a way I can't explain. It's like it reaches my soul. I'm hoping that I can do the same one day. Move a listener with my words.

I love musicals since they also show a lot of emotions. I love Phantom of the Opera, Mama Mia, Copacabana; there are so many. I just watched a movie called Teen Witch and I love the cheesy songs but I really like how the plain girl gets the popular guy in the end. If only things like that happened in real life.

I can't believe how much I've missed out on. I feel like I need to watch every film and listen to every song out there. I hate how we couldn't watch TV growing up. How we could only do things that would improve our lives in some way or benefit our parents. Thank God I had dance classes, but why would my parents keep us from watching romance? It's lovely how a girl can meet a boy and fall madly in love. Maybe that's why. They didn't want us to live in a fantasy world. They always drilled in our brains that we needed to live in the real world. And the real world is hard and mean.

I can hear my dad's voice in my head telling us that the world is ready to eat us up and spit us out if we aren't prepared for it. I look at their relationship and not once have I ever seen real affection between them. It's like they lived under an understanding. I definitely don't want to live like that, even though I know they had plans for me to.

I am re-watching Copacabana when there is a knock on my door. If it was Lake she would have knocked and walked in, not caring if I was naked or something.

"Come in!" I shout and take Lake's laptop, which I have basically kidnapped, off my knees and place it in front of me. I see Dominic poking his head in and I'm shocked that he is here.

"Can I come in?" he asks warily.

"Sure." I scoot up on the bed and move the laptop to the side of me so he has space to sit down. He lets himself in and sits across

In the Spotlight

from me. "Anything wrong?" There has to be something wrong for him to seek me out. Yes, I've been avoiding him, but it's not like him and I have been very close since I've been here, anyway. Except for the kiss.

"I was just wondering how you are? I haven't seen you since the shoot and wanted to make sure you're okay?" I see him scratching the back of his head and can tell he's a little nervous or maybe embarrassed.

"Yeah, I'm fine. I guess I'm still a little out of it since the shoot. I just hope it turned out okay. I was so nervous and the last scene..." I stop. Great, why did I have to bring it up? I feel my cheeks heat up. Great.

"You were brilliant. Trust me. The last scene..." He pauses and looks into my eyes and I feel like I'm back there.

The way he was looking at me then is how he is looking at me now. He closes his eyes and quickly looks around my room. "You were good. Won't be long till we see it. Exciting though, huh? Us being in a music video. I waited my whole life for this and now it's actually happening. It's all because of you. I just want to thank you for what you're doing" He smiles at me and it's such a beautiful smile. It lights up his whole face and I feel my cheeks flush at his words.

"I think you would have gotten here with or without my help. You are very talented. You and the guys but, yeah, I never thought I would ever be in a band let alone making a music video. If you asked me six months ago if I saw my life like this..." I shake my head, chuckling. "I would have laughed in your face and told you that you were crazy." *I would have prayed just to breath without worrying I was doing something wrong, to worry that I'm a disappointment,*

I think sadly to myself.

"You okay?" He asks, his words breaking me away from my thoughts.

"Yeah, sorry, was just thinking." I clear my throat. "Anyway, you wanted to be a rock star all your life?" I ask, trying to change the subject.

"Yeah. When I was six I heard my dad play Guns N' Roses over and over. I loved how they sounded. Loved the guitar solos. I knew that's what I wanted to be. A guitarist. My parents encouraged it. They saw how passionate I was. Me complaining non-stop helped." He laughs and I giggle with him. "They got me lessons and bought me my first guitar when I was eight. Best birthday ever." He smiles but I see sadness in his eyes. I know this doesn't have a happy ending. Then it occurs to me. He's never mentioned his parents or visited them; they've never come here.

"What happened?" I ask softly, already knowing the answer. Just thinking it makes tears form behind my eyes.

"They passed away when I was fifteen. Car accident." He pauses and looks up to the ceiling. "They were good parents. They loved each other so much and they loved me. I guess I should be grateful that I have so many good memories but I wish they were here now, to see me and that all their hard work encouraging me, spending money on my music, has gone to good use. That I'm actually following my dream." He looks back down at me and I hate how a few tears have fallen. He leans forward and uses his thumbs to wipe them away, giving me a soft smile.

"I'm so sorry. They sound amazing," I whisper.

"They were. I don't know your past but I do know you had a hard life growing up. Lake never talks about your parents. I know

In the Spotlight

it's something bad and I'm sorry you didn't grow up the way you should have. You and Lake are such good people. That's why I'm grateful for the time I had. I know wherever they are, they're proud of me." I lean forward and hold his hand.

"They are. How could they not be?" He gives me a warm smile and looks at our hands but, luckily, doesn't let go. I don't want him to let go yet.

"Leon, Chris, and Sherry were my family after. When Lake let me and Leon move in, I knew that they were my new family. I can't imagine my life without them now. They've been there for me and I would do anything for them." He's still looking at our joined hands.

"I know they love you, thank you for being there for my sister. I'm glad she found you guys." I truly am. I'm glad she found decent human beings.

"Anyway, what are you watching?" I chuckle at his change in subject. I let go of his hand, even though I didn't want to, and grab my laptop. He moves so he is at my side while I place it on my knees and he comes in for a closer look. His smell surrounds me.

God he smells amazing.

"Copacabana. I was looking at videos on YouTube and this one song showed up and I was hooked, then realized it's actually a movie." I press play and it's almost at the part that I love. It's where he sings the song to her, *Who Needs to Dream*. It's such a beautiful song. "I love this song," I speak out my thoughts and he crosses his arms and watches with me.

He stays at my side through the rest of the movie. We both laugh at certain points and at the end I can't help but cry. I hate the ending. The ending sucks. They finally get together and he dies. She grows old on her own, missing her true love. I grab a tissue from my side table and wipe away the tears. I look up at Dominic and he's staring at me. He grabs the tissue from my hand and dabs under my eyes softly.

"You're a romantic aren't you?" He smiles at me.

"Yeah, I guess I like to believe people get their happily ever after's. I hate how he dies." I feel myself wanting to cry all over again. Why do I have to be such an emotional wreck over something that isn't real?

"You big softie." I laugh and nudge his shoulder with mine. "What else you do you enjoy watching?" He takes off his shoes and makes himself more comfortable.

"You really want to watch more with me?" I can't help the smile on my face.

"Yeah. We're living together, in a band together. We're probably going to be stuck with each other for a very long time so I think we should get to know each other. Be friends. My first friendly duty is to watch sappy chick flicks." I laugh at his playfulness. Friends. I can do that. He shared something with me and I do need more friends.

"Okay, friends. Well friend, lets watch Teen Witch. There are some catchy songs in that film." I start loading it up.

"Play away." And we proceed to watch movies I have been addicted to into the early hours of the morning.

---★---

I wake up feeling more hot than usual. I open my eyes and try and move my body but it's being pinned down and my heart beats frantically. I've been good. I haven't done anything wrong. I feel myself start to sweat with fear when I hear a low groan next to me and I realize that it's Dominic. I'm in my room. My new room.

In the Spotlight

I take in a few deep breaths until my breathing is more under control and turn my head to see Dominic is fast asleep next to me and his body is entwined with mine. His arms wrapped around me. Just knowing he's here relaxes me. He stayed all night? I can't even remember falling asleep. I see the laptop is on the side table on his side so he must have put it there but decided to stay. I feel my heart swell that he did.

I like how my body fits in next to his. Like I was made for him. I snuggle back down and entwine my fingers with the ones that are holding onto my stomach. I feel him adjust his fingers and he pulls me in closer. I'm sure I'm smiling like an idiot. I enjoy the closeness for a little while until sleep takes me once again.

🎸—★—🎸

We are sitting in the living room watching VBox a music station on TV. It's the day of our video premier and I'm nervous. Millions of people are going to be watching it. I don't even know what to expect. I'm going to watch myself on TV for the first time. Lake is sitting next to me and Dominic is on my other side.

I was expecting Dominic to wake up and freak out that he slept next to me but he was fine. He even said that he hasn't slept so well in years and I felt like doing a little dance of joy. We started hanging out more and more over the last few days. He'll do his own thing, but will eventually come to my room and suggest a movie. I told him that me and Lake didn't really watch that many movies growing up. He never judged or pressed the issue but suggested films that he loved watching.

The movies he likes are way too boyish or scary. How can anyone watch a movie with a killer clown who climbs through drains? Or a man with knives as fingers who enters your dreams?

That is so messed up. I told him I wouldn't watch another horror ever again. I wouldn't be able to sleep at night if I watched anymore. He laughed, calling me a girl to which I reminded him that I was one.

I like seeing this side of him. I feel like we've actually become friends and he's even offered to teach me to play guitar, and in return, I would teach him to dance. He told me he loved how I moved so gracefully and would like to learn. He said we never know if he'll need to know one day for a future music video. Just thinking of another video makes my tummy go funny. I just hope I'm more fully dressed in the next one.

VBox goes to another break and we groan in frustration; we just want to see it. Robert thought it would be more exciting if we saw the final product on live TV but now I wish I said something and told him to let us see it once it was ready. The break is finished and the host is talking about a new upcoming band and butterflies erupt in my stomach. Then I hear the intro to our song. Lake screams near me but my eyes are glued to the screen.

I know it's me, but seeing myself all dressed up, I can hardly recognize the girl on the screen. I look beautiful. Hearing my voice burst through, I feel like I'm watching someone else. We all look so perfect. The song is perfect. It starts off in the club but we get flashes of me and Dominic in the BDSM scene. We look so good together which I'm shocked about. Seeing his eyes on me in the video, seeing how I look like I could jump him any moment. My body language and eyes are screaming for him. I knew I was attracted to him but to see it up close is something else entirely.

It's towards the end and I feel like I'm watching porn or something. Watching something I shouldn't be. Dominic, half

In the Spotlight

naked, pressed against my own near naked body. How he touches me. Then it's the scene with the whip. We watch as he grabs it off the wall and releases it towards me. It looks like he actually whipped me by how it cuts to my body arching. Then it's over.

"Holy fuck, I can't believe it. That was fucking amazing. I can't believe I was in a music video." Lake is jumping up and down on the couch, Leon laughing at her.

"Even with the make-up, I still looked hot. But you two," he points to me and Dominic, "you looked hot. Robert was right. People are going to think something's going on." He arches an eyebrow.

"Well it worked. I just can't wait to see it go to the charts. I hope we get in the top ten," Lake screeches.

"Fuck that! Number one baby," Chris corrects her, chuckling.

"You okay?" Dominic asks me.

"Yeah, just seeing it... It's crazy." I don't know what else to say. That we looked amazing together. That I enjoyed being that intimately close to you?

"Yeah, but if it's any consolation, you looked amazing." I smile at him and he smiles back at me.

Friends. Remember, we are just friends.

But why do I want more?

Chapter 12

Poison reached number one on the charts. Number one. We were hoping to be in the top ten, well Chris wanted number one, but we were trying to be realistic. Seeing it on TV and hearing it on the radio is insane. People are going crazy over the video. Lake had to create a Facebook fan page for the band and thousands have already pressed like. They've been commenting on how hot the video is, asking if me and Dominic are an item in real life. I guess Roberts intuition was right.

People want to know what's next, when the album is going to be released, when is there going to be another hot music video? It's absolutely crazy. Strangers messaging just to say how much they loved the song and how much of a brilliant singer I am. It's amazing how they take time out of their everyday lives just to say that.

Robert had booked us a photo shoot and set up an interview for the following day so people can learn more about us and the band. We were ushered into a grey building where the photo shoot is being held and waiting to be told what to do. Lake even dressed up in a suit so she would look professional as the bands manager. The guys are looking around in excitement and awe but I feel anxious and nervous. This is happening way too fast. I was hoping we would be taking baby steps into the music world but I feel like I'm being thrown in the deep end.

Right now I feel like I'm drowning.

In the Spotlight

I hate how insecure I'm feeling but, in three months, my life has been turned upside down and it's getting crazier each passing day. I feel like I can't breathe at times. Lake and Dominic keep telling me how amazing I'm doing but on the inside, I'm shaking.

I can hear my parents mocking voices in my head telling me how I'm going to let my new friends, my new family, down. I know if Sherry was here she would be in her element. Everyone looking at her. Everyone expecting her to know what she's doing. She would meet every task without thinking twice about it. I hate to think this but, at times, I regret saying yes. I was brought up in one controlling world and I feel like I've just been pushed into another.

Expectations to be good, to do better.

To *be* better.

I see an older man with glasses on top of his bald head walk towards us. He eyes each one of us up and down. He's wearing a pair of dark blue skinny jeans and a light pink shirt but they scream designer. They scream expensive.

"Hello, I'm the photographer. Robert has already told me what he wants for this shoot so let's get you into hair and makeup and in your outfits. I know this is all new to you but try to relax and have fun," he says, giving us a smile that doesn't help with my nerves.

"Fuck, make-up again? I'm going to grow a pussy at this rate," Chris complains.

"Joe, Keela. Take Risen Knights to where they have to be." He clicks his fingers and two people show up who I assume is Joe and Keela. Joe, who is very tall but very skinny, takes the guys away and Keela is left with me. She has short blonde hair that frames her perfect face.

"Hi, I'm Keela. Follow me." She shakes my hand quickly and

hooks her arm through mine.

"Umm, can I bring my sister please?" I stop and ask. I need Lake. I need her beside me.

"Umm, sure," she says, looking at me oddly. She probably isn't use to rock stars being a nervous wreck.

"Lake!" I shout to her. She's on her phone but rushes over.

"Everything okay?" I want to tell her no, but I know I can't.

"Can you come with me?" I plead to her. Her eyes soften and she puts an arm over my shoulders.

"Of course. I wouldn't be a good manger if I didn't please the lead singer," she jokes.

We follow Keela into a huge room with a desk and mirror full of makeup, a counter full of hair supplies, and in the far corner is a rail of clothes. Keela tells me to sit on a chair near the hair stuff and tells me someone will see me shortly. Why couldn't the people who did my hair and makeup before be here? At least I started to feel more comfortable with them.

In thirty minutes, my once straight hair is now a wavy mess and my makeup is a little gothic. Grey, smoky eyeshadow, black eyeliner, and mascara. My skin looks flawless and my lips are a dark brown. The person looking back at me in the mirror isn't me. My reflection looks like a rock star but the person she is staring at isn't. I'm taken to the rail of clothes and I groan when they show me what I have to wear.

Underwear.

Black lace matching underwear with a garter belt and stockings. No shoes.

How can they keep expecting me to wear this? Robert knows how I feel about this. He knows I have no self-confidence to wear

In the Spotlight

this stuff. I'm going to be in magazines half naked. What if my parents see me? What if someone shows them what I've done? To them, this is like porn. I can picture their angry faces looking at me like I'm dirt. Worse than dirt.

"Lake, why do I have to wear underwear again? I can't keep doing this." I sit on a nearby chair with the underwear in my hands. I just want to cry and hide under my covers.

"Sky." Lake kneels down and holds my hand. "I know you don't like this but you're thinking way too much on how people are going to see you. People wear underwear on shoots all the time. It's like wearing a bikini." *I wouldn't wear a bikini either,* I think sullenly.

"I can't do this. I'm sorry but we said baby steps, this isn't baby steps, Lake. I'm not like you. Maybe after a while I'll feel more comfortable in my own skin, but I'm not there yet. Please help me." A few tears escape.

"Right. Let me handle this. I'm not letting you do this shoot if you don't feel comfortable. Let me go have some words. I'll be right back." Lake stands up and heads to the door.

"What if they tell us to leave if we don't do it their way?" I bite my lip. That's the last thing I would want. I don't want to ruin this experience for everyone.

"Well tough. They can't make you do shit. Let me sort this." With that, she's gone.

I keep telling myself that I can be more like her but I can't. For twenty-one years I have been told to dress in a certain way, think in a certain way, and it's going to take time for me to shake that off.

If I ever can.

Then how come Lake can dress sexy, talk like a sailor and have a man who wants her? She lived in that house too, that nasty voice enters my head again.

Not long after, Lake comes in and walks straight to the rails, flipping through the clothes. She doesn't say anything until she picks out a long white shirt with a smile on her face. "I made them a deal. Would you be able to wear the underwear with this shirt over it but unbuttoned?" I look at the shirt and it looks long enough to cover my ass. I could cry that she actually did it. I stand up and hug her.

"Thank you so much. It's so much better than just wearing this." I pick up the lace.

"What are managers for? You go put all this on and tell me what you think." I go to the dressing room and put everything on. The shirt is long enough to cover most of my body. I walk back out and Lake whistles when she sees me.

"Wow, you look hot. You feel better?" I look in the long mirror and I still look sexy but I feel more comfortable going out there.

"Yes, thank you again for doing this. I was so worried that they would think I'm some sort of diva making demands."

"I explained you weren't comfortable and they understood. So let's get your sexy ass out there and show the world how hot you are." She holds my hand and guides me out.

Yeah, let's show your parents what you've become.

Shut up brain.

People are everywhere setting up the shoot, moving around lights, and I see the photographer messing with his equipment. He still hasn't said what his name is. I'm still looking around me when my eyes stop on Dominic, Chris, and Leon. They're all shirtless. I'm sure my mouth is hanging open. We walk closer and when their eyes meet me their mouths drop open too but I can't keep my eyes off Dominic. I don't think I'll ever get use to how gorgeous he is. His

In the spotlight

eyes are trained on me and I smile to myself.

"God, this life suits you Sky. You get hotter and hotter each time." Chris walks up to me and holds my hands, spreading them out so he can eye me up and down. I quickly pull away and cover myself a bit more.

"Chris, pack it in," Lake scolds him.

"Sorry Lake, but damn." Chris looks me up and down again.

"Let's get started!" the photographer shouts out and I'm glad that he did so we can get this over with and I can get back in my normal clothes. "Sky, I want you in the middle, Dominic on your right, Chris on your left and Leon, go on one knee in front." We all get in our positions. "Sky, turn to your side and look up at Dominic. Dominic, put one hand on her waist, the side that is angled towards the camera, looking down at her. Chris press your front to her back and look down to the right. Leon you look forward." Feeling two men touching me makes my heart race. The one touch I can feel the most is Dominic's.

"Hey, look at me," Dominic's voice caresses over me. I look up, staring into his eyes. "Just keep looking at me, okay? Don't look away." I do as he says. I hear clicks of a camera as picture after picture gets taken. We get told where we should stand and what to do but I never stop looking at him.

"Okay, this time Dominic, lean your forehead down onto Sky's. Sky keep your face forward but look up. Chris and Leon stand on either side of them and stare ahead at the camera." I close my eyes as I feel Dominic stand in closer. His forehead presses against mine and I can feel his breath on my face.

"Look at me," he whispers. He presses his thumb and index finger on my chin and I look up. My mouth opens a little, letting the breath I've been holding in, out. His lips are so close. I could just stand on my tip toes and they would be on his. He lets go of my chin and his hands glide down my arms, his fingers go under the shirt, touching my skin gripping onto my waist, pulling me in closer to him.

"That's perfect. Okay guys, that's all we need." Just like that I fall back down to the real world. Dominic looks down at me one more second then takes a few steps back. I miss his heat. I'm getting too used to his heat surrounding me. "You guys did great. I'll send these over to Robert and he'll pick the ones he wants to use. I hope to work with you all again." The photographer beams at us and shakes our hands.

I feel like I'm still in a fog. It felt like we were there for maybe five minutes but, as I look at the clock, I'm shocked to see we've been doing this for about an hour. Where did the time go? I head back to the room I got ready in and dress back into my normal clothes. When I'm putting on my cardigan, Keela walks in.

"That was awesome. I never would have guessed this was your first photo shoot. You looked like you've been doing this for years." Keela smiles at me. I give her a small smile in return. I don't mean to be rude but I feel a little deflated.

"Thank you. Dominic just told me to keep my eyes on him and I did. If it wasn't for him, I would have probably looked like an idiot." I try and chuckle.

"Who wouldn't want to look at Dominic? He is one fine piece of ass." I don't know why, but I hate seeing that dreamy look on her face. "Donald said you can take the underwear and shirt. He's good like that." Who is Donald?

"Donald?" I speak out my thoughts.

In the Spotlight

"The photographer." She giggles. "He's been in this field for so long he assumes everyone knows who he is. So take the underwear, you never know when you'll need them. Or for whom." She winks at me and I blush.

"I don't think so. I don't think I would wear them again."

"I think Dominic would love to see you in them again. The way he was looking at you, damn it was hot." The way he was looking at me? He was trying to calm me. I just over thought the rest. Like I always do.

"Dominic is just a friend," I tell her.

"Damn, I would love a friend like that. How can you be around him and not want to jump him? I've only been around him a short time and I'm ready to take him to a secluded room," she laughs. I cringe at the thought. She is blonde and beautiful.

Dominic's type.

"I'm not that kind of girl. But like I said, we're just friends. Wouldn't want to ruin that." *Liar* my head shouts at me.

"Yeah, sometimes that's best; you wouldn't want to ruin that friendship or, worse, break up the band. Plus, with all the groupies in the near future what guy could say no to that?" I know she's trying to be nice but does this girl not know when to be quiet?

"Yeah," I mumble.

"Well, take the underwear and shirt if you want. I hope to see you again. Good luck with your music. I hope you make it big." She winks then walks out. I look at the underwear I folded up on one of the counters and bite my lip. With one quick decision, I pick them up and put them in my bag.

You never know, right?

I leave the dressing room and the guys and Lake are waiting for me. The guys are back in their normal clothes and I chuckle as I see Chris try to charm Keela. She's fluttering her eyelashes and twirling her hair; he seems to be eating it up. I walk towards Lake and Leon and he is whispering in her ear as she giggles at whatever he is saying.

"Sky, we're going to head back. Leon and I need to... talk." She giggles again as Leon nibbles her ear.

"Yes, we got lots to talk about. Lots and lots," he huskily says into her neck; it doesn't take a genius to know what they really mean.

"Well, while you guys go and umm... talk... Sky you want to order a pizza and watch some movies?" Dominic walks over to me, putting his arm over my shoulder, squeezing me into him.

"As long as it's not a guy-flick or a horror movie." I laugh when he knuckles my head, messing up my hair.

"You are no fun. What other movies are there?" He stops messing up my hair but keeps his arm over my shoulder.

"A comedy?" I suggest.

"Okay. A comedy. Let's go guys." We start to head out but I turn to see Chris is still with Keela. Dominic turns to see what I'm looking at.

"Chris, you coming?" Dominic shouts to him.

"I'm hoping to," Chris responds and Keela chuckles at him. How can she like what he just said? "I'll catch you guys later." Dominic nods and we walk outside. I feel a chill but Dominic pulls me in closer to keep me warm.

We head back home and Leon and Lake head straight to their room. Dominic orders a pizza as I head to my room to get into my PJ's. I want to be comfortable in case I fall asleep. I do feel tired, but no way am I passing up spending more time with Dominic.

Chapter 13

I wake up the next day with Dominic at my side. He fell asleep half way through the movie and I didn't have the heart to wake him. Besides, I like sleeping next to him. I don't have bad dreams when he's near me. I like how subconsciously he reaches out to find me and pulls me in close to him. It's the best part of the day waking up in his arms. Feeling his breath on my skin.

It's the day of the interview and I'm hoping that the guys take over the majority of the talking part. They are the band and I'm just the lucky girl who came at the right time. Well, lucky if you're normal. Everyone wants to be famous. To not have to worry about money. I'm already financially okay so it isn't a motivator for me. I guess I'm so use to being in the background that it's frightening being the one up front.

Lake dresses me in dark jeans and a white T-shirt with a short leather jacket that took me twenty minutes to agree to wear. I reminded her that Mom and Dad always said people who wear leather are bad news and I don't want people thinking that of me. Lake assured me that the knowledge they threw down my throat is bullshit and leather just makes me look the part of a rock star. I do look good but, still, bad habits die hard.

Again a car is waiting for us and takes us to a hotel that, most likely, celebrities and very rich people stay in any chance they get. It screams expensive and private. Heading up the elevator to a conference room, I can't stop playing with the zipper on my jacket. Dominic had to pull my hand away and hold it to ease my nerves. He whispered to me to relax and just answer the questions honestly and we will be fine.

Easier said than done.

I just hope they don't ask me anything I'm not comfortable answering.

We are taken down a hall and to a small room with a few grey couches and a table on the far end with food and drinks. Chris heads straight there, grabbing a bottle of water and picking at the fruit. I sit on a couch and Lake sits on my left with Leon next to her as Dominic goes to the table and talks to Chris, laughing then coming back with a bottle of water for each of us and sits on my right.

We wait just a few minutes until a very short woman with short, spiky, white hair enters. She has two guys with her holding bags and heads towards us, sitting on the couch opposite us.

"Thank you for coming. Sorry I'm late, traffic was hell. Robert filled me in on what's happening in your career so far so I don't act like an idiot and ask stuff that is irrelevant. I like to pretend that I know what I'm doing," she laughs and I giggle with her. I like her already. "I'm Vera by the way." She chuckles again. "I'm going to set up two recorders, so just pretend they aren't there, and these two next to me are my PA's; Steve and Eddie." They give us a quick wave. "They're going to write notes as we talk. I want you to feel comfortable and just go with it. Just say whatever is in your head. Honesty is best though. You want the fans to know the real you. Any questions before I begin?" We all shake our heads.

"Okay." She plays with the recorders and places them in front of us on the coffee table. "Right, why don't you introduce who you are, and give your age and marital status." That's easy. We each answer. Chris had to make a show that he is single and wanting any girl to try and change that.

"Dominic, you're the one that created the band. What made you want to be a musician?" I tense up, knowing now that he did this for his parents. Without thinking, I place my hand on his. He looks down at our hands then back up at me, giving me a small smile.

"My dad used to play rock music all the time when I was growing up. I knew I wanted to be a part of that world. They encouraged me to follow my dream and I did," he pauses taking in a deep breath. "They passed away and I told myself that I would still follow my dream." He looks at the ground but I don't let go of his hand.

"I'm so sorry to hear that. Well, you sure did follow your dream; your new single is already in the number one spot in the charts," she says, trying to change the mood.

"Yeah, they would be so proud of you. You earned it to be here," I jump in. I turn my head towards her and she is staring at me with a smile.

"How did you meet Leon and Chris?" she asks Dominic.

"We've known each other since we were kids. We went to the same school and I guess we had music in common and have been inseparable ever since."

"I heard you had another lead singer before Sky took the spot. Are you happy with the new change?" she asks everyone.

"Hell yeah. Sherry was so full of herself. Sky works hard. Even though she hasn't done this before, she puts her whole heart into it. I honestly don't think we would have gotten this far if it wasn't for her," Chris answers. I beam at him and he gives me a wink.

"Do the rest of you feel the same?"

"Yeah totally. Her voice is amazing and I'm glad she agreed to sing for us," Leon pipes in.

"She's brilliant, what more is there to say?" Dominic shrugs but smirks at me.

"Sky, the guys seem to be happy that you joined when you did. What's it like to be the new lead singer? How are you handling this crazy life?" She swipes her hand around the room, indicating the music world.

I giggle. "Well it took me by surprise that's for sure. I wasn't expecting to be in a band, no less a lead singer. At times it feels overwhelming but I have my big sister who looks out for me and the guys have been amazing, bringing me in with open arms. They've been patient and helping me when I need it."

"So the manager is also your big sister. Have you two always been close?"

"Yeah we have. I've always looked up to her. I wanted to be just like her; I still do. I don't know what I would have done if it wasn't for her being there for me. I love her to bits."

"Sky grew up with music in her veins. She was always the lead in plays. Always getting the solos. She was made for this world. I've always been her number one fan," Lake joins in.

"That's nice, being able to work alongside of one another. I heard, Lake, that you are also dating the drummer, Leon?"

"You heard right. He's my man. We've been together for about five years now. He helped me follow my dream, even though I didn't know it was my dream at the time. He helped me be me. I owe him my life for loving me so much." She smiles up at Leon and he leans forward and kisses her softly on the lips.

In the Spotlight

Vera asks more questions about each of us and I have fun answering each one directed at me. We have a good time laughing and it's been a joy hearing stories about the guys growing up and the mistakes they made along the way. But I knew it would be too good to be true, for it to be sweet sailing.

"So, I think what the fans have been dying to know is if there is any kind of romance between the lead singer and the guitarist? Are you just as hot off the screen as you are on?" I feel myself blush; my face feels like it's on fire.

"We're just good friends," Dominic answers. "We've gotten close over the months, being in a band together and living together."

"So, no chemistry between you two? I saw the video and, man, it was hot." Vera fans herself. "You're telling me that it's just good acting?"

"Like I said, we're close."

"I bet you are." She winks.

"One last question. You ready to leave your home town for life on the road?"

"Hell yeah," Chris answers.

"Yeah, it's part of the job," Leon replies.

"We'll go where we need to go. We want to get our music out there. I'm looking forward to seeing more of the world," Dominic says.

"Sky what about you?"

"Well, it's going to be new to me but, as long as I have the guys and my sister, I'm sure I will be just fine." God, I sound cheesy.

"That's it guys. That was brilliant. Think we covered a lot. Help yourselves to the food. I'm sure we'll see each other again." She shakes our hands and I watch her pack up her stuff and leave the room.

"God, that was crazy. I think I know you guys so much better now," Lake laughs and heads to the table of food; I follow her since my stomach is starting to grumble. "You did good, Sky. Proud of ya." I smile at her.

"Thank you for answering the family life part. I didn't know what to say. I was frozen." Vera asked each of us about our parents and I didn't know if I should be honest or lie. Lake, though, answered saying we aren't close to our parents and they don't really approve of our career paths and luckily nothing more was said.

"What are you two whispering about?" Leon asks from behind us.

"You, like always." Lake licks her lips and Leon's eyes follow the movement. Geez, do they ever cool off?

"You two are starting to get too sickly for me," I joke as I hold my stomach.

"Oi, you." Lake pushes me and I laugh. "Not my fault we can't keep our hands off each other."

"I'm going over there before I throw up. Try not to eat each other." I walk away and hear Leon whisper that he wants to eat her and I groan.

"You did amazing," Dominic says as I sit back down next to him. I pass him a bottle of water that I picked up before leaving the table.

"You don't need to keep praising me when I do okay," I chuckle. "But I do like a good praise." *Yeah, because you never got it growing up.*

"I just like you to know that you're doing well. I don't want you to ever think you aren't brilliant."

In the *Spotlight*

"Thank you." I smile at him.

"Anytime." He winks at me. "You wanting to head back home? I can start giving you those guitar lessons before Robert gives us more chores." I try and act neutral but the smile on my face has a mind of its own.

"I would love that."

"Great, let's go," he responds and we stand.

"Lake, we're heading back home," I shout to her. Leon surprised her with a room here so they are staying, but Lake looks back and forth between us, biting her lip.

"Okay. Dominic can I have a quick word?" she asks, trying to keep the smile on her face but it seems off.

"Sure. Be right back." I nod and sit back down.

🎸 ★ 🎸

Dominic

I watch Sky sit down and I head towards Lake. She looks at Sky and back to me. I hate the way she's looking at me. I feel my blood boiling, knowing what she wants. I haven't even touched Sky. Okay, that's a lie. I kissed her. Fuck me, I miss her lips. The music video, the photo shoot. It took so much will power to not drag her somewhere and taste her. Feel her.

Devour her.

Her big, dark blue eyes look at me with so much trust. I love being around her. She's finally gotten out of her shell when she's around me. I watch her laugh, cry, smile at the silliest things. Watching that film, Copacabana; watching her cry at the end. It was like she was experiencing their pain. She is beautiful on the inside as well as out. Who could blame me for wanting to be around her? Wanting to be close to her.

"Lake, don't even start with this shit," I whisper shout.

"Don't think I haven't noticed you hanging out with Sky more and more. Don't you dare hurt her, Dominic. Don't ruin the band. We're actually getting what we worked so hard for. Don't think with your dick, okay?" she whispers loudly back

"Lake, I'm her friend, which means I'm going to be around her. She only has you and half the time you're with Leon. You want her to be alone most of the time?" I pause. Lake looks back at Sky with sadness in her eyes. "You have your life, too, but she needs more than just you. You can't be with her all the time. We just hang out. It's been three months; thought you would know that I wouldn't dare hurt her." I would rather chop off my own arm before I would ever hurt her.

"You're right. I'm sorry. Just be nice to her okay? Just seeing how she is with you and seeing the music video and the shoot, you can't blame me. I'll back off. But," she points her finger at me, "you touch her, you fuck with her; I will cut off your dick." This girl is messed up.

"Right. I'm off. Enjoy your room."

"We will." Leon picks up Lake and pins her to the wall. Fuck, can they not at least wait until we're gone?

"Ready?" I ask Sky and she stands up. She looks over at Lake and Leon and seeing that blush form on her chest and face is so adorable.

"Yeah, let's go." She walks out of the room, well, practically runs out.

"You ready for your first lesson?" I try and make conversation and seeing her face light up as she smiles hits something in me that I can't explain. I love seeing her happy.

In the Spotlight

"I'm so excited. Maybe in time I'll be as good as you."

"I'm sure you will. You could even play on stage to some of our songs when you're ready."

"I don't think I'll ever be that good, to play in front of thousands." She looks down at the ground. I hate that she puts herself down so much. I want that smile back. I stop in front of her and place my thumb on her chin, tilting her head up. Her skin is soft. "Don't think you can't do something unless you try. If you work hard enough, anything can happen. I'm living proof." She smiles at me and I'm surprised when she leans up and kisses my cheek. Feeling her lips touch my skin causes a stir in my pants. What the hell? How does an innocent kiss make my dick hard? What am I, fourteen?

"Thank you," she whispers, biting her lip. I hate how much I want to kiss her right now.

"Anytime," I answer. I try and think about anything but my dick and the most amazing person next to me.

Chapter 14

Sky

We've been in Dominic's room for about thirty minutes, him trying to teach me how to play guitar, and I swear I think learning how to play is like learning how to fly a plane. I watch Dominic's fingers caress the instrument so fluidly, he makes it look so easy. I try and copy and the sound the strings make is awful. It doesn't help that he keeps chuckling at me.

"You laugh at me one more time, I swear I will hurt you," I groan as I try again and the strings just make another bad sound. "This guitar hates me, that's the reason why I suck, it hates my guts." I face the ceiling.

"It doesn't hate you. First of all, it has no feelings; second of all, you just need more practice. You're not going to be the best in just a day." I groan again but more loudly. Yes, I have moved to the point of acting like a baby.

"What's the third point? It always comes in threes."

"Third point is; you could just suck at it," he says, trying not to laugh.

"I can't believe you said that. What happened to praising me so you know that I'm doing okay and all that jazz?" I place my hand over my heart as if I'm offended.

"I praise you if you've done well at something, but this," he points to the guitars. "you kind of suck at." I place the guitar I'm

In the Spotlight

holding down and stand up.

"You think you're so hot because you can move your fingers like a pro? Maybe you just have magic fingers, ever thought of that big guy?" I say teasingly but Dominic lays his guitar down and when his eyes land on mine, I feel frozen to the spot. How did we get from laughing to his smouldering eyes piercing me to the spot?

"You have no idea how good I am with my fingers." He walks slowly towards me and out of instinct, I walk back. I don't get far as I hit a wall, stopping me from going any further. "You want to experience how good my fingers really are?" He stops just a few inches away from me, his heat wrapping around me like a blanket.

"Dominic," I whisper, but it sounds unlike me as I hear it leave my lips. He leans his head down and strokes his cheek with mine. Feeling his stubble along my skin causes goose bumps along my body.

"You always smell so good," he whispers into my neck. He steps in further, his body touching mine. I swear I can feel his hard erection press against me and a whimper leaves my mouth. He glides his fingers down my arms and when he gets to my wrists he raises them up and pins them over my head.

"Dominic," I whisper again. I just want him to touch me. Kiss me. Do anything. He stays where he is but presses his hardness against me and I arch into him. Wanting more of him. Like I've just burned him, he drops his arms and takes a few quick steps back.

"Fuck." He pulls his hair as he turns around facing away from me. "Fuck." I don't know what happened. What did I do? What do I do?

"Dominic?" I speak up and his body tenses at the sound of my voice.

"Sky, you need to go," he says sternly. I try to walk towards him so maybe I can comfort him. Assure him what we did was okay. It was more than okay. I want more. "Sky. Leave," he raises his voice and I flinch.

I feel like he just slapped me. Tears start to fall but I don't want him to see them. I run out the door and into my room, falling on my bed and crying into my pillow. Why does he do this to me? He wants to be my friend but he touches me all the time. The way he looks at me from time to time says more. Am I just imagining all of it? Am I *that* naive that I'm just seeing what I want to?

Maybe he just doesn't want you. Maybe he just wants to fuck you but knows he can't. That nasty voice echoes through my head. Is that what it is? He just wants to sleep with me but can't? He said friends though. *Yeah because you're in his band, what else did you expect?* I cry all over again, confused about what is going through Dominic's head.

I stayed in my room for the next few days, trying to build up some strength for when I see Dominic again. I know if I don't show my face around the house soon, Lake is going to think something is wrong. I take a long shower, since I'm sure I'm starting to smell, and head down to the kitchen to get something to eat. Lake is there, making dinner and my stomach grumbles like a monster, echoing through the room.

"You hungry?" she laughs. I wrap my arms around my stomach, embarrassed it made that sound.

"Yeah, sorry."

"Don't be sorry. Dinner will be ready in ten minutes. Don't know when it'll be the last time we have homemade food so I want

In the *Spotlight*

to cook as much as I can." She checks the oven.

"Yeah, I don't think I can eat take out forever. I would get bored of it and no way do I want to ever get bored of food." I chuckle and she giggles with me.

"Yeah, well let's hope we stop at some hotels and get decent food there. Like hell I am getting fat. I worked hard on this body and no way anything is going to ruin it." She places her hands on her hips and poses as she sweeps her hand up and down.

"I think I've gained enough, too. I just don't want to have a heart attack by the time I turn thirty. Could you imagine if Mom and Dad saw how we eat now? They *would* have heart attacks." I say, laughing.

"Yeah they would be all *'Do you have any idea what crap is going down your throat? Do you know what that is doing to your body? You are not going to eat until you've lost two pounds'.*" We laugh but then stop. The last part isn't that funny. I remember when I gained a couple of pounds once. They didn't let me eat for two days. I was so hungry I even ran a couple of miles to help lose the weight just so I could eat again.

"Do you ever wonder what we would be like if they didn't treat us like they did?" I look down and play with the hem of my shirt.

"Sometimes, but I like to think that we've become good people, despite them. We appreciate what we have now. I appreciate doing what I want, when I want, without being judged or punished. They had too much control over us. No one should ever have that much control." I nod in response.

"I just think maybe I wouldn't be this shy, naive girl. This girl who won't take a step out of her comfort zone. I just think maybe if I was treated differently, I would be able to experience life more without getting so scared." Maybe Dominic would like me if I was different.

"Sky, I was where you are now when I left that place. I was cautious, I didn't know who to trust. I had all their rules drummed so far into my brain that it took me ages until I said fuck it and did something. I am so grateful for Leon. He was very patient with me. He knew I was different. He said he could sense it. I told him how I grew up after I learned to trust him. It even took us over a year to have sex." I look up at her in shock. The way they are always touching each other, kissing each other, you would think they were like that from the very beginning.

"You waited that long?" I'm still looking at her with my mouth hanging open.

"Yeah, I did. I was so scared. I kept thinking, what if he uses me? Sleeps with me then runs away, leaving me alone. But one night we were talking and he looked into my eyes and that's when I knew. He had me. He had my mind, body and soul. He told me he loved me months before we had sex but people throw those words around and don't mean it. But you know, if he hadn't fallen in love with me, I would probably still be under our parent's claws. Married to a man they chose, ready to reproduce babies to enter that kind of world." She shudders at the thought.

"What if I can't find someone? What if I stay alone or, even worse, marry a guy our parents choose? What if all this," I swipe my hands around the room, "is just temporary? What if it's all a dream and soon I'll wake up, back with them? What if I don't get my happy ever after?" I start to cry and I feel Lake's arms wrap around me.

"You will. You'll meet someone who loves you unconditionally. You'll meet someone who you think about constantly and vice versa.

In the Spotlight

It will happen. I can feel it. Just be patient; you'll find him, and like hell will I let him take you away from me. I will not let you live the rest of your life married to a man who just sees you as arm candy while fucking his secretary behind your back. You deserve more than that. You will fall and there will be someone who will catch you." She places her hands on my cheeks guiding my head up to wipe away my tears with her fingers.

"Lake. I think I..." I was about to tell her what I was feeling for Dominic when we hear a commotion at the front door. Lake and I run to see what is going on and I feel a sharp pain through my entire body.

Dominic is pinning a girl with very dark hair against the wall, kissing her vigorously. I watch as he starts kissing her neck, pressing his lower body into hers. Her moans echoing through the room.

"Fucking hell, Dominic. Go take your play thing to your room. We don't want to see that shit," Lake shouts. Dominic stops, having not realized anyone was there. He turns his head and his eyes soften as they land on mine. I'm sure he can see the pain looking back at him. Quick as lightening, his face turns emotionless.

"Baby, let's go take this to my room," he huskily tells her. She nods her head as she unwraps her legs from around his waist and he helps her stand. I watch as they walk past me, not even giving me a second glance. I hear banging then I hear a door slam.

"Fuck, I knew it was too good to be true," Lake says, shaking her head before going back into the kitchen. She puts on her mitts and starts taking things out of the oven. I was starving before but I think I just lost my appetite.

"What do you mean, too good to be true?" I ask, leaning my arms on the counter opposite her.

"Well, before you came he used to bring girls back here all the time. I told him that when you moved in, he had to tone it down. Anyway, the last couple of months I haven't seen him with anyone. He could be fucking them at their places but I thought maybe he was growing up. Guess I was wrong." Yeah, I guess you were.

Lake plates up our dinner and Leon joins us. I hate that I'm missing Dominic's company. Whenever we eat at home, we all eat together. I eat as much as I can handle but my thoughts keep going to the guy I thought I was falling for. Lake was right at the very beginning. He would hurt me. I can't let him break me further. I'm already broken but I'm putting the pieces back together.

─── ★ ───

Dominic

"Yes, fuck me harder! Please!" the girl beneath me screams out. I'm ramming my dick so hard into her, my bed is banging against the wall, but right now I don't give a flying fuck. I went to a bar to numb my thoughts and it worked. Luckily for this girl, she met me at the right time. I needed my dick wet and she was willing to accommodate. There was something about her I couldn't put my finger on, but I had to have her.

"Scream my name," I growl.

"Dominic!" she screams. I pull out of her, flipping her around so she's on her hands and knees, and enter her again with one hard thrust, causing her to moan into the pillow.

Her dark hair spills across the creamy white skin of her back. I place my hands on her tight ass and dig my fingers in. Fuck, I'm going to come soon. I need a fucking release. Why the hell did I wait so long? A voice in my head is trying to tell me something but I let the alcohol mixed with the pure ecstasy I'm feeling drown it out. I

In the Spotlight

lean forward and start rubbing her clit. Her walls start to squeeze my cock and it doesn't take her long until she is screaming out her orgasm. I kneel back up, grab her hips and start thrusting in and out of her until I find my own sweet release. It doesn't take long before sleep takes over.

— ★ —

I wake up to the mother fucker of all headaches. I try to open my eyes but they feel like they weigh a ton. When I finally manage to tear them open, I wish I hadn't. The sun is streaming through my room. Why didn't I close the curtains? I'm about to stand up when I feel movement next to me. I look across the bed and all I see is dark hair.

Sky?

What is Sky doing in my room? I look around and there are clothes everywhere; *her* clothes. Shit. Did we sleep together last night? Fuck, if I took her virginity and can't remember doing it I am the biggest asshole of all time. I know I've been craving her but, fuck. Flashes of last night come through my head. Her on her hands and knees. Her saying my name. I'm trying to get my head around it when I feel her hand stroke up and down my arm. I turn my head with a smile but it falls when I see that the girl next to me isn't Sky.

"Morning," she purrs. What the hell? I place my hand on my forehead and try to think. I was at a bar drinking and a girl, this girl, talked to me. A few more drinks. Fuck. I fucked her. "Your head sore? Want me to make it better?" Her hand trails down, trying to get to my dick, but I stand up before she has a chance to touch it.

"Listen, this was fun, but it's time to go," I try and say calmly but I just want her to leave so I can think clearly on my own.

"No problem, sugar." She stands up, fully naked, not caring

that I can see her. Well, I did fuck her so why be shy now? She gets dressed and I open the door to show her out when Sky's door opens as well. I look across to the girl I wished was in my bed. She looks at the girl leaving my room then back to me. The pure adoration she normally looks at me with is gone. Her eyes are now vacant and I start to feel an ache in my chest.

"Sorry about last night," the girl, I have no idea what her name is, says. "We didn't mean to give you a show." Then it comes back to me. Entering the house, having this girl against a wall. Looking up and seeing Sky, her eyes full of pain. No wonder she has such a blank look on her face right now.

"It's fine. I hope you had a good night. I'm off for a run, see you around," she says to the girl, not once looking back at me as I watch her go.

"She seems nice, very pretty." The girl starts walking down the hall towards the stairs.

"Yeah, she is," I say quietly then follow the girl to make sure she actually leaves.

Chapter 15

Sky

I went for a run to clear my head and, even though I tried to push them away, thoughts of last night and this morning kept creeping back in. Seeing that girl made things clear. Dominic and I aren't meant to be. What did I really expect though? That the first guy I saw would be the one?

I think I've read too many books; lived in some sort of fantasy bubble. It hurt, yes, but it was my fault not Dominic's. He told me he wanted to be friends and I made it more than what it truly was. I still want to be friends. I like hanging out with him. Plus, we *are* in a band together and will be going on tour soon.

Lake woke me up this morning, telling me that we're going to be meeting the band members of Absolute Addiction. They have had ten number one hits, four albums and are well known to the music world. I looked them up on Google and listened to their music on YouTube. Their music is a little heavier than ours but they are good. Luckily the drummer is a girl so I have someone I can talk to; well hopefully, if she likes me.

I'm just hoping she isn't another Sherry. I don't want to be touring for a month or so with someone who wants to be a complete bitch to me. I hate that swearing is sneaking into my vocabulary. Being around the guys, and Lake, who swear all the time is definitely rubbing off on me.

Running back home, I tell myself that I can't be angry. I'm hurt, but I'll get over it. If Dominic tries to talk to me, I will assure him that we are fine. I'll need a little time before we can go back to how we were, but it's something I want to do.

I walk into the house and everything is quiet. I head to my room and look at Dominic's door before heading to mine. I guess thinking about something is different than actually doing it. I take a long, hot shower and dress in a light blue summer dress. I'm just in one of those moods to feel girly. The dress does go past my knee and I wear a short white cardigan to cover my arms.

I'm leaving my room to find Lake when once again Dominic's door opens and I get a flashback of that girl leaving.

Stop this. You are acting like he was your boyfriend, grow up, my head scolds me.

Dominic stands there in a pair of black jeans that hang on his perfect hips and a black T-shirt hugging his tight body. Why does he have to look so good? He stands there looking at me and I feel out of place. Why would I ever think we would fit? He screams bad boy and I scream... school teacher.

"Sky, hi," he clears his throat. "I want to apologize about last night and this morning..." I put my hand up to stop him from whatever he was going to say. I can see he feels guilty but there's nothing to be guilty for.

"Dominic," I say his name and when his eyes focus on mine, I see something in them, something that's going through his head that I can't explain. I only said his name. "Listen, you don't need to apologize. This is your house too and if you want to bring people back, that's fine. It was more of a shock than anything. We're fine, okay?" I stutter out. He looks into my eyes and doesn't say anything

In the Spotlight

for what feels like minutes but I'm sure it's just seconds.

"You sure you're okay?" I nod my head. "I don't want to lose our friendship. I know some of my actions may have led you on and I'm so sorry about that. I like being around you, I really do, and I hope we can continue that." He scratches the back of his neck.

"I like being around you, too. I'm not used to being around men and I guess that when I saw you with that girl I just felt a little off. I felt like you were mine," I chuckle. "Friends don't own friends. But yes I want to keep our friendship. We're in the same band after all." I try to lighten the mood.

"Yeah we are. So friends then? He places his hand out for me to shake. I smile at him and place my hand in his. I hate that as soon as my skin touches his, I still feel that electric current flow through me.

"Friends," I say softly. I notice his hand stays holding mine a little longer than normal but I try not to over think it.

My new motto, *try not to over think.*

"You ready to meet the headlining band of the tour?" I ask, trying to make conversation as I head downstairs.

"Yeah, I heard all their stuff and it's awesome. I can't believe we'll be working next to people who are going to be legends." He smiles brightly, I guess he's a fan of theirs then.

"You never know; it could be us one day. Touring as headliners with a new band being the opening act, thinking how awesome it is playing along with us." I wink at him.

"Yes, that's the dream. I would love for us to be that big. Having that many hear our music and wanting more. What else could a guy like me ask for?" Hmm, nothing I suppose.

★

Leon drives us to Delta Records and we head straight to the elevator that leads up to Robert's office. I groan inwardly when I see Carly sitting behind her desk and realize I must have accidently let it slip when Dominic gives me a funny look. I just shrug at him, acting like I don't know what he's giving me that look for.

We're asked to sit and after a few minutes we are guided into the office. My eyes pop open when I see the band, acting like they own the place. I watch as the drummer, Kym, helps herself to some alcoholic drink. The guitarist, Lloyd, lies on the far couch with his arm over his face. Robert is talking to someone who is slouched down in the chair, his back to me, and I assume it's the lead singer, Jensen. Travis, the bassist, is leaning his arm against the window looking down.

"Holy shit," I hear Lake say quietly beside me. Yeah, they scream sex. We look like puppies compared to them.

"Risen Knight, welcome. Come meet the band you'll be working with." He smiles at us but looks down at Jensen, giving him a stern look.

"Holy fuck, I just want to say I'm a huge fan of your music and I'm looking forward to working with you," Chris basically fan girls at them. Kym chuckles and shakes her head.

"Jensen, Travis, Kym, Lloyd; don't be so rude, come and meet the band you'll be working with," Robert says sternly and the band groans as they stand up and walk towards us. But my eyes are stuck on Jensen. He's about the same height as Dominic but has longer hair, and the eyes that are staring at me are a very light green. They look unreal.

"So you're the opening act? Think you can handle it?" Travis asks.

In the Spotlight

"Yeah, we can. Music is our life, we know what we're doing," Leon speaks up and I notice he's put his arm over Lake's shoulder, showing that she's his.

"So, who does what?" Kym asks, taking a sip from the glass.

"I'm the drummer," Leon says first.

"Guitarist," Dominic answers next.

"Bassist," Chris winks.

"I'm..." I don't get to finish when Jensen cuts me off.

"Let me guess sweets, you're the cheerleader? The groupie?" He looks me up and down and I take a step back, feeling a little uncomfortable. "I swear sweets; you look good enough to eat. Want to take a turn on a real band?" He licks his bottom lip. Did he just say that?

"She's our lead singer." Dominic stands in front of me, shielding me. They all laugh.

"She's your lead singer?" Kym laughs, pointing at me and I feel the heat on my cheeks.

"Come on, be serious, who's the singer?" Travis butts in, chuckling.

"She is. I swear if you make her feel like shit, I will gut you like a fish. You hear me?" Lake pushes Jensen's chest but he just chuckles at her.

"So this goody, goody is the lead singer of a rock band? Well. This should be interesting," Jensen says and sits back down in the seat he had been occupying.

"Guys be nice. Their first song reached number one on the charts. Did you do that?" Robert pauses. "No, you didn't, so shut the hell up. They're going to be the opening act so grow the hell up and accept it." He looks at each member.

"Whatever," Kym says downing the rest of her drink.

"You know how rock stars can be," Robert says, trying to comfort us, but I feel like crying. They were laughing at me. I know I don't look like a rock star, but it's my voice, not my appearance, that matters. "They let fame get to their heads and think they're all that. When they aren't!" Robert yells out the last part.

"If you say so!" Lloyd yells back.

"Anyway, glad you all met. Let's talk details of the tour." Robert walks around his desk and sits down. Lake holds my hand and takes me to a chair on the side of the room away from the band and when I look up, Jensen is looking at me. I mean *really* looking at me.

"I don't like that guy," Dominic says as he sits down next to me. I look away from Jensen and turn to Dominic who is glaring at him.

"I thought you did. You said you thought they were amazing." I nudge my shoulder with his.

"I guess when you see them in person they aren't what you expect them to be. I just hope we stay down to earth. I don't want to ever think I'm too good for someone." I nod, agreeing with him.

"You won't." I smile at him and he smiles back. I look back at Robert, who is still talking, but feel eyes on me. When I look out of the corner of my eye, Jensen is still drilling holes into me. Why the hell does he keep looking at me?

🎸 ★ 🎸

We've been rehearsing for the last five days and for the first time since I've been in the band, I'm enjoying myself. Robert liked the idea of having dancers join us. He liked how I danced the night he first saw me. I have an amazing choreographer who constantly praises me, telling me how flawlessly I move. I'm dancing with five guys to *Poison* but there are both men and women for the rest of the

In the Spotlight

set.

I've worked my ass off, giving my all to my performances. Singing and dancing is what I can do. All the way through, I made sure I danced my heart out. It's been drummed in me to do better, be better, and I think I'm accomplishing that. I guess certain habits are hard to break.

We're playing our first gig tonight in our home town at a stadium, on an actual stage, live in front of thousands, and the thought alone makes my heart plummet with fear. I just hope nothing goes wrong. I'm standing in the middle of the stage, watching crew members set up lights and instruments, and I look out at all the empty seats that will soon be packed full of people. I can hardly even see the ones at the far back. I wonder why people would pay so much money to see a band if they just see them as ants.

I'm wearing yoga pants with a long tank, waiting for the signal that we can start rehearsal. This will be the first time we'll be doing this on stage. There is one bit during the song *Poison,* that I do something that's a little dangerous. I just hope nothing bad happens. We've rehearsed that single move over and over, but it's still a little scary. I watch workers sort out the long stairway that Dominic will be playing on top of.

"Aww, don't you look cute up there," I hear Kym's voice and my eyes look for her. I find her walking down one of the aisles with the rest of her band. "I hope you're not getting stage fright?" She fake pouts at me then smiles. They all sit down a few rows away from the stage. Why are they even here? We're scheduled to have the place first. They're just trying to spook me.

"Sky!" Dominic shouts over and I turn to him walking towards me. "Don't listen to them. Ignore it, you got this. Show them what you're made of." He winks at me and I nod, taking in a deep breath.

A couple of minutes later we're told we can start. Dominic gives me a nod and walks over to the stairs and I walk away from the main stage over to the wing. The five male dancers, Martin, Dale, Graham, Adam and Bryan, give me a quick hug wishing us all luck and I take in another deep breath before sliding the head piece into place. I hear the intro of the first song and start to sing.

I sing a few lines before starting a slow walk to the middle of the stage just like I did the first time I sang this song. I ignore everyone around me; I just let the music and words take over. I stop and keep my eyes on Dominic as I sway my hips slowly to the music. The drums kick in and I sing my heart out.

The song goes slower and I start to walk towards him again. I pick up my tank a little, showing off my midsection and releasing it, teasing him. I walk closer to Dominic, he walks back playing his guitar, walking up the stairs and I follow him. I stop at the bottom as he goes to the top.

I take my first step up but then the dancers come out and one grabs my hand, twirling me out, before another grabs my other hand. I'm lifted then thrown in the air, landing in another man's arms as he swings me around before lowering me to the ground, his hand still in mine. I feel a set of hands pick me and swing me under his legs. I'm swung back up and dipped backwards, so much adrenaline rushing through me that I don't have time to think, but just *do*.

The dancers finally let me go and I sing the last bit of the song walking up the stairs slowly, keeping my eyes on Dominic as I get close to him. I pull his shirt towards me, singing to him. My hand glides up and I grip his hair, pulling his head near mine. He keeps

In the Spotlight

playing and I keep singing. I lean my mouth close to his. I let go and take a step back, giving him a wink, then splay my arms out and fall on the last word. I feel such a high as I fall, feeling butterflies in my stomach, then I'm caught by the dancers.

The song ends and they set me on my feet. We hug each other happily and I have a huge smile on my face. We did it. Nothing went wrong. Dominic runs down the stairs and picks me up, twirling me around in a circle and I feel so good I let out a huge laugh.

"You were amazing." He beams at me.

"No, we all were. We were perfect." I push his shoulder.

"That was fucking awesome." Chris says, rushing over.

We're all talking over each other, so full of excitement that our first song went smoothly and that we can go straight to the next. Absolute Addiction walks up the few steps to the stage, looking shocked.

Yeah, eat that, I think to myself.

"Wow," Is all Kym manages to say, looking at me like I have two heads. "I was not expecting that. Your voice. I have chills." I shrug at her then look at the ground.

"You did awesome. If that's just with one song, I can't wait to see and hear the rest," Travis adds in.

"We were wrong. We shouldn't have judged so quickly. We just saw you," he points at me, "looking like a good girl. A nun. Who would have thought you would have a voice like that? Your voice definitely suits the music. You were brill. Congrats." Travis walks towards me with his fist out. I look at Dominic and he has a huge smile on his face, looking at me with so much pride. I walk towards Travis and give him a fist bump and giggle after.

"We're thrilled you'll be opening up for us." Lloyd walks over and shakes our hands. I swear I think Chris is going to pass out at any second.

We all start talking and they keep going on and on about my voice. I like that they like me and have finally crawled out of their stuck up asses, but I am *not* all that. There are people who can sing just as good as me or even better. Adelle comes to mind. I look around and see Jensen leaning against a wall near the wing of the stage looking at me. He's in the shadows, looking like a fallen angel. His angelic face is hidden in the dark, not wanting to be with us in the light. He screams *stereotype bad boy*.

He lifts his hand and gives a come here signal with his finger. I look behind me and everyone is distracted, talking to each other, but I don't know. I turn my head back around and bite my lip. I hate that I'm tempted to follow him. I hate how my body is screaming for me to just do it. I feel like someone has a rope around me, pulling me towards him. I look back at Jensen again and he's still standing there, his eyes still trained on me.

I give one final glance behind me and walk away. Jensen walks further into the shadows. We should be rehearsing the next song but I'm curious as to what he wants. I walk past the curtain and only see darkness. I can't see him. I walk further in before my arm is being pulled and I'm being pinned against a wall. Jensen leans his body against mine.

"I knew there was something about you." He strokes my cheek. "I couldn't put my finger on it but I felt it," he whispers near my ear and I feel my body shiver. "I couldn't keep my eyes off you. Seeing that tight ass move across the floor. Hearing your voice... I felt like it was piercing through me. I got so fucking hard seeing you up there." I look into his black eyes, the only light coming through is from the stage. "You really are a good girl aren't you?" He rubs his nose against my neck smelling me.

"Jensen," I say softly. Why am I not pushing him away?

"I want you, Sky. I want to be so far inside you that you scream my name." His stubble is scratching my neck. "You smell so good. Fuck, I want to taste you." He presses his erection against me and I feel that similar ache build inside me. I shouldn't feel like this. I only ever felt like this towards Dominic. Why is my body acting like this?

Remember, he was a dick when he first met you. He just wants to screw you and leave you like he probably does to every single girl he meets. With that thought, I push him as hard as I can. He looks shocked. Good. I'm not one of those girls who spread their legs for anyone.

"Yes, I *am* a good girl, which means I don't just sleep with anyone." He doesn't know I'm a virgin and I don't plan on announcing it. "You'll need to find some other easy lay." I try and walk away but he grabs onto my elbow and pulls me into his chest.

"Is that a challenge?" he huskily asks into my ear.

"No, it's a promise. I'm not a whore and you're an asshole; I don't get with assholes. Enjoy the rest of the show." I turn and give him a wink before walking back onto the stage. Everyone is still talking but Dominic notices me coming back. He looks pissed when he sees Jensen walk out behind me.

Crap.

We rehearse the rest of our songs and everything goes perfectly. We nailed it. It's time for AA to go up and rehearse so I decide to leave even though Jensen insisted that I stay to hear him play. I can tell by the way he looks at me that he isn't used to women saying no to him.

I head back home to grab a shower and a sandwich before I have to go back. I relax into the couch and put on Supernatural, cringing when the first thing I see is the name Jensen. A freaky ghost scene is playing when I'm startled by the front door slamming and Dominic stomping in, glaring at me.

―――★―――

Dominic

When I noticed Sky was gone, I was worried, but then I saw her coming from behind the stage with Jensen and my blood boiled. What the fuck did he do to her? She looks fine and the way he is looking at her; she must have knocked him back. At least that's something, I guess, but all the way through rehearsal I noticed him staring at her. Looking at her like he's just waiting for his chance to fuck her.

I know his type; he'll just use her and throw her away like yesterday's trash. He even tried to make her stay to watch them play but again she said no and I know he doesn't like hearing that. Yes, I'm a little jealous that she went with him, but I did tell her we are just friends, and it doesn't help my case that I fucked some stranger. I'll look like a dick if I tell her she can't go near him.

I went for a walk to try and clear my head but, the more time I spent alone, the angrier I got. I've turned into one of *those* guys. I can't have her so I don't want anyone else to have her. I head back home and see her lying on the couch, watching one of her shows, her hair splayed around her.

She looks like an angel and I'm sure I must be the fucking devil. She's wearing some short shorts and I hate how comfortable she's been around here lately. She used to make sure all of her skin was covered, but now it's like she's teasing me even though she isn't

In the Spotlight

aware of it.

"You okay?" She sits up, looking concerned. I hate that I just want to walk over to her and kiss her; lay my body on top of hers. I feel my dick stirring just thinking about it.

"Yeah, I'm fine. You okay? I saw you were talking to Jensen." I see her skin blush and jealousy rises again. Fuck my life.

"Yeah, he was trying to get me to hook up with him but I told him no." Thank the holy fucking Jesus for that.

"Good for you. I don't want you to get hurt, that's all. Sorry I sounded like a whack job just then." She looks down and nods her head. God, how I wish I could know what she's thinking. "You ready for tonight?" I ask, sitting next to her.

"Yeah, after rehearsing today I feel less nervous. I just hope they like us." She looks up into my eyes. I love how her big dark blue eyes always look straight into mine.

"They will." They will love you.

Chapter 16

Sky

I'm in one of the dressing rooms and Lake is helping with my hair and makeup. I thought I would be more nervous than what I'm feeling right now but, for some reason, I'm more excited than anything else. Rehearsing today really did help and the feedback from AA, telling me and the guys how amazing we are, made me feel like I can actually do this.

Dominic and I hung out on the couch, talking about the rehearsal, thankfully never bringing up Jensen again. I know he feels protective of me but I'm starting to think he views me as a sister. Knowing that has finally given me the push I need to try and move on. I've been thinking about Jensen, but no way could I go there.

If I was ever going to let a guy into my heart, I want them to be all in. I want a relationship; well, to work towards one anyway. I'm not going to give up my virginity to a one-night stand. It's a gift and like hell I'm giving it to just some pretty face with a hot body that makes me feel funny things.

I'm wearing black skinny jeans and a black top that hangs over one shoulder and is longer on one side, showing a little of my stomach. My hair is wavy and I'm wearing dark makeup to complete the look. I look like the rock star people are expecting and I hope I don't disappoint them.

In the Spotlight

"Sky, I need to tell you something." Lake puts the hairbrush down finishing off my hair and I look up to her smiling warmly at me. "You have been so amazing these last couple of months. Working so hard with the band, doing things out of your comfort zone. I just want to say I have never been prouder. I feel like each day you are changing into this stronger person. You don't ask for permission to do things, you do what you want, you're starting to speak your mind. I just want you to know that I appreciate everything you have done to help this band get where it is. I love you so much." She grabs my hands, pulling me in for a tight hug.

"I love you too." I don't know what else to say. I don't feel like I've changed much but if she sees it, it must be true. "Thank you for looking out for me, for being there for me." I see tears glaze her eyes and hug her again. A knock sounds at the door, the person on the other side telling us we are on in five minutes.

"You go out there and rock their socks off." I chuckle at her comment and we head towards the stage. Before the crew has a chance to start fussing over my head piece, I hear my name. Turning, I see Jensen leaning against the wall. Does he always need to lean against something? Does he always have to look at me with those dark eyes?

"I'll be right back." Lake nods and walks off, talking to the crew. Jensen eyes up my outfit as I walk towards him and when his gaze finally lands on mine, I can see the desire there.

"Jensen," I say his name and just like with Dominic, his eyes dilate.

Do I say names strangely or something? Men are weird. When I'm close enough, he grabs hold of my hand and pulls me towards him before pushing me against the wall he was leaning on. He surprises me when his lips land on mine. His lips are soft but the kiss itself is rough and hard. He is showing me how much he wants me. Just like that, he's the second person I have ever kissed.

My body reacts to him and I kiss him back with the same intensity. I let out a moan in his mouth and he growls in return. He pulls my hair back exposing my neck, biting and licking it. I arch my body towards him, gripping his hair into me. I'm so lost in the kiss I forget that we are surrounded by people. I like how he's kissing me like he wants to devour me. He pulls back, both of us breathing hard. Pure instinct has me slapping his face hard, causing a sting across my palm.

Don't ask me why I did it. I'm turned on but I'm also angry at the same time. I thought he would be angry that I hit him but his eyes go darker and he licks his lips like he wants to savor the taste. We both just stare at each other until he pushes me against the wall again, this time harder, causing that ache between my legs to intensify.

"Fuck, I want you so badly. I *am* going to have you," he promises, pushing himself closer to me.

"Never going to happen," I say, trying to control my breathing. I feel his fingers go under my top, caressing the skin there before moving to stroke the part on top of my jeans.

"I do like a challenge." He pulls my jean hoops so I fall into him, causing his erection to press into my core.

"I am not a challenge. I just have self-respect. I am not going to sleep with you. Get that through your thick head," I seethe at him.

"We shall see. Have a good show." He kisses my lips again quickly and walks away, giving me a wink. My whole body is shaking. I can't believe what just happened. I press my fingers to my

In the *spotlight*

lips and I can't help but smile.

God what is happening to me?

— ★ —

Dominic

Watching them kiss is like being kicked in the stomach over and over. Seeing her grip his hair, kissing him back. I feel like some creeper watching them but I couldn't look away. She said no again but since we're going on tour with them, he knows he has plenty of chances to try and get in her pants. I watch Sky leave and quickly run after Jensen. I need to speak to him. I want to kick his ass but that would do no good. I see him entering their bands room but I quickly yell out his name before he goes in.

"I thought you had to get on stage?" He looks at me, confused, wondering why I'm here and not ready to play in front of thousands.

"I need to speak to you about Sky," I say sternly, crossing my arms and he does the same.

"Go on then, tell me how I'm not good for her. To leave her alone. That she shouldn't go near a guy like me." He rolls his eyes. I just want to punch his face in. How the fuck did I idolize this dick?

"Yeah, all of those reasons, but I know you won't listen. I know what you're thinking; I'm the same way. You see her as a challenge, you want to prove that you can get her to say yes."

"You telling me to stay away so you can have her?" he interrupts me.

"No, we're good friends, very good friends. She's a good person. She doesn't deserve to be fucked over. She's an innocent, pure person. I'm telling you now to leave her the fuck alone so she doesn't get her heart broken."

"What, it's not like she's a virgin." He chuckles but when he sees my face his eyes widen. "Fuck, she's a virgin? How can that be? Have you seen her?" He shakes his head. Yeah I have, but I know I would hurt her in the end, just like I know this guy would. She deserves better than men like us.

"She believes in true love, happily ever after's. She has a good heart, and I don't want to see that heart shattered into a million pieces. I am telling you now that she needs a man who will fall for her. Who will catch her when she falls. Not just a quick fuck to boost your ego. You feel me?" I look him in the eye so he knows how truly serious I am.

"Yeah, I get it. Fuck. I thought she was just playing hard to get; you know like women do?" I nod. "She isn't like other girls is she?" I shake my head.

"No, she isn't. She's one of a kind." I hear my name being called. "I need to go but I hope you understand that you can't give her what she needs. So leave her alone," I say, then turn around and walk away, praying he will listen.

★

Sky

We rocked.

We played our hearts out and the audience loved it. They screamed and shouted, demanding more. I'm full on sweating, my clothes clinging to my body, but I don't care. I push my hair away from my face, smiling at the crowd. We did it. We played our first show and they are begging for more.

We whisper amongst ourselves and decide to play one more song, even though it's not rehearsed. We're on such a high, we aren't ready to come back down. We do a cover of Amy Studt's *Just a Little Girl*. I feel it's fitting since it talks about people underestimating you and that there is a lot more to you. I feel like I'm singing this song to Jensen and his band. The crowd eats it up and we leave the stage high fiving each other.

Jensen and his band saunters on to the stage like they own the place and if I thought the screaming was bad before, now it's deafening. I'm almost off the stage when I feel my hand being tugged and I turn to see Jensen smiling at me. I look into his eyes and they seem different. His smile isn't one of his cocky ones, it's an actual smile and it makes him even more beautiful. Why don't men smile more? It makes them seem more human.

I'm dragged into the middle of the stage and Jensen doesn't let go of my hand. I see flashes going off and women screaming at us. I have a huge smile on my face, shaking my head. God, this is crazy.

"Did you enjoy Risen Knights?" Jensen screams into his mic and the crowd screams louder. "What do you think of their lead singer, Sky?" He points his mic into the crowd and they scream even louder. "How many of you think she should give me a good luck kiss before she walks off stage?" I look at him and he turns, a huge smile on his face. The crowd is chanting *"Kiss, Kiss, Kiss!"* over and over. I cover my face with my hand, shaking my head, not believing he is doing this in front of thousands of people.

He turns his body so he is fully facing me and his hands cover my cheeks as he looks down at me softly. How has this guy changed from an egocentric ass to this warm, sweet man in such a short amount of time? He strokes my bottom lip with his thumb and leans down, kissing me so softly, so gently. Nothing like how he kissed me before. He pulls back and he has such an adorable smile that I can't help but smile back up at him.

"Now you ready to rock?" he yells back to the audience and with that, I wave to the crowd and walk off, not believing he did that.

"Holy shit, Jensen Ryder kissed you in front of everyone! I bet that will be all over the internet within seconds!" Lake is screaming at me.

"I can't believe he did that," I say in disbelief, shaking my head.

"Who cares? He's hot. I saw how he was looking at you, he has it bad," she shrieks. I look over and see Dominic shaking his head before walking away. What is that about?

"Right, I need a shower. I stink."

I go to my dressing room and head for the small shower. As the hot water falls down on me I still can't believe we did it. It all feels like a dream. I quickly dry myself and put on a dark purple dress that hits my knees. It hugs my top half and flares out past my waist. I'm about to put on a cardigan, but I hold it in my hand, take a deep breath, and leave it.

I blow dry my hair and put on some lip gloss before heading to a room we were told to go once we were ready. The guys are already there helping themselves to the food and drinks on the table. I see a wide screen TV on the wall showing AA playing. I watch them for a moment and they are really good, so in-sync with one another, but my eyes are glued to Jensen. His voice is so raw and masculine. He flirts with the fans, smiling and winking. I'm pretty sure I saw someone throw their panties at him. Fans actually do that?

I grab a bottle of water and talk to Lake but my eyes keeping wandering back to the TV, watching the band play. After they sing their last encore I watch them exit the stage. They join us about ten minutes later, all showered and dressed themselves. I feel eyes burning into me and keep telling myself not to look but my damn body messes up and I turn my head. He's looking straight at me as I

In the Spotlight

knew he would be. Lloyd and Kym are talking to him but he isn't paying attention to them. He is solely looking at me.

I am in deep trouble.

I just don't know if it's trouble I wouldn't mind getting into.

Chapter 17

We drive to the club in a limo. A freaking *limo*. It's huge and I can't stop looking around as everyone chats. Jensen makes sure to sit next to me and he smiles when he sees me looking around in amazement. I've seen my parents ride in a few, but I've never seen one as long as this.

We show up at the club and the bouncers let us right in. A girl who looks the same age as me walks us to the VIP section that is up some stairs and roped off so no one can enter unless you're on the list.

We have our own bar and can see down to the dancefloor. A few women scream when they see Jensen and the band and a few even try to touch them. They just smile and wave. Jensen makes sure to sit next to me again and Lake is on my other side.

A woman wearing a tight white blouse and a short black skirt comes to the table with glasses of champagne for everyone and I was going to decline but, since everyone was toasting, I felt like I should join. I've been trying to do what my sister always tells me. Just let go and have fun. So that's what I do. My first sip of alcohol isn't as bad as I thought it would be. It's very sweet and I enjoy it.

The woman, our server, comes back after we finish the champagne and asks what we want to drink and everyone orders a beer, except Lake who asks for a gin and tonic. When the server looks at me, I falter, not knowing if I should just get a coke or

In the Spotlight

something a little stronger.

"Do you not drink?" Jensen asks me. I feel a little embarrassed that I don't have any idea when it comes to alcohol.

"I've never really drank before so I'm not sure really what to get." I look down and start playing with my hands and he reaches out and grabs them, giving them a squeeze. When I finally look up, his head is turned, studying me.

"How about a cocktail? It's a fruity type of drink; I think you'll like it." I nod. "She'll have a cocktail, something with passion fruit." The girl nods her head and walks off to get our order.

"Thank you, I bet you think I'm a weirdo." I chuckle.

"Not at all. It's nice to meet a girl who isn't just after a party all the time. Look at Kym, she drinks like a fish and never knows when to stop," Jensen says and the way he is smiling, I know he is just making fun.

"I like the buzz, so sue me." Kym throws a coaster at him. "So you've never drank alcohol? Not even once?" she asks me and I shake my head.

"The champagne was my first. I was brought up not to so..." I shrug.

"Wow, well I hope you enjoy your cocktails." I hope so, too.

When my drink arrives, I take a hesitant sip and am surprised that I actually like it. It tastes more like juice than anything else. For the rest of the night I try different flavored cocktails and after a few hours, I feel relaxed and happy and Lake looks the same, telling everyone how much she loves them. I head to the bar, wanting to order another round for the table, when Kym comes next to me, smiling.

"You want to try a shot?" she asks me. A shot?

"What's that?" I ask, smiling back at her.

"It's a mini drink; you down it in one go. We'll start off with a lemon drop." I nod my head. I'm in the kind of mood where I feel like saying yes to everything. She orders our shots and where mine is yellow, hers is clear. She taps my glass with hers and I follow suit, swallowing in one go. I feel the burn go down my throat and cough, not used to the sensation.

Lake, Kym and I have a couple more drinks and shots and I feel so wired, so awake, so full of energy. I look down below and see everyone moving to the music and I want to join in. I grab Lake and Kym's hands and drag them down the stairs, them giggling behind me.

We head to the middle of the dance floor and I start moving my hips to the music. Lake eventually goes back to Leon but Kym stays with me. We are laughing and swaying, our arms up in the air, and I shriek when the next song comes on and its *Poison*. I hear my voice singing through the system.

Kym shrieks with me like we're teenagers and I start to dance. Kym presses herself into me, dancing slowly, so I follow her lead. She smiles at me, her short brown hair shining in the lights, her skin bronzed compared to my paleness. I look into her chocolate brown eyes and before I know it, her lips are on mine.

We keep swaying to the music, her body moving with mine. She cups my cheek and strokes my neck. My head feels so fuzzy and blurred. Her lips and touch are gentle; treating me as if I'm fragile. Her tongue presses against mine and I know I shouldn't be doing this, kissing a girl, but it feels so nice.

She pulls back and smiles at me and all I can do is smile with her. We dance for the rest of the song and, as it ends, she tells me

In the Spotlight

she's going to the bathroom. I want to go with but I tell her I'll stay here. She nods and leaves and I dance to the next song, not caring that I'm on my own. I just close my eyes and follow the beat of the music. Music has always moved me but, right now, I feel like it's in my soul.

The next song comes on and I feel arms go around me, pulling me so that my back is to their front. I keep my eyes closed and lean my head back, knowing instantly that it's Jensen when his smell surrounds me. His hands are on my hips, his body moving with mine. I can feel his erection press against my ass and I moan, hoping it was drowned out by the music, but I'm sure he heard it.

He moves my hair off my right shoulder and his touch causes goosebumps all over my body. His stubble scratches my cheek but I'm starting to like that feeling. I feel his breath coming in heavy near my ear. I don't know if it's the alcohol or my need but I start grinding my ass against him and he growls in my ear. My panties grow wet. His grip on my waist tightens.

His hands glide further down and then he lifts one side of my dress up. I open my eyes and look around to see if anyone can see, but no one is paying us any attention. Everyone looks too drunk and in their own worlds to notice the two of us. I feel his fingers slide up my thigh close to my soaked underwear. I so badly want him to touch me there but I can't. I'm not this type of girl. I step away from him and turn to look at him. We stare at each other, our breathing coming in fast.

"I have to go," I tell him and walk away.

He calls out my name but I ignore him and head outside to get some fresh air. My head is all over the place and I can't think clearly. I walk around the corner, being sure to stay in sight of the bouncers, and press my back against the wall, sliding down into a crouch. I can't believe I was going to let him touch me there. That I wanted him to. I wanted him so badly to touch me. I can still feel the ache between my legs. I hear footsteps coming my way and look up to see Dominic standing there, giving me a warm smile, putting out his hand for me to take. I place my hand in his and he pulls me up into a hug.

"Let's go home." I nod in response. I do feel really tired now and my bed is exactly what I need.

Dominic

I've noticed a big change in Jensen and wish I never said anything to him. He seems softer with her now, staying close to her, and his dickhead attitude has changed. I don't know if it's a game or if he is really trying. No matter which one it is, I hate it. I see Sky looking at him like she used to look at me.

Seeing her get drunk for the first time is something I will never forget. She looks so cute, giggling and smiling. Relaxed and stress free. I keep my eye on her to make sure she doesn't do anything silly, but when she goes to dance with her sister, I relax myself and enjoy having a few. When I see Lake return, I stand near the balcony and look down, watching her sway her sexy hips.

I swear I don't think I've ever been as turned on as I am right now, watching her kiss Kym. I know it's the alcohol, Sky would never have kissed her otherwise, but God it's hot to watch.

Kym leaves and I watch her dance alone, badly wanting to join her, but Jensen must have thought the same thing and I watch him walk towards her, her back to his front. I should look away but something is telling me to stay just in case. I'm glad I did as I see her

In the Spotlight

walk away from him a few minutes later. I followed to make sure she's okay. If that dick touched her in any way, I swear I will kill him.

I find her kneeling down against a wall, looking so lost. When her eyes land on mine, I see how relieved she is knowing it's just me. I take her home and she falls asleep against my shoulder during the drive. I pay the cab and carry her like I did when Sherry hurt her. I walk up the stairs and head to her room, lay her on her bed and cover her with the sheet. I'm about to walk out when she calls my name. I turn and she sits up, pulling her dress over her head and throwing it across the room. My mouth hangs open and I can't stop staring at her perfect creamy breasts that are covered in black lace.

"Will you sleep next to me. Like we use to?" Her deep blue eyes look into mine, pleading with me.

How can I say no to her? I nod my head and close the door, taking off my shoes and shirt. I lay down next to her but she asks me to get under the covers. I do and she moves herself so her ass is curved into me. I try so hard to keep my dick at bay. She grabs my arm and wraps it around her waist, entwining her fingers with mine.

"I missed this," she says so softly, I hardly hear her.

"Me too." I lay my head down, listening to her breathing.

"Friends forever right? Forever and ever?"

"Always." I kiss her neck.

"Even if I was taken away?" she mumbles. I lean up looking at her but her eyes are closed.

"What do you mean, taken away?" I ask her softly. No one will ever take her away. "Sky?" I hear her breathing evening out. She fell asleep. What did she mean, taken away? Who would take her away? Does she mean if she ends up with Jensen? I want her to be happy; I did promise I would be her friend.

Sky

I wake up the next morning with the worst headache ever. I sit up and notice I'm in only my underwear and when I look next to me, Dominic is fast asleep, mostly clothed. Last night's events come rushing in like a flood. Oh God. I rest my feet on the floor and see painkillers and water on my nightstand. Dominic must have put them there. I take the tablets and down the water, feeling a little better.

I look back over at Dominic and he looks so peaceful. Some of his hair has fallen into his eyes so I sweep it away and stroke his cheek with the back of my hand, causing him to smile in his sleep. God he's so cute when he's sleeping. I walk on shaky legs to the bathroom to relieve myself and brush my teeth since it feels like a skunk died in my mouth.

I head back to bed and lay on my side and instantly Dominic moves himself so he's cuddling me again. He's still sleeping, his breathing nice and slow, so I close my eyes and let sleep take over once more. I don't know if it's a dream or not but I'm sure I hear Dominic say to never leave him as I drift off.

Chapter 18

When I wake again, Dominic is sitting up, coffee in hand, wearing a cute smile that shows off his dimples. I sit up and the sheet falls down before I realize that I'm still in my underwear. Dominic's eyes dilate and I quickly cover myself while he does his best to look anywhere but at me.

"I thought you'd like some coffee to feel more human," he chuckles at me. I take the cup and the first sip is heaven.

"Thank you." I take another sip.

"Anytime. We're leaving for the tour bus in forty minutes so you better get moving. I look at him and see his hair is wet so he must have already had a shower. I can smell alcohol and cigarettes all over me so I'm in desperate need to wash all of last night's events off me.

"What time is it?" I yawn and stretch out my arms, making sure I don't spill my hot beverage.

"Just before six." I groan. I knew it was way too early. "I'll leave you to it." I lie back on my bed and place my drink off to the side. I throw a pillow over my head and groan into it. Why did I drink so much? Oh yeah, because I'm an idiot. I decide to have my first drink, well bender really, the night before I start travelling all over the state.

I walk to my shower and make sure the water is scalding hot before jumping in. I groan again when I remember kissing Kym and then almost letting Jensen feel me up in front of a club full of people. How am I going to face them again? Hopefully they feel just as embarrassed as I do and forget that it ever happened. Then a flash comes back.

Dominic.

I remember when I caught him getting a blowjob, he never mentioned it again. He never even acted like he saw me there watching them. I wonder why, even now, he has never brought it up. Maybe he's just a gentleman and knows that I would die of pure mortification if he said anything.

I dress in a white and black summer dress with a short black cardigan and leave my hair up in a high ponytail. I don't bother wearing any makeup besides some lip-gloss. My lips are so dry; I need to make sure I keep myself hydrated today.

A car pulls up right on the dot and takes us to three huge buses. One has Absolute Addiction on it, that bus is bigger than the other two. I see crew people, or are they called roadies? I need to ask about that. They are putting instruments and equipment on one bus so I guess the other is where we will be staying throughout the tour.

We climb out and I see Lake pressing her back against the car, wearing sunglasses; at least I'm not the only one who's feeling rough. I see AA come out of their bus and whistle at us and I know they aren't going to let us forget anything about last night.

"Sky, never knew you had it in you girl," Lloyd laughs at me. I look at the ground but feel an arm go over my shoulders and look to see Dominic pressing me into his side.

"Come on, back off, she isn't like you. She doesn't drink alcohol like it's water," Dominic retorts back.

"I have to admit, that girl can kiss. It's like her lips gave me this

In the Spotlight

electric current through my system. I swear, if that was a drug, I would take it every day," Kym says, looking at me like she wants to kiss me again. I feel Dominic tense beside me. Yup, this is so embarrassing. "Who was your first kiss?" she asks, and I don't mean to but, I look up at Dominic through my lashes and he's looking back down at me. I think he knows; the way his eyes widen; I know he knows. *Yes, you were my first.*

"Some guy." I shrug and she nods.

"Well, must be some guy, I'm surprised he let you go." I watch Kym get back on her bus and the guys start talking to a few roadies.

"Was I your first kiss?" Dominic asks me. I take a step back so I can see him.

"Yeah, you were," I say softly. He shakes his head at me.

"But... I know you're a virgin but come on, you're beautiful; you're smart, funny, sweet. How can it be that no guy has ever kissed you?" I know he's shocked but I can't help but giggle when he says all those nice things to me.

"You think I'm beautiful?" I smile at him. He looks at me and chuckles, shaking his head.

"You know you are." I don't.

"Thank you," I whisper as he steps towards me and I wrap my arms around him. With him holding me, right now there is no other place I would rather be.

"Ready to see our new home?" He puts his arm around my waist and we walk towards the bus we will be sleeping in.

I hear my name being called and see Jensen looking at me. I feel my face start to burn up. I can't be around him right now. He is looking back and forth between me and Dominic. This may be childish but I turn around and walk inside the bus, ignoring him. I'll talk to him when I'm ready, if I ever am.

The inside of the bus is huge. There is a massive TV on one wall with a black leather couch in front of it; the opposite side has two booths. Further down has a small kitchen area and down towards the far end is what looks like bunks and two doors. I walk down and peek inside the doors and one is a room with a double bed and the other is a bathroom with a shower. Wow, they've thought of everything. I walk to the bunks and wonder where I'll sleep and who will get to have the room.

"Fuck, this bus is awesome!" I hear Chris shout as he gets on the bus.

"Wow, can't believe we'll be staying on this thing." Lake looks around. "God, you're all going to get on my nerves by the time this tour is over." She sits in a booth and Leon sits next to her, pulling her towards him so her head is resting on his chest.

"Umm, there's a room with a big bed down there." I walk towards them and sit opposite to Lake and Leon, pointing down the bus.

"Think we should flip for it?" Chris asks as he sits next to me.

"Hell no." Lake glares at him. "I don't trust you and your coins. I think it should be me and Sky who sleeps in there since we're girls. We need our beauty sleep away from you pigs. No offense baby." Lake kisses Leon on the cheek.

"Thanks." Leon chuckles at her.

"Why should you get the bed just because you're girls?" Chris crosses his arms pouting like a child.

"Exactly. We're girls. Plus, Sky is the lead singer so she needs rest and to be away from you guys who will probably be fucking your groupie whores in the bunks and like hell I want to hear any of that."

In the *Spotlight*

"What, you think *we* want to hear his ass banging a chick?" Leon shivers and I bet he's imaging Chris doing exactly that.

"Sorry baby, but we need the bed. If we go to any hotels, I'll make it up to you." She licks his lips and smiles at him. I have to look away so I don't have to watch them sucking face.

Again.

— ★ —

I'm sitting in the booth, looking out the window as I watch the scenery fly by. I've never really travelled and I'm finding that life can be really beautiful and breath taking. I'm lost in my own world when I feel someone sit next to me and look over to see Dominic smiling at me. I smile back at him.

"You enjoying yourself?" he asks me.

"Yeah, a little bored though. I can't believe we're actually going on tour. I've read about this stuff in books but can't believe we're actually doing it. It's crazy. I can't wait to see more of America though."

"Yeah, I keep thinking that I'm dreaming all of this and at any second I am going to wake up and find out it isn't real. That I'll wake up and Sherry will still be the lead singer, bossing us around." He chuckles.

"Yeah, I wake up at times thinking I'm back home and you have no idea how relieved I am that I'm not there." I shake my head and look back out the window.

"Well, since we're going to be on the road constantly, I was thinking about me teaching you guitar again; you know, to help time fly and all that." I turn around and laugh.

"You do remember last time you tried to teach me? I sucked. I sucked really bad. Are you willing to go there again?" I raise my eyebrow, and he laughs. I mean a huge, belly, full laugh. I try and not think about after he tried to teach me, how close him and I were to kissing again.

"Yes, and I'll take my chances. You never know, you may get better and be half decent by the time this tour is over." I think about it and decide, why not? It may be fun.

"Okay, let's do this. At least it will help with the time." I stand up and Dominic goes to get his guitar. We sit on the couch so we have more space.

"That's the spirit." He shakes his head and starts tuning his guitar.

I look around the bus and see Chris sitting up front listening to his iPod. Leon and Lake are in the back sleeping. At least they better be sleeping. There is no way I'm sleeping on a bed that they just made love in. I watch him play with some of the strings and then pass it to me when he's happy with it. I put the strap around my neck and place the guitar on my knee, making myself more comfortable with it.

"Let's start from the very beginning. We won't move on to the next step until you are happy with it. Deal?"

"Deal." I shake his hand and quickly pull it away so I don't feel that electric pull I always feel when his skin touches mine.

🎸—★—🎸

Hours fly by and I'm finally to the point that, when my fingers sweep over the strings, it doesn't sound that bad. I listen to everything Dominic says. Seeing him talk about it, going over every detail, you can see the love he has for it. He talks so passionately and he never once gets frustrated with me. I take my time digesting all the information and think maybe when this tour is over, I will have improved immensely.

We finally stop the lesson when the driver tells us that we'll be in Seattle in just under an hour. I lean back on the couch and rest my head on Dominic's shoulder, now feeling exhausted. My mind was so distracted learning to play that I never realized how tired I actually was. Dominic wraps his arm around my shoulder and pulls me in closer. Before I know it, I've fallen asleep.

After what feels like ten minutes, I'm woken up by Dominic telling me that we've arrived. I look out the window to see the other buses pulling up and check out the place we will be playing next. It looks so much bigger than the place we played last night. It's just after twelve in the morning, and I wouldn't mind getting some more sleep, but everyone wants to go to a club and have a few to say we drank in Seattle. Right after we play, we have to move on to the next place, so once AA is off the stage and have completed their meet and greets, we are on the bus going to our next stop.

I use the bathroom to brush my teeth and hair so I look a little less like a zombie. The guys are waiting outside so I join them and walk straight to Dominic who naturally puts his arm over my shoulder and hugs me into him as he talks to Lloyd. I place my hand on his chest and listen to them. I never realized how relaxing Dominic's voice is. It's so soothing. Maybe it's because I'm sleepy.

I'm listening to them go on about their first experience playing something in front of anyone when I look up to see Jensen leaning against his bus drilling holes into me. Kym and Travis are talking to him but he, once again, isn't listening. I'm surprised his friends don't think he's rude since he never pays them any attention.

"You ready?" Dominic asks me and I look away from Jensen and back to Dominic who is smiling at me. He's always smiling at me. Even though Dominic and Jensen are both very attractive in their own ways, I realized that Dominic is lively and full of light, whereas Jensen is a moodier type who likes to hide in the darkness, the shadows.

"Yup, but I'm not drinking. I think I had enough last night to last me a life time." I cringe just thinking about taking a sip of anything alcoholic.

"That's fine. You're a bit of lightweight. Think next time you should know your limit," he teases me and I smack him on the chest. We all walk to a club that isn't far away. I notice that we have a few huge men walking with us. "Who are they?"

"They're our body guards, well AA's body guards, since fans go mega crazy," Dominic answers my question.

"Wow, they must be really famous to need body guards. Do you think we are ever going to need them?" It's insane thinking that people need protection, but I've never seen anyone go crazy, so who am I to judge?

"Probably. We're still new but if our album does well on the charts, our lives may get even crazier. We could have crazy fans, groupies sneaking on the bus, sneaking into hotel rooms. Hey, some may even think they love you so much they want to get a lock of your hair to make a voodoo doll." Dominic chuckles at me. This time I elbow him in the chest and he bends over a little, touching the spot I hit him.

"Serves you right." I laugh at him and walk on.

"You'll pay for that." I hear him behind me so I turn around and see him start to run towards me so I scream and run off, passing Lake and Leon who are laughing at our display. "Stop now or it'll get worse." Dominic smirks at me.

In the *Spotlight*

"Not a chance." I stick my tongue out at him. He squeezes through people to try and grab me but I dodge him and I'm now in front of Jensen who looks angry. I don't have time to think twice about it as Dominic nears me again so I shriek and run off but then I feel arms around my waist, lifting me off the ground.

"You should have listened," he says before he starts tickling me and I'm screaming and laughing. I'm sure if anyone nearby is asleep, I probably have woken them up by how loud I'm being.

"Stop, please! I'll pee myself!" I'm still screaming and his fingers tickle all over my sides. I am almost bending down on my knees but he follows me down, not stopping.

"Say 'Dominic, you are the mighty king of rock and you play like a God'." I snort at him and he tickles me harder until I scream out the line he wants me to say. He eventually stops and my body feels like I just worked out. "See, it wasn't that hard." He pulls me in close to him. I almost elbow him again but stop since I definitely don't want to be tickled again.

"You are such a meanie."

"A meanie? Is that even a word?" He snickers at me.

"Yes it is. It's in the Sky knows it all vocabulary, look it up." I stick my tongue out at him and in a flash his fingers grab my tongue.

"Be careful where you stick out your tongue." He lets go and I feel the fun mood slip away. It's gone back to serious. We walk the rest of the way in silence, me still tucked under his arm.

🎸—★—🎸

We've been here for an hour and I'm ready for my bed, well Lakes' and my bed. It's been a long day and my body needs to rest, especially knowing I'll be playing in front of a brand new crowd soon. Jensen looks at me now and then but hasn't said a single word to me. Maybe he's still pissed off that I ignored him this morning.

I go to the bar to order myself another coke when a guy wearing an expensive looking suit walks up to me. He's cute, probably in his thirties. He's smiling at me so I return it before looking back to the bartender, hoping I can get his attention.

"I'm sorry, but may I ask if you're the girl from that new band? Risen Knights?" I look at him, shocked that he recognizes me.

"Yeah I am. I'm Sky." He shakes my hand.

"I saw your music video and I have to tell you, wow. I didn't recognize you at first, but when I saw your eyes, I knew it had to be you. You definitely don't look like the girl on the screen." I bet I don't.

"It's acting, isn't it? I'm not that girl you see. You know how it is. You have to give what the people want." As soon as those words leave my mouth, I regret it. That sounded so bad but, with the guy still smiling warmly at me, I don't think he noticed.

"True. I have to say, your voice is amazing. Heard you're playing here tomorrow night." Well more like in fifteen hours.

"Thank you. Yeah we're opening up for Absolute Addiction. Will you be coming?" Again, why don't I think before I let words leave my mouth?

"Yes, I have tickets and backstage passes. My sister loves Absolute Addiction so she's dragging me along. Now I'm glad she is." He smiles at me and it clicks that he's hitting on me. I look down, seeing the baggy blue jeans and long sleeve top that I have on. I don't even look that pretty, but he's looking at me like I'm wearing a glamorous dress. "I'm Miller by the way." He shakes my hand; I notice he holds on a little longer than normal.

"Nice to meet you. I hope you enjoy the show."

In the Spotlight

"I'm sure I will." We smile at each other and I notice Miller is looking behind me. I turn around to see Jensen standing there.

"Is there a problem?" he asks, but his eyes are trained on Miller.

"No problem, just telling Sky how great of a singer she is." He smiles at me.

"I bet you were. Well if you don't mind, we're having a band hang out so I'm going to steal her away." What the hell? I turn to look at Miller, apologizing with my eyes.

"It was nice meeting you, I hope to see you again." Miller shakes my hand, smiles at me and walks away. He was so nice and Jensen talked to him like he was garbage.

"What is your problem?" I yell at him.

"What? He was looking at you like he wanted to fuck you on this bar," he growls at me.

"What, like how you used to look at me you mean? It's okay if you do it, but not okay when another man does it? I'm not yours so back off." I push his chest but it's like pushing a wall and he hardly moves.

"You may not be mine, but like hell I'm letting another guy try and sweet talk you just to get in your panties." He leans in towards me, blocking me in against the bar.

"Like I told you, I'm not a whore. Just because you think a guy wants to sleep with me doesn't mean it will happen. Besides, I can look after myself." I try and walk under his arm but he grabs my elbow and pulls me into his body.

"I'm just looking out for you," he says, his voice softer.

"No, you're not. You're claiming your territory." I push his arm away and walk back to my seat, pissed that I didn't get my drink.

Miller was just being nice and Jensen had to act all caveman. Men.

I'm listening to Chris and Leon when I hear a commotion and turn to see Jensen standing on the bar, holding a microphone. What the hell is he doing? Is he drunk? Everyone goes quiet but a few girls yell out their love for him. Suddenly a song comes on and he starts singing. He stares at me as he sings Jason Derulo's *In My Head*.

His voice is so sultry and smooth. The song is about a girl being in the guy's head and how he sees them together. I also notice some sexual innuendos. He walks up and down the bar and his moves are flawless. You can tell he performs professionally. Girls on the dancefloor are going crazy. He jumps off the stage and walks towards me with determination in his eyes. When he gets close, he puts his hand out for me to take.

I look up at him and he is so adorable that I take the offered hand and he helps me up, twirls me out and twirls me back in, continuing to sing to me. He's actually singing to me. He pulls me closer to his body and I move with him. This guy can dance. I'm giggling at him, shaking my head at him actually doing this. I notice when the words *you fulfil my fantasy* come out, he looks straight into my eyes, telling me that I really do.

The song ends and people cheer. He is wearing a huge smile that makes him look years younger. He places the mic down and, before I know what's happening, he dips me back and his mouth moves close to mine.

"I really like you, Sky," that's all he says before his lips are on mine in a soft and gentle kiss. I wrap my arms around his neck and kiss him back. "I know I didn't make a good first impression but I really can't get you out of my head. Please, will you try and give me a chance?" I pull back a little and look into his eyes.

In the *spotlight*

I nod and he smiles at me, kissing me again before lifting me back up. The whole place is cheering and he smiles at everyone, bows, and then points at me. I take a little bow as well and he pulls me back to him, kissing my cheek. I look around me and see Dominic watching us. There is something in his eyes I can't explain but he gives me a small smile and starts to talk to Chris.

―――★―――

Dominic

He did it, he actually did it. He got through her walls and she let him. I watch him sing to her, and seeing her face light up like it did was like a kick in the teeth. I should be happy for her, happy that she's happy. Seeing his lips on hers, I can't help but remember how they felt against mine. I was her first kiss and now he's claiming her. Claiming her in front of everyone. I wasn't expecting to feel so hurt. It hurts she said yes; it hurts that she's letting him into her heart.

What have I done?

Why am I only realizing *now* that I made a mistake?

I fucked up.

Now that she is with someone else, I realize how badly I want it to be me.

Now I have to live knowing that I made the biggest mistake of my life by keeping her at arm's length. I know this is going to be my biggest regret.

I guess the saying is true; you don't know what you've got till it's gone.

Chapter 19

Sky

Jensen insists on me joining him on his bus but I decline since all I want to do is sleep. I have a feeling he wants to do anything *but* sleep. I know he was disappointed by my answer but, if he wants to be with me, he has to learn that just because I'm letting him in, doesn't mean I'm going to start changing what I believe.

He held my hand all the way to my bus and stops near the door. He places his hands on my cheeks as he leans down to kiss my lips softly. I was expecting it to be more urgent, rough, but it's not. He smiles at me, walking backwards so his eyes are still on me. I gave him a small wave and walk up the few steps. I hear a shriek and see Lake running towards me.

"I can't believe you're dating Jensen! It's all over YouTube. He serenaded you. Oh my God, your first boyfriend is a famous rock star," she says in one go without taking a breath. I look around and the guys are all staring at me like I'm some sort of alien. I look at Dominic and he's on the couch, strumming his guitar, not looking at me.

"How could I say no to that? He was being sweet and I think that cockiness is just what he thinks people expect from him. I just hope it works out." I shrug and sit down in a booth. I can't believe I said yes, but the smile on my face is showing me that I did the right thing. I like this side of Jensen.

In the Spotlight

"This tour is going to be amazing, I can feel it. My baby sister is going out with the lead singer of Absolute Addiction. I'm going to post it on our Facebook page." Lake kisses my cheek and goes to her laptop.

I tell everyone I'm going to sleep and head to my room. We have to be up in a few hours to do some rehearsing and right after, I want to catch up on some more sleep before we go on. We just started this tour and already I know I'll be losing lots of sleep. I change into my PJ's and lie on the bed, staring at the ceiling, when I hear a knock on the door.

"Come in." I sit up and when the door opens I see Dominic standing there. "Everything okay?" I ask him.

He doesn't say anything but walks to the bed and sits next to me.

"I just wanted to make sure you're okay?" My whole body softens at the sincerity in his eyes. I know he sees me as family but, apart from my sister, I don't think I have ever had someone else care for me like this.

"Yeah, I'm fine." I smile reassuringly at him and he gives me a warm smile in return.

"I know this may be out of line, but I just want you to be careful when it comes to Jensen. Me and you have gotten close these last couple of months and I would hate to see you get hurt. It would break me if he hurt you in anyway, or pushed you to do anything you didn't want to do." I can tell he's upset and I place my hand on his. His eyes look down at our hands and he entwines them.

"I'll be careful, thank you for looking out for me. I know you think he's an ass, but I've seen a different side to him, a playful side. I've never had a boyfriend but, trust me, I wouldn't do anything I'm not ready to do. I just want to see where it goes. If it doesn't work out, it doesn't work out. At least I know I'll have you at my side." I nudge his shoulder with mine.

"I'll always be by your side. But if he does hurt you, I'll kick his ass, just to pre-warn you." I giggle.

"If he does hurt me, I won't stop you."

"Right, I'll let you get some sleep then." He is about to stand when I hold his hand tighter and bite my lip.

"Umm, I know you probably want to sleep on your own, but do you think you could lay next to me for a little bit? Until I at least fall asleep?" I look into his eyes and he looks like he is struggling with something and I hate that I have put him in a weird position.

Maybe it's because I'm with Jensen and it won't be right, but before I can tell him it's okay and that he can go if he wants, he nods his head. I shuffle to the side of the bed to give him some room and he lies down. We are both on our backs, staring at the ceiling. I want us to sleep like we used to.

"Dominic?" I whisper out his name.

"Mm." He turns and looks at me.

"Can we sleep like we normally do?" It takes a few seconds before I feel his body turn and he helps me to my side, wrapping his arm over my waist, and entwines his fingers with mine again. I know we shouldn't be sleeping like this but when he is near me, he fights away my nightmares. But most of all, I just like knowing he is near me. I feel his breath on my neck and I finally close my eyes and let sleep take over. I hate that when I wake up again, he is gone.

⟵ ★ ⟶

I'm walking towards the stage for rehearsal when I feel my arm being tugged and I'm pinned against a wall with Jensen's lips on mine. His fingers fist in my hair, his body presses against mine. His tongue licks my bottom lip and I open my mouth, giving him access, and he growls in the back of his throat. He takes a step back, our breathing coming out in fast pants.

"I don't think I will ever get sick of kissing you." He comes close again and kisses my lips softly before pressing his forehead against mine, looking into my eyes, searching for something. "You really are different than other girls, aren't you?" I hate that he's comparing me to the women he has been with before but I can see a compliment in there as well.

"Is that a good thing?" I ask him and he smiles at me, kissing me again.

"Definitely."

"Sky, we need you on stage!" someone yells out to me. I turn my head and see everyone is staring at us and feel my cheeks heat up.

"I love how easily embarrassed you get. Your creamy white skin turns into a lovely shade of pink. I wonder what other places would turn pink." His eyes have gone hooded.

"I need to go," I whisper. He nods.

I walk a few steps when he tugs my arm and twirls me around and slams his mouth on mine again, leaving me breathless with a hard kiss. He lets go and takes a few steps back, giving me a wink. I have to walk on stage with wobbly legs and all eyes on me.

Great.

The rehearsal went great and luckily I left without running into Jensen again. I know that sounds mean but, I know he would have asked me to stay and watch him and right now all I want to do is catch up on some more sleep. I head back to the bus and can hear soft music playing inside. I take a couple of steps and see Dominic with his head down, singing a song about falling to pieces. I think I recognize it as The Script's *Breakeven*.

    His voice is beautiful and I can't move. I know he's lost in the music, like how I am when I let the words take over, and can't see me. He gets louder and I feel like his voice, the words of the song, hits me right in the heart. A few tears fall down my cheek as I continue to listen. Why is he singing this? Why didn't he ever mention that he could sing? He could have been the lead singer as well as the lead guitarist. I have so many questions but I know I could never ask. There must be a reason he hasn't said anything and I don't want to pry. I know what it's like to hide something. I continue to listen to him and wish I could crawl inside his head and see what he is thinking.

    He finishes the song and I don't know if I should walk away or walk up to him, pretending I never heard him. Pretending that in my eyes, he is even more perfect than he already was. I go for the latter and walk up the steps humming so he can hear me. I watch him strum the guitar, not looking at me.

    Please look at me.

    I sit next to him and watch his fingers strum and I want to change the atmosphere that is choking away the light we are normally in. I start to hum and before I know it I'm singing. I sing *Breathe* by Michelle Branch, letting the words easily fall from my mouth and, finally, Dominic looks at me and starts to play along. I smile at him and when the song gets to the chorus, I stand up and spread my arms out, my head falling back as I let the power of music take me over.

    I move around the bus, twirling, singing, swaying my hips. I

In the Spotlight

jump on the couch and Dominic stays where he is but not once do his eyes leave me. I finish the song and a huge smile is on my face. I love how music can always make me feel so alive, so happy.

Dominic stands up and walks towards me, his guitar forgotten. He's in front of me and puts his hand around my neck, moving in closer, and I feel my heart yammering in my chest. His thumb strokes my skin back and forth. I close my eyes and hate what I'm about to do.

I step back.

I walk away from Dominic.

I open my eyes and he's looking at me, knowing why I did it. I'm with Jensen. Dominic opens his mouth to say something when I hear my name being called and see Jensen walking towards us. I give him a smile but I'm sure he notices it's a little forced. He looks back and forth between us and his eyes have gotten darker, angry.

"What's going on?" Jensen asks.

"We were just goofing around." I shrug, trying to act indifferent, but he doesn't seem convinced, especially because Dominic is standing there still looking at me. It's like he's in some trance.

"I bet you were." I look at Jensen and I swear that sounded like him calling me a liar. I could have kissed Dominic, but I didn't since I'm with him.

"What is that supposed to mean?" I ask angrily. He looks at me and his eyes soften.

"I'm sorry. I was looking for you. Want to hear me rehearse some songs?" I want to say no but, after what he almost walked into, I feel like it's my duty to say yes. It's what girlfriends do right? We haven't put a label on what we are but I assume that's what this is.

"Sure." Jensen holds my hand and we start to walk away. I quickly look behind me and Dominic is still standing there. I whisper "I'm sorry", like he did all those months ago when I first moved in with him, and he gives me a nod. I walk back to the stage and sit in the third row as I watch Jensen play.

After hearing Dominic sing, I can't get his voice out of my head. I watch Jensen and see how he plays to the audience, his smirks and smiles. When Dominic played, it was like he was in another world. Lost in thought. I shouldn't compare, maybe if Dominic was singing in front of people, he would act different too.

I stay there till the end and Jensen comes and sits with me and we talk. He gives me all of his attention, asking me questions about my favorite color, food, movie. He does bring up my parents and I tell him it's a sore subject so he drops it, not asking for more information. It's times like this that I am happy to be around him. I enjoy talking and laughing with him, but only when my mind is fully on him.

That's when it clicks. I'm still holding back, keeping that space in my heart for Dominic. But Dominic and I will never be. Jensen is a guy who treats me like I'm precious, who is willing to show the world he wants me; is right here in front of me, trying to get to know me. I deicide there and then that I am going to try harder. I can't keep holding onto hope for something that will never happen.

Jensen is talking to me but I put my finger to his lips to stop whatever he is about to say and I stand and straddle him. I watch his eyes go wide with shock. I sit on his lap and press my lips to his. I'm nervous since it's normally the other way around. I normally wait for him to kiss me but, this time, I want to take control. I bite his lower lip and feel his hands grip my waist. I press myself forward

In the Spotlight

and can feel the friction between us, causing me to arch myself into him.

His hands go in my hair and he starts nipping and licking my neck. I look at him and start to grind myself against him, back and forth, and that ache between my legs starts to increase. I slam my lips on his and kiss him with everything in me. I keep pushing myself against his hardness, back and forth, back and forth. His fingers have moved to under my tank and are digging into my skin, but the pain intensifies the pleasure I'm feeling.

I'm so lost in the sensation that I startle when I hear clapping, looking up to see Kym watching us in one of the seats in the back. It feels like cold water is splashed all over me. I sit up and jump back into my seat, looking at the stage, not wanting to look anywhere else. I try and get my breathing under control and notice Jensen looking at me, licking his lips.

"Please don't stop. It was so hot, I feel like fingering myself so I can get off, too," Kym shouts out. I quickly stand and walk away, wanting to be alone. I tried to do something spontaneous, but I still should have made sure we were alone, that there was no one watching. For the first time, I wasn't thinking, just going with it, and it bit me in the ass.

"Sky, wait!" Jensen calls out but I keep walking till I'm pulled back into his chest. "Ignore her, she's just jealous. I think she has a girl crush on you." He rubs his nose against my neck. "Do you want to continue this back on the bus? We have at least an hour before the show starts." I turn around and see he has *that* smile on his face, not the smile I like. It's the smile of the dick rock star.

"I'm going back to my bus. I want to rest before I need to get ready."

"Rest with me." I shake my head.

"I don't think rest is in your plans. I'll see you soon." I press a kiss on his cheek and can tell he's pissed off. Does he not realize that I feel mortified?

"You really going to go and leave me like this?" He points to his hard bulge.

"I told you, I'm not that kind of girl. It's only been a day, I'm not going to just start getting you off," I say sternly.

"What was that back there then?" He points back where the seats are. "You were happy enough to be that kind of girl back there." I walk back to him and push him.

"You are a dick. I wanted to try and get out of my comfort zone and you throw it in my face. I was trying to please you in a way that I can. Obviously that was a mistake." I walk away. I hear him calling my name but I ignore him and head back to the bus.

Chapter 20

I sing that night with so much more emotion. I'm angry and pissed off. I'm feeling emotions I've never felt before. My parents treated me like a doll; they did things that hurt me physically as well as emotionally, but not once have I ever felt like this. The crowd seems to eat it up, screaming out my name, wanting more. I push myself, trying to get rid of this pent up frustration. I dance with the male dancers more seductively than usual. I glide my body from one guy to the next, knowing Jensen is watching. I feel his eyes burning through me but I don't care.

We sing our last song and I walk past Jensen on my way off the stage, pretending he doesn't exist. Maybe I'm acting like a child, but I don't care. I go and get ready and make sure to wear a dress that could pass as lingerie. It's nearly see through, depending on the lighting, and usually I would never wear something like this, but tonight I want to piss Jensen off.

I'm in a back room, talking to some of the fans, taking photos and signing posters. A few of the male dancers surrounded me and I enjoy the attention. Dominic comes over and joins us and, as usual, hooks his arm around my shoulders. I'm caught up in laughing, my head thrown back, when I feel the familiar tingle of someone watching me. When I look up, Jensen is standing near the door, glaring at me. I smirk back at him and continue like he isn't here.

A while later, I sneak off to use the toilet quickly and after I relieve myself, I open the door only to be pushed back in, my back pressed into a wall. Jensen's lips land on mine while his hands pin my wrists over my head, holding them both in one of his hands as he uses the other to slide down my arm, to my waist, to the hem of my dress.

I feel him lift it up as his fingers tickle back and forth on my thigh. My breathing is coming in fast; I'm so turned on and I want him to keep touching me. My whole body is vibrating with so much need. I dig my nails in his hand, wanting to scream out for more. His hand slides up further, nearing my now soaked panties, and I hold my breath, waiting for him to touch me there. A place no one has ever touched.

Like he can hear my thoughts, he begins stroking over my underwear, right on my clit. He rubs harder and I moan out with pure pleasure at the feelings it causes in me.

I need more.

The arm holding my wrists starts to shake and I love that I'm not the only one who is worked up by this.

He pushes my underwear to the side and spreads my wetness through my folds before his finger enters me. I want him to release my hands so I can hold onto his shoulders for support. He enters another finger and I almost buckle.

"Fuck, you're so wet. So fucking tight." He releases his fingers and I whimper with the loss.

He releases my wrists and lifts me so I am sitting on the counter and lifts up my dress until it's around my waist and his thumb is at my clit rubbing a spot that makes me scream out his name. I'm close to something that I know will be amazing. I close my eyes and just feel but then a voice screams out in my head that I'm letting some

In the Spotlight

guy I hardly know touch me in such an intimate place. My head is screaming at me to stop but also to feel that release its crying out for. The first voice wins out and I push Jensen away from me.

"You've got to be kidding me. I could feel how close you are. I could feel how your pussy was squeezing my fingers and you just pushed me away?" I look at him with anger building inside me.

"Stop talking to me like that. If this is how you're going to be every time I won't let you do anything sexual, I'm walking away. Just because most girls you know don't mind all this stuff doesn't mean I don't," I seethe at him. I jump off the counter and straighten myself up.

"It seems like just a few minutes ago you didn't mind what I was doing. Look how you're dressed, the games you were playing, using other guys to make me jealous. You think you're not like the other girls? You need to look in the mirror, baby," he mocks me. I look at him and it kills me that I can't deny what he is saying. He's right. I've known him for a short while and already I'm turning into someone I don't like.

"You're right. I can't do this Jensen. You bring out a side of me that I don't like." I walk around him and he grabs my hand, entwining our fingers together. I turn my head and he is looking at me like I just shattered him.

"Please don't go. Please don't leave me," his words are soft and I can see desperation in his eyes.

"You hardly know me, Jensen," I say his name softly, all the irritation washing off me.

"I want to get to know you, I'm sorry I'm being like this. I'm just so used to this life, so used to girls being a certain way with me. Please, can we start again?" I should have said no, I should have walked away, but a part of me couldn't.

"Okay," I say softly and he wraps his arms around me, holding me. I don't know how long we've been in the bathroom just holding one another but I know we have to show our faces before my sister starts worrying where I went. "Jensen?" He looks down at me. "Can I have your jacket please?" He smiles at me and takes off his leather jacket, helping me put it on.

We walk back towards our friends and enjoy talking and laughing. We need to get back on the road so we say our goodbyes to the fans that got VIP passes and head back to the buses. Jensen puts his arm around my waist and when the buses come into view, he stops me.

"Can you stay with me? No funny business, I just want to sleep next to you." I nod my head and he gives me a huge smile, kissing my lips softly.

I walk towards his bus and turn my head to see Lake giving me a thumbs up. I wonder why she is okay with me being with Jensen but not Dominic? I remember I heard her tell Leon that he was a player and would hurt me. I'm sure Jensen was a bigger player, even though those are thoughts I don't want to be thinking about.

Stop thinking about Dominic, you're with Jensen now.

I walk onto Jensen's bus and it seems like it's twice the size of ours. There is a round couch with a TV that basically takes up most of one wall with a few game consoles and games. I see a few guitars around. The bunks look more spacious too. Jensen holds my hand and pulls me down the bus.

"Woooo, you're finally going to tap that!" Kym shouts out, jumping on the couch.

"Shut it, Kym," Jensen shouts at her and she just pokes her

tongue out at him before winking at me. I feel my cheeks blush.

I follow Jensen to a door that I assume is his room, and see a huge bed taking most of the space, covered in black sheets. There are note books everywhere but, apart from that, the place is tidy. I sit on the bed, unsure what to do now. I'm just praying that he keeps to his word and doesn't expect anything to actually happen, especially after I got us both worked up in the bathroom.

I watch him as he goes to some drawers that are opposite the bed and takes out a big black T-shirt that has AA stamped on it and throws it to me.

"I figure you'll feel more comfortable wearing the shirt instead of the dress." I appreciate the gesture and he guides me to the small bathroom that is joined to the room. I change and when I come back out, he's lying on the bed with the sheets over him. He really does look like the bad boy parents warn you about.

I walk around to other side, feeling self-conscious, and get under the covers. Why do I suddenly feel so nervous to be around him?

Because it wasn't long ago you let his fingers touch your nether region. My head mocks me.

I lay there stiff as a board and Jensen laughs next to me. I turn my head and he's laughing so hard I can't help but laugh with him. We laugh for a few more minutes until we start to calm down and, with that, I start to relax. Jensen puts his arm around my shoulder and pulls me in closer so my head is on his chest.

"You looked like you were comfortable," Jensen says sarcastically and starts chuckling again and I softly hit his chest.

"Hey, it's not my fault you make me feel like this." I snicker to him.

"I want you to be comfortable around me, like how you are with Dominic." I almost tense up but control it since I don't want him to think something is wrong.

"We weren't like this when we first met. We hardly talked, we hardly even looked at each other, but when I joined the band we knew we had to get along. It took time, but we're close now." I feel Jensen's fingers stroking my arm as he listens.

"How can anyone who just met you not want to be around you? When I first saw you, I felt this aura around you, this pull, and I'm sure every guy who sees you feels the exact same way." Except Dominic.

"I think you need glasses." I try and laugh off the comment.

"You're gorgeous. You have amazing dark blue eyes that look like the night sky, a smile that could melt any guys heart; you just radiate innocence." I blink at him.

"Thank you," I whisper.

"I read online that you weren't the original lead singer, how did that happen?" I turn my head and he smiles kindly at me and I tell him about Sherry, about me stepping in at a gig last minute and that's how we met Robert. "Wow, so you sang one song and your life changed. Guess you were at the right place at the right time." Depends how you look at it.

"To be honest, I didn't want to be in the band. I didn't know what I wanted in life other than just to enjoy it. I'm glad that I did though since I get to stay close to my sister."

"And you would have never met me," he jokes and I chuckle.

"And there's that. This life is so crazy, so insane at times, but I do love music, I love how when I sing I feel like I'm a completely different person." I think about every song I have sung so far, how it takes over me.

"When I see you onstage, seeing you sing, it's like you're home. You look like you're in your own world; you move and flow with the music, its mesmerising, it's like you're at peace with the world."

"What about you? Tell me how you got into music, how you became the famous rock star we all adore?" Jensen turns, leaning on his elbow so he's facing me.

"I fell in love with playing as soon as I got my first guitar. Travis and Lloyd were looking for a singer back when I was in high school so I auditioned in their garage and they liked me. We played gigs and we got spotted. Nothing exciting I'm afraid." He pushes some hair over my ear.

"What about your parents, do they support this life of yours?" I see him tense up and I hope I didn't bring up a sore subject. What is it with these music types having a bad history with their families?

"They wanted me to be a doctor or a lawyer. They didn't mind me playing as long as I put my academics first, but when I got the opportunity to play professionally, they didn't approve and basically disowned me. Travis and Lloyd have been my only family ever since."

"What about Kym?" I stroke his stubble on his jaw.

Jensen laughs. "Our original drummer got into an accident and couldn't play anymore and we were lucky enough to find Kym. She plays like a demon possessed when she's behind those drums; it's her passion. She's a good person but she loves to wind people up. I think she likes winding you up the most seeing as how you react so easily." We both laugh, knowing it's true.

"I like it when you're like this." I swipe his hair away from his eyes and he leans towards my touch.

"Like what?" he whispers.

"Like a normal person, not the rock star, or the sex obsessed guy. How you can talk to me so tenderly, so openly. How you can look at me without only seeing sex." I smile softly at him and he looks into my eyes.

"I like being like this too, it's nice to just talk. I like how you don't expect anything from me." I cup his cheek.

"I do expect something from you though." I look into his eyes.

"What's that?" He grins at me.

"To be like this around me, to be kind, sweet, not acting like you're the biggest thing ever in front of your friends. Just be you." I kiss the corner of his mouth.

"How do you do that?" he asks me, shaking his head.

"Do what?" I beam at him.

"Look at me with those deep, dark blue eyes of yours and make me want to be a better person? You draw me in so deep, it's like my soul has known you for ages." I look at him, not knowing what to say.

"I don't know what to say to that," I speak out my thoughts.

"You don't need to say anything. Just sleep. Night my sweets." I chuckle at the name he called me when we first met.

"Night, Jensen." I hear him suck in a breath and I turn to my side as he holds me. It doesn't take long before I hear his breathing even out.

Tonight has been a rollercoaster from beginning to end. From being so angry to feeling all mellowed out. I feel like I've met a side of Jensen that I will enjoy hanging out with. I just hope I know what I'm getting into. I feel a little worried about that side he brings out in me, but I can't fully blame him. It's my choices and decisions; how

In the Spotlight

I dress and act. I try and clear my thoughts and hope sleep takes over me soon.

🎸 ★ 🎸

I'm singing on stage, Jensen in the wing watching me. I feel his eyes on me with each step I take. The song ends and I run towards him and he lifts me up, telling me how amazing I was and kisses my lips like he hasn't kissed me in days. I am breathless when he puts me down. I look up and see my parents standing behind me, looking at me in disgust.

Jensen turns his head to see what I'm looking at when my parent's walk towards me and I cower into his arms. They stop just a few paces away from us, eyeing Jensen up and down.

"This is who you're going to waste your life on?" my mom screams at me and I flinch, remembering how her voice could be.

"Mom..." I try and defend myself.

"Don't you dare 'Mom' me! Do you have any idea what you're doing to this family? What you are putting us through?" I feel a slap across my face. I touch my cheek and feel liquid and see blood on my fingers. Mom always knows how to hit me without leaving a mark, but I guess this time she doesn't care.

"You are coming home. You have been whoring yourself for the whole world to see. Kissing girls, grinding against every guy you see on stage. You make me sick." Dad grabs my wrist so hard, I'm sure he could break it.

"Jensen," I turn and plead to him but he looks at me with the same revulsion as they did.

"They're right; I can't be with someone who throws themselves at every guy who is willing to touch you. I'm sorry, Sky, but I don't want a girl like that. I thought you were different but I guess I was wrong. A good girl wouldn't let me kiss and touch her like you let me do to you." he says with disgust and I feel tears start flowing down my cheeks.

They drag me off the stage, pulling me along so that I am jogging just to keep up with them. We make it outside where a car pulls up and my Mom climbs in first. I don't want to go with them. That wasn't the deal. I start kicking and screaming but my dad holds on tighter, causing me to scream out in pain.

"Sky!" I hear Dominic's voice. I turn and he is running to me. "Sky where are you going?" His voice is panicked.

"Dominic, help me please!" I shout out to him. I stretch out my other arm and try to reach him, but his fingers barely touch mine when I am dragged into the car. I am banging on the window trying to get to him. I feel my arm being pulled so hard that it almost comes out of the socket until I'm facing my father. His eyes blaze red like fire.

"You are coming home; we are going to teach you how to be the girl we raised. You will be punished like the whore you are." I feel his fingers tightening on my arm.

I jerk awake, covered in sweat, trying to breath in as much air as I can. It's been months since I last had a nightmare. Jensen is on the other side of the bed, sleeping peacefully. A part of me wants to wake him up but I know I can't. I head to the bathroom and look in the mirror to see a frightened little girl. I look paler than normal. I splash some water over my face to try and calm myself down. *It was only a dream.*

I go back in the room and grab a fresh t-shirt from the drawer and take a very hot shower, trying to get rid of all thoughts of my parents. I look at a scar on my side, seeing just a faint white line, and

In the Spotlight

memories come back in a flash I crumble down on the floor and cry. I don't know how long I've been sitting there for but I feel arms wrap around me, holding me. Reassuring me that I'm safe and no one will harm me. I pray to the God's that it's true. Jensen is fully clothed but he continues to hold me, stroking my hair, soothing me, and we stay that way until the water turns cold.

Chapter 21

The next day, Jensen doesn't bring up my melt down, which I really appreciate. I could never tell him about my past or the dream I had. There are some things I'm not ready to share. He held me all night and I woke up with his arms still around me. We have a day before we have to get back on the road so Jensen wants to surprise me and take me out for the day. Our first real date. Well, *my* first date. Ever.

I was told to dress casually so I got help from Lake who giggles and shrieks the whole time. I put on a light blue summer dress that hugs my curves and flares around my knees. I know it's the right choice when Jensen's eyes soften when he sees me. He holds my hand and guides me to a fancy car that looks expensive, and I'm shocked to see that he got a personal driver to take us.

A car follows behind us, holding Jensen's bodyguards; that's something I still need to get used to. I look out the window watching the world fly by, the whole time my hand held firmly in Jensen's. My eyes go wide when I see a movie theatre and I beam at him. When we walk in, it's completely empty apart from a couple of people who are in uniform.

"Welcome, Mr. Ryder, is there anything else we can do for you?" a man in his late fifties asks.

"No thank you." Jensen captures my hand again and guides me to one of the rooms which is also entirely empty. How did he do this?

In the Spotlight

"Lake told me you loved movies so I booked the place out so we would have some peace and quiet. I'm sure you can imagine how crazy it could get if people saw I was here. Plus, it's a bonus of being a famous rock star," he answers my thoughts with a wink.

We take a seat in the middle and a person comes with two huge boxes of popcorn, two large drinks and basically every bag of sweets you can think of. I put the popcorn between my legs and wait for the movie to start. I'm surprised when I see the title and it's *Calamity Jane*, a musical.

"We're actually watching a musical?" I look at him, shocked.

"Lake said you loved musicals and I thought you would like this one." I smile at him and press a kiss to his cheek.

When the movie starts, I watch intensely, not wanting to miss a single bit. The way Calamity sings, her voice is so beautiful, and I love the story line. The songs are fun and catchy and this is definitely something I want to see again. Jensen never complains once and half way through, he held my hand again, entwining his fingers with mine.

I've never felt so moved or touched by a movie. I'm glad they got their happily ever after. We walk back to the car and I quickly throw my arms around him, knowing he did all this for me. Watching a movie, I know most guys would hate.

"Thank you so much for this, it was amazing." I go on my tip toes and kiss his lips gently.

"I'm glad you enjoyed it. I was anxious about the movie choice, in case you didn't like it, but I watched you watching the film and it was like you've never seen a movie on the big screen before." I look at the ground, unsure what to say and he lifts my chin looking at me like he thinks he said something wrong. "Have I upset you?" I shake my head.

"I've never actually seen a movie on a big screen," I say, embarrassed.

"I'm glad I could change that. It's a memory I will always cherish," is all he says before kissing my knuckles and taking me back to the car. I thought we were going back to the bus but we take a detour to McDonalds and I laugh when we wait in the drive through.

"I can't believe you're taking me to McDonalds for lunch." I laugh but I can't wait to eat a Big Mac. We eat in the car, laughing and talking about anything as the car just drives us anywhere and everywhere.

We park up at a beach and we take off our shoes so we can walk on the sand barefoot; I love feeling the sand between my toes. We walk to the ocean and along the shore, talking about him and the gigs he has played at, life on the road when they first started.

It's been a perfect day. When we start to walk back, I see a blanket on the sand with a picnic basket. I gasp when I notice it. How did he plan this? Being a famous rock star clearly has some advantages. I sit down and watch Jensen take out some fruit, bread, cheese, chocolate and a couple of bottles of water.

I pick at the food as I watch people around us; children building sandcastles, people playing fetch with their dogs. Watching people doing normal things. Jensen stands up and sits behind me, so that I'm now sitting in-between his legs. I rest my head on his chest as we watch the sun start to set. Seeing the different colors in the sky is so mesmerizing. I've never been on a date before, but this has been so romantic and thoughtful and after yesterday, we needed this.

In the Spotlight

"I loved being near the ocean when I was a kid," Jensen says, and I don't respond, just let him open up to me. "I used to build forts and fly my kite, back before life got hard; before pressure got put on me." I entwine my fingers with his and he tightens our joined hands.

"I know what pressure is like, I was brought up to be the perfect daughter, the perfect girl but the thing about perfect, is that it doesn't exist." I feel the wind against my face.

"You're perfect to me. I'm happy how you turned out; you are special and definitely one of a kind." I chuckle at him.

"At least I'm special." I elbow his stomach.

"You are," he whispers in my ear and kisses the side of my head.

"Thank you for today, it has been beyond words." I turn my head and he leans down and kisses my lips.

"I'm glad. I wanted to make it... special." I chuckle.

"It was." I won't forget this day.

We stay there till the sun fully sets and when it starts to get cold, Jensen helps me up and folds the blanket. He picks up the basket and we walk back to the car, our hands still joined. I lay my head on his shoulder and soon, sleep takes over. The next thing I know, I'm being lifted. I open my eyes to see we are back at the buses and I'm sad that the day has already ended.

"I didn't want today to end," I groggily say.

"Neither did I, but we will have more days like this." I snuggle back into his chest as we walk on to his bus. He helps me take off my dress and put on one of his shirts before helping me into his bed without it being sexual. The whole day he has been the perfect gentlemen. We talk about the day; out favorite parts of the movie and about the ocean. I fall asleep again feeling content, happy.

The next day we are rehearsing when I hear my name being called and my blood runs cold. I turn to see Sherry staggering towards the stage. I look to Dominic who rushes to my side; Jensen was supposed to be here but he and his band are doing an interview for Rolling Stone right now. I'm glad he isn't going to witness this.

"Look at you, Sky. I guess fame really does change you. You looked like a nun last time I saw you, now look at you." She swipes her hand up and down my body. "I guess fucking with a lead singer of a famous rock band changes things," she laughs. I look at her appearance, seeing dark circles under her eyes. Her skin looks paler but not in a healthy way.

"What are you doing here Sherry?" Leon walks to my other side.

"I came to see my once-upon-a-time family. We grew up together and you kicked me to the curb without a backward glance. Thanks for checking up on me, doing great as you can see." She sniffs and wipes her nose.

"We don't have time for this; you made your bed after you attacked Sky, you changed and that's not our fault. Just leave, okay? We don't want to cause a scene." Dominic says.

"A scene? Don't you fucking worry about making a scene. That's why I'm here; I need some cash and I know you guys are doing very well. I need a few thousand to cover some expenses." She sniffs again. I see that her eyes look a little too wide.

"Why the hell would we give you our money?" Chris chuckles.

"Because if you don't, I'll go to the papers, magazines, anyone who will hear my story. You've mentioned that there was another lead singer, so maybe they'll want to hear some stories from behind the scenes. I can tell them all about how you and I fucked, Chris. Or

In the Spotlight

about how I fucked the lead guitarist three days before the choir girl showed up on your door step." My body tenses up, hearing her say that she slept with Dominic a few days before I arrived.

"Why are you doing this? You really want to hurt us that much?" Leon shakes his head in disbelief.

"You all fucked me over, so yeah, I would. I'll answer every dirty question they can think of, so it's up to you." I look at Dominic and he is grinding his teeth.

"Fine, I'll give you the fucking money." He spits out.

"Dom, you know she'll just come back for more," Chris whispers in his ear but I hear it. I look at Sherry, remembering her looking flawless and confident and seeing her now, her body looks like she's shaking.

"I just printed this out. I heard what she said and made this up." Lake walks towards us with a piece of paper. "It's a contract, we give her the money and if she tells anyone anything about us, we will sue her ass and whoever she tells the story to will have no choice but not publish whatever rubbish she spews out." Lake walks towards Sherry with a look of disgust. "Sign this." I watch Sherry's hand shake as she signs her name. Lake gives her a check and Sherry accidently drops it. When she bends down to pick it up, I see a small plastic bag with white powder in her pocket.

Is that drugs?

"Fuck, Sherry, you're doing drugs?" Dominic looks at her with pity. "We promised we would never touch that shit." He says with sadness in his eyes.

"Well, sometimes people forget the promises they made to one another. Have a nice life guys, thanks for bailing me out." Her voice shakes and, in that moment, I do feel bad for her.

"Don't leave like this." Dominic takes a few steps forward.

"Goodbye Dominic." She gives him a small smile and leaves. I wrap my arms around my middle, hating what she has done to her life and I hate how I feel somehow responsible.

Chapter 22

Since our date, Jensen and I have been inseparable. I sleep over on his bus and all we do is kiss, cuddle or just talk; not once has he pushed for anything more. He watches as I rehearse and vice versa. It's rare to see one of us without the other close by. It's been two weeks since we started the tour and we are starting to get a larger fan base. Lake said we have over thirty thousand likes on our Facebook page.

I woke up in Detroit next to Jensen and wanted to surprise him with breakfast in bed. I saw a café not far away when we were driving up and decided to get something to eat and drink for when he wakes. I write him a quick note letting him know I would be back in case he wakes up and worries that I'm gone.

I put on my jeans and his black t-shirt, tying my hair up in a high ponytail. My hair has gotten longer, now reaching my waist, but I like it. I walk off the bus and everyone is still sleeping. I start walking down a path until I see the sign 'Bev's Café' and walk inside, ordering some bagels, croissants, and coffees. The lady behind the counter is super nice and I leave with a pep in my step but it quickly fades when I hear a few girls scream nearby.

I'm suddenly surrounded by a group of girls, screaming and shouting at me, some taking pictures. I try and walk past them but they're blocking my path and won't move. They shout questions at me; asking if I'm from the band Risen Knights, am I with the lead singer Jensen, am I leading Dominic along. It's so much that I start to feel claustrophobic and am having difficulty breathing properly.

"Can you please let me through?" I try and squeeze by but it's like they can't hear me. I feel my hair being pulled and my shirt is grabbed.

"You don't deserve Jensen. You're using him," One of the girls say. She's behind me and I can't see her face.

"Let her go!" another girl shouts and I'm being pulled back and forth. I fall to the ground, tears streaming down my face, and the girls are basically on top of me. I'm trapped.

"What's it like being with Jensen?"

"Are you sleeping with Dominic too?"

"Are you wearing his shirt?"

"Can we meet him?"

Questions are being thrown at me right, left and center and none of them care that I am on the ground, sobbing, trying to stand up. I feel my shirt rip and it's like I'm in another nightmare but I can't wake up from this one. I tuck myself into a ball and pray someone will save me. All of a sudden there are arms under me and I'm being lifted from the ground.

"It's Dominic!"

"Dominic, are you in love with Sky?"

"Are you jealous she's with Jensen?"

"Marry me Dominic!"

I tuck my head into Dominic's chest as we walk through the crowd and I see a few body guards trying to get the crazy fans away. I have one arm around Dominic's neck as I fist his shirt in my other, crying into him.

"I got you. You're safe," Dominic tries to soothe me but I can't

In the Spotlight

stop the tears. "You should all be ashamed of yourselves!" Dominic shouts out.

I am back on my bus and being taken down to my room. The door opens with a bang as Dominic places me down. I feel him sit me up and take my shredded top off and then place another over my head before he tucks me under some covers and holds me.

"Where's Sky?" I hear Lake somewhere on the bus and she comes into the room, running to my side to hug me as soon as she sees me. "What did those bitches do?" she whispers.

"I wanted to surprise him with breakfast and the next thing I knew; I was being trapped by a group of girls. They were all talking at once; they wouldn't listen to me when I told them to let me go. Someone grabbed my hair, pulled at my shirt. It was horrible," I sob into my sister and she strokes my hair.

"Fuck. You're okay now. Shhh, you're safe," she says over and over again, rocking me back and forth.

After some time, my tears have finally stopped but I want to stay in my sister's arms. Dominic is still next to me, watching over me. I don't know what I would have done if it wasn't for him.

"Thank you, Dominic," I say, but my voice comes out hoarse.

"I'm always here for you, you know that." I feel the bed dip and his hand palms my head and brings me into his chest. "I just wish I had gotten there sooner," he whispers to me.

"How did you know she was there?" Lake asks him and I feel his body tense up.

"I was on my laptop when my Google alert beeped; someone was recording what was happening. I saw Sky getting hurt and I ran out there, taking some guys with me. This world sometimes makes me sick. Recording someone getting attacked and doing nothing about it?" I feel him shake his head.

"Thank you, for getting her," Lake says tenderly.

"I told you, I would never want to see her get hurt."

"I know." I feel something in the air change and I'm about to say something when my bedroom door bangs open again and I see Jensen standing there, looking anxious. When his eyes land on me, he runs to my side and lifts me into his lap.

"You shouldn't have left; you should have told me what you were planning." Jensen rocks me.

"I wanted to surprise you with breakfast." A few tears slide down my face, he cups my cheeks and wipes away the tears with his thumb.

"You're so sweet, but so stupid for what you did. You are a rock star now; you can't go somewhere without having security with you from now on, okay?" I nod and he pulls me back in, holding me before lifting me up and I wrap my legs around his waist. "I'm taking her back to my room, thank you for looking after her."

"You going to be okay, Sky?" Lake walks to me and holds my hand that is around Jensen's neck.

"I will be, thank you." I smile at her.

"Just be careful okay? I don't want to go to jail for kicking some crazy woman's ass." I chuckle and nod my head. We are near my door when I quickly turn my head around and see Dominic watching me.

"Thank you, Dominic, for saving me."

"Anytime." I feel Jensen's body stiffen but then relax when he walks me off the bus, towards his.

"If she goes anywhere, make sure someone goes with her," he barks out orders to someone. I'm taken to his room and he lays me down, spooning me, and holds my hand. I don't know if it was the whole ordeal, or what, but I'm suddenly very tired and worn out. I'm about to fall asleep when I remember the breakfast I got must have fallen to the ground at some point.

"I'm sorry I didn't get you breakfast," I groggily get out.

"Don't be stupid, I'm just glad you're okay." He glides his fingers up and down my arm and, not long after, I fall into a deep sleep.

I wake up not sure what the time is and see that I'm alone in the room. I lift my head and it feels like it weighs like a ton of bricks. I need some painkillers; my body is aching all over. I'm still dressed so I walk to the door and start to open it but stop when I hear Jensen talking about me.

"I can't not be with her. I really like her, okay?" he seethes out to whoever he is talking to.

"I get that you like her but, come on, she isn't part of this world yet. She needs to get used to being in the spotlight, not get thrown in the deep end because you see her as some sort of challenge," I hear Lloyd's voice.

"I don't see her as a challenge. I like being around her, I like seeing me through her eyes."

"That's very nice to hear but you aren't that guy Jensen. You're going to end up hurting her at some point, I know you man. Just end things now, before anything else happens. Look at today for example, she needs time to get use to this life. We had the chance to gradually get here, she's being forced. Do the right thing," Lloyd sighs.

"I'm not letting her go," Jensen whispers shouts at him.

"Do what you want but remember, we're meeting up with

Trigger tonight. Do you really think Sky will be okay being around that scene?"

"Fuck. I'll just tell her to hang out with her friends tonight."

"So you're going to tell the girl who got attacked to go back to her bus even though she's been living with you for two whole weeks? Good plan," Lloyd says sarcastically. Who is Trigger? What's happening tonight?

"What do you want me to do?" Jensen says dejectedly.

"Do what you want but, Sky is a good girl, she doesn't need to see this shit."

"That's why I'm going to make her stay on her bus. She'll understand and plus, she'll get to hang with her sister. It will be fine."

"If you say so." I walk back in the room and lay back down on the bed, wondering why Jensen is getting all wound up about tonight. I hear the door open and Jensen lies next to me, kissing my neck and falling asleep while I stay awake with several different scenarios running through my head.

🎸—★—🎸

I'm sitting on the couch with one of Jensen's guitars, practicing the notes Dominic taught me. I'm determined to be able to play at least one song by the time this tour is over, which is in two weeks. AA will be going to Europe to finish the rest of their tour and I'm not sure what is going to happen between us, but I'm not going to ask yet.

I'm humming another Michelle Branch song; she is now my personal favorite singer. Jensen sits next to me and I know he is going to talk about me going to my bus tonight. I don't mind, it would be nice to spend more time with my sister and Dominic since

In the Spotlight

I've been less sociable recently. I just want to know who this Trigger guy is.

"Sky, I need to ask a favor from you." I put the guitar down and look at him so I can see every expression and emotion through his eyes.

"Okay, ask away." I watch him rub his stubble and look at the ceiling like he's trying to figure out how to word what he's going to say.

"This guy I know from another band is coming to hang out with me and the guys tonight. I would love for you to be here, but he likes to party a little harder than normal." I look at him confused at what he means by *harder*. He can see the confusion on my face and continues, "He likes to drink heavily and have girls basically naked around him when he parties. I don't want you to see that kind of thing." Wait, so there are going to be half naked, drunk girls around and he wants me to be okay with that?

"So, you want me to leave you alone, with a guy who likes to have naked girls around him, on your bus so you can hang out with them, but you don't want me there to witness it all?" I shake my head, not understanding this.

"I want to hang out with *him*, not the girls," he tries to defend himself.

"But there are going to be drunk, half naked girls around and you want to be alone with them?" I stand up, feeling pissed off. I got attacked today and he wants to hang out with groupies?

"You know what? Do what you want. I'll see you later." I grab my jacket and walk towards the exit.

"Sky, don't be like this." I spin around and point at him.

"Listen to it my way then, huh? If I was hanging with a girl who enjoyed having half naked guys around and I told you to leave me alone with them, would you be okay with that? Knowing I'm alone with these guys?" I see his eyes darken. "Exactly. You don't like it, but you think I should be okay with it, even after I went through a day of hell? You enjoy your party; I'll enjoy hanging out with my sister and friends." I walk out of the bus wishing it was a real door so I could slam it shut.

※

I tell Lake and Dominic what happened as soon as I walk on the bus. They knew something was wrong since I looked like I could kill someone with just my stare alone. Come on though, it's not right what he did. Would any girl be okay letting their guy hang out with someone who needs half naked girls surrounding him? I just feel insecure. He's been by my side every day and now he wants space to what? Party?

I'm sitting with Lake on the couch playing zombies on the game console, trying to distract myself from thinking about what's going on over there. I saw a limo pull up but I couldn't see who got out, or how many. It's completely bugging me; I can't believe I have turned into one of those jealous girls. I should trust him, but there is a voice buzzing in my head telling me that I can't, not fully. I died again on the game and Lake takes the controller from my hands and stands up with her hands on her hips.

"Right, this is annoying me as much as it is you. I'm not going out with the guy but my head is full of some nasty images of what may be happening over there. You are my baby sister and I love you, I need to see with my own eyes that he isn't being a dog."

"What are you wanting to do? Go over there and spy on them?" I chuckle at her but her face doesn't change. Oh my God, she's

In the Spotlight

serious. "We can't go spy on them." Can we?

"Yes, we can. We'll just pop our heads in and if everything is okay, we'll come back here and enjoy some quality time killing zombies. Deal?"

"What if there *is* something going on though?" I rub my face with my hands. I'm not sure if I would rather sit here not knowing or go and end up seeing something with my own eyes.

"Then I'll kick his ass and you'll dump that sack of shit like yesterday's garbage. No one is messing with my sister, so pull up your big girl pants and let's go." I stand up, feeling my stomach flutter with butterflies.

"Okay," I barely get out. We grab our jackets and head towards the door when Leon asks us what we're doing.

"Going to make sure Jensen is being a good boy and not getting his dick wet," Lake says casually and kisses his lips softly.

"Okay, if you think that's best." He looks at me and I can see he's worried. Even *he* thinks maybe Jensen is up to no good.

Great, now I'm worried.

"It is. We need to know; it's driving me crazy." Lake grabs my hand and pulls me off the bus. We head towards Jensen's and can hear music coming from the inside.

"What do we do now?" I ask her. She is looking at the bus door, knowing we can't get in without being noticed.

"Okay, get on your hands and knees and I'll see what they are doing." She can't be serious.

"The windows are tinted; you won't be able to see inside."

"The front ones aren't, now come on and get on your hands and knees." I can't believe I am actually doing this.

I bend down and get on all fours and Lake stands on my back.

Damn she weighs a ton. She gets her balance and asks me to lift higher and I try, hoping she doesn't hurt my back in the progress.

"What do you see?" I ask impatiently.

"Hold on." I wait a few minutes then I feel her jump off me. She's looking everywhere but at me.

"Well, is he cheating on me?" I bite my lip and she shakes her head, biting her nails. I know she does that when she is debating on something. "What's wrong then, what is he doing?" I start to get annoyed that she suddenly went so quiet.

"I think we should go back; he's not cheating on you which is a bonus." She tries to pull me away but I know there's something wrong and she is hiding it or waiting till we are away before she tells me, but I need to know now.

I don't know if it's just the adrenaline, or that voice in my head that is screaming at me to see for myself, but I run to the bus door, open it, and walk up the few steps until I can see what's going on. There is a guy I don't recognize who has a girl on each side in nothing but panties, their breasts in his face.

Kym is sucking face with a girl in the corner; Lloyd isn't here but I see Travis smoking something that I'm sure is illegal. But my eyes are trained on Jensen; the caring guy who has opened up to me; the guy with a sweet side who worries and treats me like I'm glass. Except for today and now I know why. I watch as he snorts a white line of powder up his nose then leans back, inhaling in.

Drugs.

He's doing drugs.

Like he can sense me, his eyes open and land on mine. I see shock in them before his signature smirk appears. The guy I thought I knew turns into the dick I first met. He eyes up my body and I wish

In the Spotlight

I wore something different than my short shorts and tank with a leather jacket.

"Baby, you come to please your man?" I look at him, *really look* at him, and all I see is a mess of a guy who is high as a kite, I think the expression goes.

"You made me leave so you can do drugs?" I ask him.

"I couldn't do it in front of you could I? Miss High and Mighty, Miss 'everything is black and white'. I'm just getting a buzz; all rock stars do it." He can't be serious.

"Come on Sky, let's go." Lake takes my hand and tries to guide me away.

"There goes my girl, everyone," he claps his hands, "who is harder to get into than one of my own concerts." He laughs at me and I feel sick that he just brought up our personal life in front of these people. I hear snickers come from the boob twins.

"Don't you dare try and laugh at my sister." Lake storms up to the girls. "You're sitting here with your tits out for these guys to look at you and snort drugs off you. You're pathetic. I bet your parents are real proud of what you've become. At least my sister doesn't open her legs to every Tom, Dick and Harry who gives her attention just to be used and tossed away." Lake walks back to me and grabs my hand again.

"I'd like some sister/sister action if you're interested, Lake?" Jensen says, looking at her like he could devour her.

"You make me sick. Come on, Sky." I'm pulled away from the bus to the sounds of their laughter.

Lake walks me back and takes me to our room and I just sit there, feeling so stupid. What did I truly expect from him? He's a rock star who is used to a certain lifestyle; a lifestyle I will never be a part of. I can't be with someone who takes drugs; I've heard what it does to people. I just want this tour to be over so I don't have to see him ever again.

    Lake tries to talk to me but I tell her I want to be alone. I lay on the bed, images of us flowing through my head like a movie. Him, holding my hand every chance he got. Talking about anything and everything. Our first date. I feel like he is two different people and I definitely don't like the one I just saw. I know now that person will always be there.

Chapter 23

I wake up the next morning to banging on the bus door. I groan into the pillow before standing, hating that I had only a few hours of sleep. I get off the bed and am heading to the door when I hear raised voices coming from the other side. I peek out the door and see Jensen standing there with dark circles under his eyes, his hair messier than normal. Lake is standing in front of him blocking him from going any further.

"What do you think you're doing, banging on our door this time of the morning? Are you inconsiderate as well as a drugged up asshole?" Lake growls at him.

"I just want to talk to Sky. I need to apologize about last night." He rubs his eyes, looking tired.

"I don't want you anywhere near my sister, you get me? You stay the hell away from her. I thought you would be good for her but I was wrong. Now fuck off before I do something you'll regret."

"I'm not leaving until I talk to her." He walks towards her but she doesn't move a step.

"Go away or I swear I will get the guys to kick that pretty face of yours in. FUCK OFF!" she roars and I flinch at the volume of her voice.

"Sky! Sky! I'm not leaving until you talk to me!" He shouts out to me. I groan and open the door, his eyes landing on me. I shake my head at him. What the hell is he doing here?

"Go away, Jensen," I tell him, staying where I am. "I just want to talk, please." He looks defeated but I don't care. I meant what I said; I can't be with someone who can do drugs like it's nothing.

"I don't want to talk to you. You ditched me after I was basically attacked so you could do drugs. You chose *drugs* over me. The way you talked to me was disgusting. I can't be with you knowing you can be like that. Please just go."

"Please, Sky, I don't know what I was thinking. Please, just give me another chance. I messed up." I look at him and he is pleading to me but I shake my head, I can't do it.

"I'm sorry but I can't." With that, I go back to my room.

"You heard her, now leave," I hear Lake tell him.

"I'm not giving up Sky; I *will* make it up to you," I hear him yell, then finally, there's silence.

I lay back on the bed and hate that I have two more weeks of this. Lake comes in the room and sits with me. She is about to say something when her phone rings and she answers it; I can hear Robert faintly in the background.

"Yeah, she's okay; Dominic got to her and brought her back." There's a pause. "Yeah, that's fine. We will meet you then." She hangs up and looks at me. "That was Robert; he was checking in to see if you were okay, he wants us to meet him when we get to New York. He has some news for us." I nod my head. Great, more band stuff. "I'm sorry for taking you last night. I thought the worse was him being with another girl; I wasn't expecting him to be doing drugs." Yeah, you and me both.

"It's not your fault; at least I know now. I can't be with him knowing he does stuff like this. I just can't."

In the Spotlight

"I don't blame you, I would be the exact same. Let's just get this tour over with and see what Robert has in store." I nod my head and lay back down to try and sleep for another hour before I need to get ready for rehearsal.

─ ★ ─

I went to rehearsal and Jensen was there, sitting in the third row like always, watching me, but I wouldn't look at him. I've made a couple of dance mistakes which isn't like me, but I know it's because my head is distracted. I apologize to the guys that it's taking us a little longer than normal. They understand completely, saying we all have off days. I make sure to leave with Lake, knowing Jensen will try to talk to me if he ever sees me alone.

I go back on the bus and was shocked to see the place covered in every flower imaginable. A note with my name on it confirms that they're from Jensen, begging for my forgiveness. I smell the daisies in front of me and walk to my room, trying not to cave to the sweet gesture. I also receive emails from him, pleading for me to talk to him, but I don't reply.

We play the show and luckily there are no mistakes, but my whole heart wasn't in it, which made me feel guilty; people spent a lot of money to see us, well us and AA. I'm leaving to head back to the bus when I hear my name being shouted and turn to see Kym heading towards me.

"Sky, do you have a minute?" she asks me. I look behind her and notice she's alone.

"Sure, what's up?"

"I know you don't want to talk about Jensen, but he's messed up about what happened last night. He was going on and on about you all night, well until he acted like a complete ass, but it was the drugs talking, not him."

"It doesn't matter, Kym; he was doing drugs. I know you're going to say all rock stars do it, but I can't be with someone who does. You know me, I'm a good girl, I can't be around someone like that." I try and make her understand.

"I know. I just want you to know he really is sorry. I'm sure he'll give up that shit for you; he's crazy about you. He's back to the guy he was before fame took over and that's all because of you; you're a good influence on him, and it's not like he does it all the time, just here and there."

"I'm sorry, Kym, but I've made up my mind. This tour is over soon for us anyway and it will be harder to see each other after that. I don't know where this career is taking us, but I'm sure it won't be down the same path. I'm truly sorry and hope we can still be okay, although I'll understand if you don't want to be friends since Jensen has to come first."

"Hey, we are always going to be friends. Like I said, I know he can be an ass. He messed up a good thing. Just don't be too hard on him, okay? He's never been dumped before. I think it's ruined his ego a little bit." We both laugh.

"Thanks Kym."

"Anytime." She hugs me and walks back towards the stage. I'm about to head out the back door and head towards the bus when I hear my name coming from the stage and curiosity gets the better of me. I head back to see Jensen standing in the middle talking into the microphone.

"Like I was saying, I messed up a good thing with Sky, the lead singer of Risen Knights, and I wanted to tell her how truly sorry I am, I know I messed up. This is a little out of the norm for us, but

In the Spotlight

we're going to play a song just for her, hoping she can find it in her heart to forgive me and give me another chance." The lights go low and the guitars start to play and his voice comes through. He's singing Bryan Adams *'Please Forgive Me'* and it's all too much. I walk away, hearing his voice flow through the halls until I slam the door behind me, drowning it out. Why is he making this hard for me?

I walk on the bus and see Dominic where he always is, sitting on the couch with his guitar, strumming away a melody. I sit next to him, neither of us saying anything. It's like he knows I just need his company, not words. I listen to him play for a bit before grabbing a spare guitar. I sit next to him and watch his fingers, trying to copy the movements. We stay like this for the rest of the night.

I wake up the next morning, noticing the bus is moving. I look out the window and see the sun high in the sky; I must have been tired to sleep for this long. I get in the shower and sit down, letting the water spray over me as I try to get my thoughts together. My head is so messed up. I thought relationships would be easy at the beginning; not full of all this drama and confusion. It's been two weeks, *two weeks,* and already I feel like it's too much.

We head to New York and for the first time since starting the tour, we're actually staying in a hotel room. I look around the foyer of the hotel thinking how amazing it is. AA got the penthouse on the very top floor and we are on the floor below but I don't care; at least I'm not anywhere near Jensen. I can still feel his eyes on me whenever he's close by, but I try to ignore it.

We head straight to our floor and I can't believe how massive our suite ends up being. There is a living room that looks twice the size as ours at home and I see four doors that I assume lead to the rooms. I pick one and enter and run straight to the bed, laying on it, feeling like I'm on a cloud.

I've missed having so much space. I quickly change my clothes and head to the sitting area where everyone is at and notice Robert is there already. He smiles at me and I sit next to Dominic, who wraps his arm around my shoulder. I notice Robert watching us.

"Right, well, I bet you are all wondering why I'm here. I heard the tour is going amazingly, and that the fans are loving you. I wanted to be the first person to tell you that the album has reached number one on the charts." I look at him with my mouth hanging open. Number one? No way.

"Holy shit, number one? You hear that guys? We're fucking number one!" Chris jumps up and down on the couch.

"There is also going to be a movie from the eighties that's being redone, *Teen Witch*, and they want you to choose a song to record a track for it." Oh my God, I love that movie. I turn my head to Dominic, eyes wide in shock, and he is smiling at me, remembering that I made him watch it.

"I've actually seen that movie, I really enjoyed it," I speak up.

"Well, that's good. Now we have to record a song for it. I was thinking something along the lines of what you're already doing, something raw and sexy." I roll my eyes at him. Why does everything have to be sexy? Why can't songs just be powerful and moving?

"What about the tour?" Lake asks, taking notes.

"Well the tour for you guys is going to end a week early so we can get this under wraps. Don't worry, the remaining venues have been informed and have readjusted. So, back to the song, have any of you written any new songs or are there any you wouldn't mind doing a cover of?" I bite my lip and raise my hand like I'm back at

In the Spotlight

school. "Sky?" Robert smiles at me.

"Well, like I said, I like the movie and at the beginning of the original there is a song that is really good. Maybe we could sing that? Change it up to make it sound more like us. I think putting an original song to the remake would be a good thing." I fumble with my fingers. Why is it that when I need to speak up, I feel like a child?

"Do you have the song so I can listen to it?" he asks me. I quickly go to my room and grab my laptop and wait as it loads up. I go to YouTube and enter the name of the song and press play as I wait for everyone to hear it.

"I like it," Leon speaks up.

"Me too," Lake adds, smiling at me.

"Well okay, we'll do this one, then. Lake, email me the singer and song title so I can get the copyrights and we'll start recording in a week. Start practicing in your spare time." With that he stands up and leaves.

"So, what is the song called?" Lake asks me.

"It's called *Never Going to be the Same Again* by Lori Ruso." I can't wait to sing this song. I love that movie.

"I can't believe, out of all those movies out there, they chose a film you made me watch." Dominic is smiling, shaking his head.

"What can I say? Just lucky I guess." I stand up and head back to my room and start learning the words, even though I'm sure I know them by heart already.

─ ★ ─

I must have fallen asleep as I wake up to see it's dark outside. I look at the time and it's after one in the morning. I grab my laptop and see ten more emails from Jensen. I must be glutton for punishment since I read them all. At first, they are him apologizing and promising to make me happy but then they start to sound like gibberish. Has he been drinking? Then I remember hearing Kym say how messed up he is and not to be too hard on him.

I sit there contemplating on what to do and I know I won't be able to get back to sleep anytime soon so I quickly brush my teeth and hair and muster as much confidence as I can. I head to the elevator and push the button for the top floor. I get to the door and wonder how I'm going to get inside without a key but then notice it's a little ajar. I poke my head through and it's dark and quiet. Maybe they're all sleeping.

I walk further in and notice bottles of alcohol everywhere and start to get a bad feeling in my stomach. I'm wondering which one of the rooms Jensen's in when I hear some noises and head that way, my heart feeling like it's in my throat.

I push the door open that I heard the noises coming from and my eyes blur with tears. A girl with platinum blonde hair is completely naked, standing up bent over the bed with her ass sticking out as Jensen rams inside her. Groans of pleasure echo throughout the room. Jensen is completely naked, his hair and body covered in sweat.

I should be running but I'm stuck to the spot. He was messaging me, asking for another chance, and he's here with this girl? I take a step back to leave and knock over some empty bottles. Jensen turns his head and when he sees me, he stops fucking the girl, causing her to whimper, begging him for more.

We both stand there staring at each other and when I'm finally able to take a step back, I run out but can hear Jensen running after me, calling out my name. I get to the door and Jensen slams it shut, his body pressed against my back. I almost throw up when I smell

In the Spotlight

that girls' perfume all over him.

"What are you doing here?" he asks me.

"I came here because I was worried about you. I shouldn't have bothered; you seem fine to me." I try to open the door and he shuts it once again. "Let me go," I spit out.

"What did you expect from me?" he slurs. "You've completely ignored me, haven't answered my emails. I would have called you if you had a fucking phone," he raises his voice. I turn around and shove him as hard as I can and see the girl walk out, wrapping herself in a sheet.

"I ignored you for one day, *one day,* and you're already sleeping with someone. It just shows you how much time I'm worth until you move on." I glare at him.

"Sky, come on." He tries to touch me but I step back. If he touches me I swear I will hit him. I've never felt so embarrassed and small.

"Don't you *Sky come on*. I came here for you and you fucked up again. Listen to me, I'm fucking swearing. You bring out a dark side of me that I don't like. This time, leave me the hell alone." I try and leave but he blocks the door again.

"Don't you start blaming me for the girl you're turning into. You always had that side in you. Do you know what? I can't handle living on this pedestal you have me on, wanting me to be damn perfect and for what? You don't even let me fucking touch you. No wonder I grabbed a girl who was willing to open her legs." God he makes me sick.

"Well, enjoy your life having meaningless sex, enjoy being alone, because that's what's going to happen. You're going to be alone. These girls only like you because of your title and soon, your looks and the music will stop and you are going to end up with nothing but memories and regrets. At least I have some self-respect," I spit out every word.

"Yeah, your self-respect is you being a virginal prude," he growls.

"Well I'd rather be that way than some disgusting prick who probably has every sexual transmitted disease out there. You are a worthless piece of shit. I hate you, you mean nothing to..." I don't even get to finish my sentence when I feel a slap across my face, causing me to tumble to the floor. I look up at him, pressing a hand to my cheek.

"Sky, I didn't mean..." He tries to walk towards me but I crawl backwards away from him.

"You leave me the hell alone." I stand up and get to the door.

"Sky, don't leave me." I look at him, still standing there naked, like he's a complete stranger.

"I don't even know who you are." I feel tears that were building up fall once again.

"Sky..." He walks towards me but I walk backwards until my back hits the wall.

"I'm leaving," I hear the girl say who is now dressed in a tight red dress. "Come on, Sky." She holds my hand and we walk out the room; I don't look back.

"Thank you," I say between my sobs.

"I should be apologizing; I didn't know he was yours. I wouldn't have gone near him. I just saw a rock star and my pussy did the talking. I'm so sorry." I nod my head, understanding. She walks me to my room and tells me again how sorry she is.

The suite is the same as when I left, dark and quiet. I'm almost to my room when the light switches on and I see Dominic standing there, looking at me. When he sees my hand pressed against my cheek he comes running over. He removes my hand and his eyes darken when he sees what's underneath.

"That mother fucker!" he roars.

"Dominic," I try and say his name but it barely comes out.

"What the hell is going on?" Lake is rubbing her eyes and when she sees me she runs over. She strokes my cheek and I wince in pain. "What happened?"

"You mean who? I'm going to kill him." I watch as Dominic puts on his shirt and makes to walk out the door, but I run towards him, jumping on his back to try and stop him. "Sky, get off so I can teach that bastard a lesson." But I only hold on tighter.

"Dominic please, don't leave me," I whisper in his ear. He stops moving, taking in a few deep breaths. He grabs my leg and turns me so I'm now wrapped around his front. He pushes my hair back and looks at my face.

"He hurt you," he whispers.

"I know." I hold him, pressing my face to his neck, smelling him. God, how I've missed him. I haven't been this close to him since I started dating Jensen. Dominic sits down on the couch with me on his lap. Lake grabs some ice and puts it in a towel handing it to Dominic to put on my cheek, causing me to wince at the contact. I look into his eyes and can see the anger brewing there but I can also see tenderness towards me.

"Always my hero," I whisper and he looks into my eyes, giving me a small smile.

"Always."

Chapter 24

Dominic slept by my side all night, his body entwined with mine. I wake up to the sun shining through the room. I turn to see Dominic is still fast asleep and I can't help but smile; always my protector. He warned me about Jensen but I didn't listen. I told myself I could handle it, that I saw a side of him that I thought was good, but it wasn't enough.

He laid his hand on me; I wouldn't let him do it twice. I saw the remorse as soon as he did it but no man should ever lay a hand on a woman. I know I spewed some nasty stuff but I didn't deserve that, especially not after what I saw him doing. In the past, I used to think I deserved my punishments but, now seeing things in a new light, I know that's its wrong.

I get up, desperately needing the bathroom. When I look in the mirror I gasp at my reflection. The left side of my cheek has a dark blue-grey bruise. I touch it and wince. How am I supposed to perform with this on my face? Tears build behind my eyes but I don't want to let them fall; he doesn't deserve them.

I use the bathroom and head out, not wanting to disturb Dominic. I head to the kitchen and make myself a cup of tea and sit on the couch, staring off into space. I think about the last five months and how so much has changed. I think about myself and how I've changed; I'm not sure if it's in a good or bad way.

I'm still sipping my luke-warm tea when Lake joins me. She

In the Spotlight

strokes my cheek with tears in her eyes and I cringe. I place my cup down and hug her. I know she's blaming herself; she feels responsible for me even though I'm a grown woman. She always blames herself but, in her eyes, I will always be her baby sister.

"I'm so sorry, I shouldn't have let you go anywhere near him. I was so impressed with him being famous that I couldn't see past it. I feel so self-absorbed." She holds me tighter.

"It's not your fault. I thought he was different behind all that money and fame but I guess a guy so used to that life isn't easy to change. I just can't wait to get off this tour and away from him. I just don't know what to do in the meantime. I can't go out there with this on my face." I point to my cheek. Lake holds my chin and guides it side to side, inspecting it.

"I think with some concealer and foundation we should be able to cover it up. It should heal in a few weeks but will lighten considerably before that. Let's go play make up." I smile at her and nod my head. We had just gotten up when there is a banging on the door. I don't know why, but it causes me to cower. I don't want to see Jensen. I know he won't touch me again, but I can't bear to see him after last night. It's too fresh in my mind.

"Leon!" Lake yells, holding me behind her like a shield. Leon, Dominic and Chris all come running out. My eyes go to Dominic who is standing there shirtless with just his boxers on and I scold myself that I was in bed with him all night and didn't notice.

For goodness sake woman, your ex just hit you and is banging down your door and you're thinking about another guy half naked already?

"What the hell is going on?" Leon walks towards us and his eyes widen when he sees me. "Holy hell, Sky! Lake you didn't say it was that bad." Leon comes and hugs me, and I'm surprised at the contact since he has only showed physical affection once towards me and that was when I first met him.

"It was just red last night; it must have gotten worse while she slept." Lake looks at us with happy tears in her eyes seeing Leon holding me like this, like family. "Now go kick the dicks ass that is banging on our door. I don't want him near her or I swear I will be put away for life for murder," Lake tells him. Leon glares at the door, hoping to hurt the person on the other side with a look alone.

Leon leaves my side and heads to the door and Dominic comes to me, Lake and him blocking my view. Chris comes over and puts his arm around my shoulders, looking at me with concern, but I give him a small smile to show him that I'm fine. I hear the door knob turn and my body tenses up. I know Chris felt it when he pulls me in closer to him. Leon doesn't have a chance to say anything before the door bangs open and Travis and Lloyd saunter in.

"Where is that bitch?" Travis seethes and I flinch. Why is he calling me that? I've done nothing wrong.

"Who the hell do you think you are?" Leon pushes Travis so he doesn't enter our suite.

"Fuck you! That bitch did something last night, the place is trashed and there are empty bottles everywhere. We found him lying in his own vomit. Now where is that whore of a singer?" I jump when I see Leon punch him and watch as they land on the floor, tackling each other. Lloyd joins in, causing Dominic to as well, followed by Chris. Punches are getting thrown everywhere.

"STOP IT!" I scream, tears flowing down my cheeks and they stop at the loudness of my voice, hearing the pain through them. "Stop it. I'm here okay. Leave them alone." I manage to get out, the

In the *Spotlight*

tears blurring my vision. Lake puts her arm around my waist as I face Jensen's friends. All the guys stand, cuts and bruises covering them. All this over me. I shake my head, thinking that maybe if I never joined this band, this drama wouldn't be happening.

"Look at you. I guess you got what you deserved then?" Travis smirks at me and I start to cry harder. "Some bitch hit you for being a two-faced whore?" He looks at me with a look I recognize; disgust.

"You piece of shit." Dominic punches Travis again.

"Stop it!" I yell again.

"You think she deserved getting hit by Jensen? You are one sick fuck," Leon spits out.

"What the fuck are you talking about?" Lloyd looks at me and back to Leon.

"Jensen did that." Leon points to my face. "Not anyone else," Leon tells him and comes to my side, pulling me into his chest as I cry.

"You're lying!" Travis roars.

"Go ask him; if he's conscious. She went there last night to give him another chance and she caught him fucking some girl. Some words were said then he hit her," Dominic adds.

"He wouldn't do that, he adores her," Lloyd says but I can see he's unsure.

"Adores her so much he was fucking someone else? Yeah that's pure adoration," Dominic says sarcastically.

"Sky is this true?" I look at Lloyd and nod my head. He puts his hands in his hair and stares up at the ceiling.

"You don't believe her, do you?" Travis asks Lloyd.

"Come on man, look at her. You know as much as I do how much of a good girl she is; she wouldn't lie." Lloyd turns to me. "I'm sorry Sky, for what he did. We'll leave." Lloyd heads to the door.

"What, and that's it? What about Jensen?" Travis glares at me.

"He did this to himself. She's done nothing but be herself. Leave her alone," Lloyd warns him and they both turn and leave. My tears have stopped but I feel like I've been in a war. I sit down and the others sit as well, just thinking about everything.

"Well, at least you all look messed up and not just Sky," Lake tries to make a joke and I chuckle at her.

"I'm sorry you all had to get hurt because of me," I speak out.

"Don't be stupid, we're a family, we look out for one another," Chris says and I smile at him. My family.

"Right. Sky, come with me and we'll cover up the bruise. Guys, try and clean yourselves up, you look like shit." The guys laugh.

"I could never look like shit. I'm a God," Chris says before heading back to his room. I follow Sky to the bathroom so she can work her magic.

🎸―★―🎸

When Lake is done with me, you can't tell there was ever anything wrong unless you really look closely. We went through rehearsals and thankfully never see anyone from Absolute Addiction. We have tonight and two more stops. The next four days can't come quick enough.

I've kept myself in my room, practicing for the new music video for *Teen Witch*, letting the music take me to a place where I can forget all the drama that is happening around me. Some of my thoughts today have gotten dark, asking the *what-ifs*. I just want to clear my head and in no way do I want to leave the comfort of my room for a run, so this is the next best thing.

After a while, I notice Dominic leaning against the door frame,

In the Spotlight

watching me. I continue singing and when I get to the last words, he comes over and sits next to me on the bed. He looks at my cheek and glides a finger over the covered bruise. It's still a little sore and I wince slightly, hating that I did. I love how comforting his touch is.

"I still want to kill him." He looks into my eyes, showing how serious he is.

"I know," I whisper. "Please don't though." He entwines his fingers with mine and holds it in his lap.

"I don't want him to get away with it." He shakes his head and lies down on the bed.

"He won't. He'll have to live with this, knowing what he did; he'll punish himself," I say and lay down too.

"I just can't believe he did it." He looks up at the ceiling. "I'm sorry he hurt you."

"It's not your fault, and remember, you were the one who warned me about him and I didn't listen." I watch him.

"I wasn't expecting this, I thought he may try and pressure you into sleeping with him or cheat, never this." He turns his head so he's looking at me. "How can anyone want to hurt you? You are so beautiful, caring, sweet, funny and kind. How could he ruin it, knowing he had you?" I look at him and say nothing, lost for words. He's called me beautiful before but it does something to me that I can't explain. "I'm just glad you're okay."

"I've got you to protect me, how could I not be okay?" I smile at him and he looks into my eyes, not saying anything. We're still staring at one another when someone knocks on my door.

"Sky, you have a letter!" Leon shouts through, breaking our moment.

"I better go." Dominic squeezes my hand and stands and I join him.

"Thank you, Dominic, for being there for me." I hug him and kiss his cheek.

"Always." He kisses my cheek, surprising me, his lips lingering a little before he walks away. I follow him out and head over to Leon who is on the couch, and grab the letter he passes me.

I head back to my room and sit back down on my bed, opening the envelope, seeing it holds a small piece of paper. My blood runs cold when I recognize the handwriting. How did they know I was here?

Your time is almost up.
Will see you soon.
M

No, this can't be happening. My breathing comes fast and I move to a corner in the room, trying to get myself under control. I feel like I'm having an anxiety attack. I look at the letter that's now lying on the floor like it will catch fire any second. My time is almost up. I feel tears slide down my cheeks; I know what my fate holds. They are going to come and get me and there is nothing I can do. I will have to leave all this behind.

Dominic. I don't want to leave him.

Chapter 25

In just two days we will have finished the tour and I can finally get away from Jensen. He hasn't tried to talk to me but I can constantly feel his eyes on me. I know he feels bad, but what he did I will never be able to forgive.

When it comes to the letter, I scrunched it up and threw it away, pretending I never read it. I don't want to think about it. I know it's childish but, if it's not there, it's like it never happened. I want to enjoy this time and I won't let them ruin it for me.

We are on the bus, driving to our last destination, and Dominic has been quiet. He didn't want to do my guitar lessons right now, which I found odd; he never seemed to mind hanging out with me.

I'm sitting in the booth, reading the information Robert emailed about what they're expecting from the music video. It's going to be set in high school, like the movie, and we will be meeting Alexandra Forman and John Yorke; the people who will be playing Louise and Brad in the movie. I'm going to be meeting actual celebrities. I still can't get my head around that.

I look over at Dominic and he's sitting on the far corner of the couch, just staring into space. He's been like this for the last couple of days, but today he's more quiet than normal. I can tell something is wrong but I'm not sure what it is. I head over to Lake, who is in our room on the bus, to ask her if she knows what's bothering him.

I knock on the door and she tells me come in. She's is sitting on the bed, going through letters and random paperwork. I hate to disturb her when she's working but I need to know. If something is upsetting Dominic I want to be able to help, like how he has helped me over and over.

"Hi, can I ask you a question?" I kneel on the floor near her so I don't mess up the papers sprawled everywhere.

"Sure, what's up?" Lake stops what she's doing and focuses on me.

"Do you know what's wrong with Dominic? He hasn't been his usual self and I'm worried," I tell her.

"Oh honey, he'll be fine. It's just a hard time of year for him. It's the anniversary of his parent's death and he always gets like this. He'll come out of it, just give him some space." My heart aches for him. It's the anniversary of when he lost his parents, no wonder he's in his own head.

"But shouldn't we do something?" I shake my head; how can she sit there acting like it's no big deal?

"Sky, he doesn't like making a fuss over it. Me and Leon try and get him out of this funk every year, but it either makes him angry to where he does something stupid or he ends up trying to drink himself to death. It's easier to just let him deal with it on his own." I stand up, feeling angry.

"Lake, if you passed away, I wouldn't want to be on my own. I would want someone there to show that they're there for me. I'm going to do something; I don't know what but I'm going to show him he's not alone." I feel determined and walk towards the door.

"Okay, but if you don't get the response you're after, don't feel bad, it's just how he is." With that I walk out and sit back in the booth, watching him sit there with this pain.

In the Spotlight

I clear my head and try to think of something I could do to help, and my head starts to hurt after a while. Every thought that enters my head sounds stupid. I keep trying to think of something when it hits me. I don't know how he will react but I want to show him that I care. I call out to Leon and Chris and tell them my plan. Chris is on board right away but Leon isn't certain. After a little persuasion though, I get him to agree.

We talk about how we're going to pull it off without Dominic knowing and I quickly get on my laptop and start searching for my idea until I find the perfect thing. I go back to my room and tell Lake what we're doing and she smiles, knowing I'm doing it because I care. She helps me put my plan into action.

I just hope he likes it and isn't angry at me for what I'm about to do.

---★---

We rehearse as normal and I leave before AA gets on stage to do theirs. I'm too busy thinking about tonight to even let any other thoughts enter my mind. I'm almost out the door, heading back to the bus, when I hear my name being called and I freeze, recognizing the voice. I turn to see Jensen walking towards me.

Why didn't I leave with Chris or Leon? I stand there gathering all the strength I have to not shake. He looks so put together, so different from the last time I saw him. He stands a few paces away from me and we just stare at one another. I arch my eyebrow to tell him to say whatever it is he has come to say.

"You're looking good," he says and I shake my head. The bruising on my face has gone to a light brown color but Lake always makes sure it's fully covered up.

"It's amazing what makeup can do these days," I say

sarcastically. I don't know why I said it; it just fell from my lips.

"Look, I know you don't want anything to do with me, and I completely understand that, but I just wanted to tell you how sorry I am. I have never laid a hand on a woman before; I don't even know what possessed me. I didn't mean to hurt you, emotionally or physically. I know I ruined it, ruined any chance I had with you." He takes in a deep breath. "I regret everything since that day those girls attacked you. I wish I could go back and tell Trigger not to come, to have stayed with you, but I know you can't change time. It's just that I know I will regret what I lost, what I did. You do still mean a lot to me and I hope in time that you can forgive me." I look into his eyes and see how sincere he is. I take in a deep breath and nod my head, deciding to be the bigger person.

"Thank you for saying all that. You did hurt me; emotionally and physically, but like you said, you can't turn back time. Maybe one day we can be friends again." He nods his head.

"You were happy though? At the beginning?" I give him a warm smile.

"I was. I enjoyed being with you, I enjoyed talking and hanging out but, please, when you let another girl in, don't be a dick. That rock star attitude stinks and is not appealing. Just be you. Enjoy the rest of the tour." I say sincerely before turning to walk away.

"Enjoy rising up the ladder, I expect great things from you!" he yells out. I smile and give him a wave as I leave. After that brief talk, I do feel lighter.

I head back to the bus and start getting things ready for tonight. My stomach is full of butterflies. Leon and Chris keep Dominic away so I can get everything done and prepared. By the time I think I have everything sorted, it's time to do our last concert on this tour. I look

In the Spotlight

at myself in the mirror and nod my head, knowing in my heart I'm doing the right thing.

Dominic and the guys are on stage waiting for the spotlight to come on. I see Dominic standing in the darkness and I want him to be back in the light. I put the head piece on and step on the stage, the spotlight finding me. The crowd screams and I feel like I'm going to pass out.

I'm doing this for Dominic, I repeat over and over.

I can do this.

"Hello Washington!" I yell in my mic. The crowd goes crazy and I giggle, turning to look at Dominic who is staring at me in confusion. I never talk to the crowd, ever. "I want to thank you for being here, for supporting us, and well tonight, we are going to do something different." The crowd goes quieter, listening to every word I say. "I know this is our last concert for this tour but, one of my dearest friends, a guy who has been there for me every step of the way into this crazy world, this guy who has been like my hero, my savior. He lost something so precious and I could never imagine what he has to deal with, how he has to live with it every day. My heart hurts just seeing him in pain. I want to help him like he has helped me. So this person, my best friend, my guardian angel; this song is for you."

A piano starts to play and I begin to sing the words. I'm singing *If You Could See Me Now* by The Script. Travis and Lloyd walk onto the stage, starting to strum as Chris joins in with Leon. I sing to Dominic who stays still, watching me. I walk over and hold his hand and can feel his body shaking; not from anger, but pain. I see a tear slide down his cheek.

I entwine his fingers with mine and continue singing. Looking around, I notice the crowd isn't screaming, just listening, showing their respect. I'm about to sing the next part but Dominic starts to sing instead. I watch him, his eyes staying on mine like I'm giving him strength to do this. During the chorus I sing with him, alongside him.

The song ends and Dominic looks at me, breathing in fast, his eyes intensely on mine. I'm about to pull my hand away when he squeezes it tighter, not wanting to let go. He pulls me towards him into a tight hug, his face in my neck, breathing me in.

"Thank you," he whispers into my ear. "Thank you for being you." A tear slides down my cheek and I nod.

"Always," I say the word he always uses with me and feel his smile on my neck. He pulls back and he gives me a smile. "Alright, Washington! Who wants some sweat on lace and chains?" I enthusiastically say in the mic and the crowd goes wild again.

We continue the rest of the concert as normal but, during some songs, I walk to Dominic and wrap my arm over his shoulder, my head tucked into him as I sing. Tonight was different from the other concerts; it was a beginning, but a voice in my head screamed maybe it's an end.

After the concert, I thanked Travis and Lloyd for joining us and they said that after the things they had said to me without getting all the information, they felt like they needed to do something to apologize. Jensen walked by me as I left the stage and I gave him a nod in acknowledgment. Kym followed behind him but stopped and hugged me; telling me she didn't want to be the only non-skank on the tour and we laughed together. She gave me a piece of paper with

In the *Spotlight*

her number on it, telling me I need to get a phone so I can keep in touch.

Dominic holds my hand while we walk onto the bus and we stay by each other's side all night to the early hours of the morning, watching movies on my laptop, not thinking about anything. I'm lying on Dominic's chest and a voice in my head keeps echoing that my time is running out. I want to keep having moments like this. I love hanging out with Dominic and I want so much more of it.

I finally drift off into a deep sleep and dream of a life where Dominic wants me to be his. I dream of being on his arm as he shows me off, to our future dates, to cuddling on the couch in our home watching movies, to him proposing, to a wedding, children. I see children with thick messy brown hair, my dark blue eyes. I know it will never happen, but that's what dreams are though; a dream.

─── ★ ───

Dominic

I can't believe she did that. For me. I know she feels overwhelmed when put on the spot, but she did it for me. She sang a song to me from one of my favorite bands and hearing her do the rap parts was so cute, but she did it without any mistakes. I miss my parents so much and that song, wishing they could see me now, I really wish they could. I wish they could have met Sky; they would have loved her.

Now, I think they sent her to me. I've become a better person in the short time I've known her. I want to be better, knowing how much of a dick I was, how much I used women to just fill a void I didn't realize was there, even though I'm sure they used me just as much. Sky is different though, and seeing her do what she did, my head can't get around it. I hear her deep breathing and know she's falling asleep. I move her hair away from her face and see even in her sleep, she is smiling. I'm almost asleep when my eyes snap open.

"I love you, Dominic," Sky whispers and I look down at her. She's still sleeping away. Is she dreaming about me? She loves me? This should scare me, make me want to run away, but hearing her say those words gives me some peace. She's in love with me, but what do I do now?

Chapter 26

Sky

We are at Washington High School and ready to film the music video. Cameras and people are everywhere. I've read over what they expect from us but, in my head, all I can think about is that I'm going to meet real live celebrities. Robert is waiting at the entrance and he comes to me first, hugging me and kissing my cheek. It feels so awkward that I instantly look at Dominic and he looks just as dumfounded as I am.

"Can I have a word with you Sky?" Robert asks me and I nod my head. He presses his hand on my lower back and guides me to an empty classroom. I wait to see what he has to say. "I'm sorry to hear about you and Jensen, you made a cute couple, I hope things haven't been that awkward."

"It was at first but I'm moving on. At least I have this today to focus on." I shrug my shoulders. He walks towards me and starts rubbing my shoulders.

"I know this may be a bit soon, but I do like you, Sky. I've liked you since I first saw you on that stage. I was wondering if you would ever want to have dinner with me?" I look at him with shock; I know he can be a little touchy with me but I thought that's just what he's like.

"Robert, I'm very flattered, I am, but I kind of like someone else and well, you're kind of my boss. I'm sorry and hope we can still continue working with each other, I don't want things to start being uncomfortable." I hold his hand so he knows I'm being sincere.

"A beautiful girl like you, you will never be alone for long. Thank you for letting me down gently, and yes we will continue working together with no weirdness, I promise. I do think you will be huge; you are already getting there as we speak." He smiles at me and I can tell he's upset, but he squeezes my hand and let's go before walking out of the room. I wait a minute then follow.

"Everything okay? Dominic asks me. I smile at him and nod.

"Yeah, everything is fine."

Robert shows us around the school, what's going to happen where. I haven't set foot in a high school since I left mine. I left with 4.0 GPA and had scholarships to a future of my choosing, but my parents told me I will marry and won't have time to work, only time to look after the home and husband. They set my future in stone and nothing would have budged them until nine months ago, which I don't want to think about.

When the tour of the school is over, we are taken to a classroom that is completely empty except for John and Alexandra and I have to keep myself from shrieking like a fan girl. I try and keep my composure but I am sure the huge smile on my face is giving me away. As soon as Alexandra sees me, she comes straight to me and gives me a huge hug. I look at Lake whose mouth is hanging open in shock, most likely mirroring my own.

"I am such a huge fan! I love your voice; would you mind signing my album?" I look at her in shock, trying to tell if she's joking, but she goes back to where she was sitting and returns with the album and a pen. I actually haven't seen the album so I look at it and see the picture is one from the photoshoot where I am looking

In the Spotlight

into Dominic's eyes and he is looking down at me. We look like we want to devour each other. I sign the album and pass it around so the rest of the guys can sign as well. "Thank you so much." She beams at me and I can't believe what just happened. Alexandra just asked me for an autograph. I look at her with her long, light brown hair and light brown eyes; she really does look like the girl next door. She's wearing tight jeans with a pale pink blouse, showing her perfect figure. She looks flawless.

"Right, ladies go get changed; guys, you do the same. Patricia and Stuart will show you where to go." Robert claps his hands to get our attention.

"I can't believe you are doing the music video for the movie! I asked for you personally but never thought they could get you. You seem to be hot property at the moment," Alexandra says.

"What do you mean hot property?" I ask, confused.

"You know; you're like, super famous now. You're all over magazines; I turn on the radio and your song is playing; you're constantly being Facebooked or tweeted. Everyone loves you." Magazines?

"What magazines?" We walk into another classroom and the windows are covered. We sit down and continue to talk as we get our hair and makeup done.

"Well first, it was pictures of you walking on and off the tour bus, then with you and Jensen, Jensen singing to you at the club." God that feels like a lifetime ago now since he did that, so much has happened since then. "Then ones with those girls attacking you, which was awful by the way; some people are so deluded that they forget we are normal people too. Oh and there's the interview with a picture of you all on the sofa and you and Dominic were smiling at each other. God, I'm so sorry, I can't stop talking; I do that when I'm nervous." She laughs.

"You're the celebrity, not me. I was a box of nerves when I walked through the door. You're like, actually famous; millions watch you." I look at her and like she said, we are like everyone else.

"Millions watch you too; your music video was so hot it was in the number one spot for three weeks and I am sure it's still in the top ten. I guess we're fangirling each other huh?" I laugh with her.

"So, have you actually seen the original movie?" I ask her.

"Yeah, I wanted to see what they expected from me. I enjoyed it and I liked the songs. Robert said you're going to do *Never Going to be the Same Again*?" I nod.

"Yeah, I watched the movie months ago and thought if we changed it up, just a little, it would go perfectly."

"I agree. I'm just happy the movie is finished. I haven't had time to myself in months, I need a break. It's so exhausting doing films. I have this to do and some interview about the movie, the red carpet, and that's it for me for a whole month. I'm taking a well-deserved vacation." I giggle.

"I can imagine you'll need the break."

"What about you? What are your plans after this?" I think about it, knowing deep down what my future holds, but I want to keep it pushed back.

"Probably do another album, release another single; the usual." I keep my head forward as the makeup artist does my eyes.

"Well, seems like you'll have a busy time ahead of you, too. Have you decided on what your next single is going to be?"

"Honestly?" I see her nod her head from the corner of my eye. "I have no clue." We both laugh.

In the *Spotlight*

We're changed into clothes and make up and I look into the mirror with Alexandra by my side and we laugh. We look the same but nerdier. I've got glasses on and my hair tied up in a high ponytail, my skin looks younger thanks to the makeup. Luckily the bruise is really faint; if the makeup artist noticed she didn't say anything.

Alexandra has messy, straight hair, going for that similar look as the original; her hair half up, half down. We are both wearing ugly clothes that does nothing for our figures. Alexandra takes out her phone and tells me we're doing a selfie. I see us on her phone and we start doing poses as she clicks away, laughing as we do.

We walk out to the parking lot, since that's where the first scene is taking place, and Chris bends over laughing when he sees us. Alexandra and I laugh with him; we do look weird. I look at Dominic and he is in a jock jacket, wearing tight jeans and a shirt. I can imagine this is what he would have looked like back in school. I wonder if he would have talked to me if we went to the same school.

Leon is in a football jersey and Chris looks like a bad boy in a leather jacket. I look towards John and he is wearing a jock jacket too, his longish dark brown hair combed over perfectly with some shielding his right eye. He's very attractive so I'm not surprised he got the lead for the part. They both complement one another.

Alexandra and I walk to a car and get in, waiting for our cue. We're talking as we wait and then we get the signal to start and the cameras zooms in on us. I forgot how engulfing this is. Alexandra drives us to a parking spot as the intro plays out and we look out the window, staring up to the school. We both get out of the car as I start to sing and grab our backpacks, looking around the parking lot when our eyes land on the guys who are pretending to talk and laugh. Alexandra focuses in on John as I focus on Dominic and both guys look at us for just a moment then look away again.

We lean against the car as I sing, watching the guys. We watch as they head to the school entrance and start to follow. We walk in and the place is full of people that are made to look like students, going to lockers, talking to friends. The guys walk down the halls like they own the place.

"Cut! Let's do it one more time and then go to the next scene." The director calls out and we do.

Once we finish the second take, we head to a classroom and sit in our seats, Alexandra sitting in front of me. The music starts up again and I start to sing. We watch a girl talk to John as they smile at one another; Alexandra wearing a look like it bothers her. I turn to look at Dominic who is across the room and he turns his head to look at me, his eyes piercing mine before he looks away.

We are taken back to wardrobe and this time we're put clothes that are very unflattering and Alexandra insists on taking pictures of us again. We get a crew member to take one of us zoomed out. When I see the picture, I throw my head back and laugh. I don't think I've ever had this much fun when cameras are involved.

We are in the school gym that's set up for a dance. I sit on a chair on my own as I watch Alexandra go to the bathroom and when she comes out, she is wearing a tutu skirt and shirt. I continue singing but almost giggle at the sight. I watch her go to the dancefloor, dancing with a guy as her eyes watch John dancing with another girl.

The next scene I'm not in. It's of Alexandra changing from a geek to the popular girl and this one needs special effects so I step back and watch. There is a green screen behind her and I watch her pretend to put some potion on her clothes and start to spin around

In the Spotlight

saying some magic words. After two takes, we are ready for the next scene.

We're back in the car but this time we look amazing. We're in designer clothes, our hair and makeup perfect. We drive up and once we're out of the car, guys surround us, helping carry our back packs and walking us towards the school entrance. We turn our heads and see the guys staring at us.

We are leaning against the lockers as guys pretend to talk as I sing and our heads turn to see John and Dominic walk down the hall, their eyes on us. I keep singing and they stop in front of us both. I look up into Dominic's eyes and I give him a smile as I sing, putting my hand on his chest and giving a little push as Alexandra clings her arm through mine and we walk down the hall towards the classroom.

The final scene is another school dance and Alexandra is wearing a tight blue dress that shows her perfect figure, her hair in waves. I'm wearing a black, strapless dress and my hair flows down my back. This time I am on stage with the guys singing for a scene, watching John and Alexandra dance, then another scene where I'm on the dancefloor, dancing with Dominic near John and Alexandra. Dominic pulls my body close to his like in the movie and sways my body side to side. Then the director says cut and we are done for the day. I smile at Dominic and he grins at me, shaking his head.

"Oh my God, today has been so much fun and so bearable with you here. I so hope we get to see each other again." Alexandra runs to me and squeezes me.

"Me too, so much better than my first music video. I can't believe the day flew by. I can't wait to see the movie." I return her hug.

"I'll get you all VIP tickets, you have to come to the red carpet. You can tell me if I was any good." She chuckles.

"I know it's going to be brilliant but, yes, I would love to come watch the first showing. Thank you so much." She gives me another quick hug and steps back.

"It is me who should be thanking you. I knew you were on tour and yet you came here. I can't wait to see the music video." You and me both. "We'll see you at the red carpet." I beam at her.

I watch her and John leave and I shake my head on how crazy quick today flew by. Dominic puts his arm over my shoulders and walks us back to the car. What do we do now? What's next for us? Robert hasn't said anything but I'm sure he will. I should enjoy the quiet time of doing nothing. Dominic and I head to a hotel where we will be staying tonight and go to my room. I run and jump on the bed, lying down as I watch Dominic do the same. I chuckle at his poor attempt.

"Today was fun," Dominic says, turning his head and smiling at me.

"Yeah it was. I didn't have to take any clothes off; I think that was a plus." I chuckle. His eyes darken and I look back up to the ceiling.

"Yeah," is all he says. We are like that for a few minutes, just lying there, the only sound is our breathing.

"Dominic?" I turn my head and smile when I see that he is still looking at me.

"Hmm?" He smirks at me.

"Can I ask a favor?" I start to fidget with my fingers and he places his hand in mine and entwines them like he always does.

"You can ask me anything." I take in a deep breath and lean

forward, pressing my lips to his and I feel his hand squeeze mine. I pull back and give him a small smile.

"Will you kiss me?" I whisper. His eyes stare into mine, not saying anything. Have I read the wrong signals? I thought since the time on the bus when I was with Jensen that he wanted to kiss me, that he liked me? God, I must have over thought it. "I'm sorry, I wasn't..." I'm cut off when his lips land on mine.

I'm caught off guard but I kiss him back, moving myself over so I am pressed into his body, fisting his hair; hearing him growl makes me deepen the kiss. I wrap my leg over his waist and my dress rolls up a little. I'm sure he can feel the heat and wetness of my panties. I can feel his erection pressed against my core and I gasp at the contact. He grips my ass, pulling me in closer, and I start to grind myself against him, feeling that ache build up.

I know I want more, I want him. I want him to take me, to own every part of me, even if it's just for tonight. I don't want my first time to be with anyone else. I want it to be with the person who has been by my side through everything, who has been my hero. Dominic starts to kiss my jaw, my neck; I lean my head back to give him better access.

His hands touch my sides, my legs, my ass, but he won't touch me more intimately. I grab his hand and place it on my breast, I don't want him to treat me like I'm fragile, I want him to want me fully.

"Please touch me," I breathe out. With that, his hands grow more urgent, touching me everywhere.

He sits me up and pulls off the dress and I'm left in my strapless back lace bra and panties. He groans when he sees me. I go on my knees and help him take off his shirt and when I see his toned stomach, I press my palm over his heart and look into his eyes, telling him I want this, even if it's just tonight.

He unclips the bra and sucks on one of my nipples and I arch my back, wanting him to take more. He does the same to the other and I whimper when he moves back, missing his heat. He stands up and takes off his jeans and boxers and my eyes bulge when I see his perfect, thick, long erection. He takes out a condom and wraps it around his dick and crawls back towards me. My heart stutters in my chest. He pulls down my already wet panties and looks at me; looks at my naked form on the bed. His eyes are dark and hooded, his breathing coming in fast.

"I imagined this like a thousand times but you are so much more beautiful than in my fantasies," he says before his lips land on mine again.

I feel one of his fingers enter me, then he adds another. I start to grind myself against his hand, not caring how desperate I look. I want him inside me so bad. I need to stop this ache that's becoming unbearable. When his fingers are soaked, he places his erection against my core and starts to push inside me. I gasp when he is only half way through; I feel so full.

"You okay?" he breathes into my ear. I nod.

"Don't stop." He thrusts one last time and he's fully inside me. I moan when I feel the pain. The pain of him taking my gift.

My virginity.

Dominic doesn't move, just stays still, letting me adjust. After a minute, the pain starts to fade and I tell him to start moving. He goes slow, kissing my neck, jaw and cheek; kissing my lips again. I wrap my legs around him, arching myself a little off the bed. I can feel more of him this way, causing us both to moan.

In the Spotlight

"Faster, please go faster," I plead to him and he does.

He starts ramming into me and I dig my fingers into his shoulders. I keep yelling out for him to go harder, faster. I say it over and over until my vision starts to blur and I scream out Dominic's name when I find that sweet release. Dominic thrusts a few more times and I feel his dick pulse inside me as he fills the condom.

"That was amazing," Dominic says in awe, chuckling a little. I laugh and lean my head on his chest.

"Yeah. It was how I always pictured it." I start to draw pictures on his stomach.

"To do it with a rock star in a hotel room?" He jokes.

"No. To give my gift to my best friend." I look up at him and he grins down at me with pure adoration. "Thank you for being my first. I know this was only one night, but I will always cherish it." I kiss his lips and smile at him. I'll never pressure him to be with me; I'd rather have him in my life as a friend than nothing at all.

"Sky, there's something..." A knock on the door cuts him off.

"Hold that thought." I kiss his him again and put on a robe. I open the door and see Chris standing there and I smile at him. I feel like I'm on cloud nine.

"Chris, what's up?"

"Umm, I didn't want to disturb you but there are people here to see you and they say they're your parents." With those words, I fall off my cloud and land face first on the ground.

"My parents are here?" He nods, looking at me confused. He doesn't know why I'm being like this, why I'm terrified of seeing them, but I put on a fake smile and tell him thanks.

"Don't tell Lake they're here, they don't get along, and it will only upset her. Can you keep it to yourself? Until I say something?"

I plead with him.

"Sure, I know what parents are like, they do your head in, but they're your parents at the end of the day." He pats my shoulder and leaves. I go to the door and open it, and like my nightmares, I see them in front of me, giving me that look I'm so used to. Disgust and shame. But this time I know I'm not dreaming.

"Hello, sweetie. You're not going to let your parents in?" Mom smirks at me and I know my time is finally up.

Chapter 27

I'm sitting in front of the mirror as I brush my hair, wondering what my parents want from me. I think back to if I have done anything wrong, but I know I've done everything right. But the fear inside me that knows I am going to be punished runs through my veins.

I take in a deep breath and stand, swiping down the long black skirt that reaches my ankles, making sure there are no creases; personal appearance is always the number one rule in this house. I'm wearing a white blouse to cover some faint bruising on my wrists that I got a couple of weeks ago when I didn't give Mr. Sherman, my father's work partner, his drink on time.

I walk down the hall, down the grand staircase and head to the lounge where I know Mom and Dad will be having their five o'clock drinks. I stand at the door and knock, waiting for permission to come in. When I'm told to enter, I walk in slowly, shutting the door behind me. They don't want the staff to hear our conversations; well hear them shout at their daughter.

"You wanted to see me?" I ask, looking down at the floor, knowing not to look at them unless permitted.

"Yes, take a seat," Mom says. I walk to the only chair that I'm allowed to sit on when in this room. It is hard and uncomfortable, but I tolerate it. My eyes still don't look up. "It has come to our attention that you have been talking to that sister of yours." Mom's voice is steady, but I know if I look up, I will see the anger radiating from her. "Care to explain to me why you are talking to that waste of space? Why you have to keep pushing us?" I feel a slap across my face; I try not to show how much it hurt. It will be worse for me if I show weakness even though I want to curl up in a ball and cry.

"Mom please." My voice is shaking; my hair is pulled back as I look into her dark eyes.

"We told you that she is no longer part of this family and yet you still speak to her?" I feel her nails start to dig into my scalp. "Why would you do this? Why talk to her?" I try and get words out but I am in so much pain I'm struggling to even think. "Tell me." She lets go and sits next to my father who is watching us.

"I miss her," I say, touching my head. I can already feel a headache coming on.

"You miss her? That is weakness, showing emotion will be your downfall. You are going to end up like her, is that what you want?" I want to say yes, but I know my punishment would be so much worse.

"No," I whisper out, looking back down to the floor.

"You are such a liar," she spits out at me. I feel tears prickle in the back of my eyes.

"Well sweetie, maybe we can make a deal with her," Dad finally talks, but his eyes look menacing. I know this isn't going to end up well.

"A deal? What kind of deal?" mom asks him, but she isn't a good actress so I know they planned this before I even entered the room.

"Yes. She misses her sister, so I think we shall let her see her. She can spend some time with her, get to catch up." I want to look

In the Spotlight

up so badly to see if this is some sick joke they are playing to hurt me.

"Why should she get to see her? She has done nothing but show shame and disappointment; why should she get such a treat?" Mom spits out.

"I think if we allowed her to do this, and she promised to come home and follow our rules and go by what we say, she should go." I see Lake in my head; seeing her, spending time with her, being away from this house sounds like heaven. Even if it's only for a little while.

"Are you willing to do this, Sky? You go see your sister then come back and you will do what you're told, do as we say?" I don't think twice; I nod my head. "Fine, we will get it sorted." I want to smile but I know I shouldn't. They may change their minds.

"Thank you," I say softly.

"Oh, and there's another catch," Mom says, walking towards me. She grabs my chin so I am looking back into her eyes. "When you come back, you will be marrying Jefferson Clarkson the Third. His family is just as good as ours; good blood and old money. Do you understand?" Marry Jefferson? He went to school with me but he never acknowledged me; he was in the popular clique, sleeping with every girl there was, now I have to live the rest of my life with him?

"Yes." I blink away a tear, Mom sees it and smiles.

"You have five months to be with your sister. You shall go to the charity events first but you can tell her that you are running away. I don't want her knowing about our arrangement, is that clear? If we find out you told her, the deal is off and we bring you back here. You won't be able to see her again," Dad says, lighting up a cigar. I know after my five months they wouldn't let me see her again anyway but at least I have five months to be free, to do as I please. My head is buzzing with all the possibilities.

"I understand."

"Good, now go. If you disappoint us from now until you go, we may take it back, don't let us down." I nod my head and stand, leaving them behind. I walk to the library and use the computer to message Lake. I'm going to see her. I'm going to see my big sister. I feel tears slide down my cheeks, but these are tears of happiness.

"How did you find me?" I ask shakily and they walk past me into the hotel room and look around.

"You honestly didn't think we would let you go without knowing where you would be?" Mom laughs and hearing it again send shivers down my spine. "Time is up Sky; you are coming with us." I'm about to say something when I see Dominic walk out and look between us. Thank God he decided to put on his clothes.

"Sky, everything alright?" he asks me, stepping to my side and I notice my parent's eyes darken but when Dominic turns, they put on their masks that show how perfect and adoring they are, even though they are anything but.

"Yes. Dominic these are my parents Claudia and Paul. Mom, Dad, this is Dominic, the lead guitarist of the band." They shake hands and I stand there, not sure what to say next.

"Dominic is it okay if we talk to our daughter alone? We haven't seen her in such a long time, we want to catch up," Mom says sweetly and Dominic nods his head.

"Sure, I'll be at the gym if you need me." He kisses the side of my head and leaves.

In the Spotlight

Because Chris is still in his room, I guide Mom and Dad to my own and smile when I notice Dominic tidied the bed, making it look like nothing happened. He's so considerate. I'm brought back to the present when I feel a slap across my face and my hair being pulled back.

"I've seen your music video, how you whore yourself about on stage, dating some punk rocker, now this Dominic is kissing you. This is what you do when we were so kind to let you see your sister? You throw it in our faces? Have you spread those legs for every guy whose given you attention? Have you turned into some whore?" she seethes in my ear. She turns me around and slaps me on the same cheek Jensen back handed me on and I fall to the ground.

"I haven't slept around; I promise; I did what I was told. I didn't expect for any of this to happen," I plead to them, tears falling and they both look down at me like I am dog muck on their shoe.

"You better not have. You are lucky no one has noticed it's you, with your hair and makeup and the using the last name your sister chose when she decided not to be part of this family anymore." I want to scream that she and dad are the ones who made her leave. "You are lucky you haven't ruined our family name. Now get your things, we are leaving." I start panicking. I don't want to leave; I want to at least say goodbye.

"Mom, if I leave now they would look for me, thinking something happened. They know I wouldn't go without saying goodbye. Please, I am begging you, please let me have this." I am literally on my knees, pleading.

"Fine, we don't want any hassle with those boys. You have until tonight," Dad says and I stand and watch Mom leave but Dad quickly turns around grabs my wrist and starts twisting it. "If you think about running, we will find you." He lets go and leaves. I fall back to the floor and sob. I cry for what I am going to be leaving and the future that I am going to have to face.

How stupid was it that I thought I could actually get away and never go back? I knew deep down I couldn't run from my past.

I don't know how long I sit there but I know someone may look for me any minute and I can't tell them what's wrong. I jump in the shower and turn the water to the highest temperature, scalding my white skin. How am I going to say goodbye? I know Lake wouldn't let me go back, she would fight, but I know if I don't go I will be ruining their futures.

I go back to my room and sit at the desk and write Lake a letter, telling her the truth, telling her about the contract that I signed with our parents. That if I stayed, I would be destroying everything she worked for. I put the letter in an envelope and put it on my pillow, knowing she would come back here to find any evidence of what happened.

Then I sit there and try to think of how to say goodbye without Lake doing something stupid. I look through my bags and find Kym's number. I go to the phone near my bed and dial and it rings a few times before she answers.

"Hi Kym, its Sky."

"Miss me already?" She laughs and I chuckle with her.

"I need a favor." I feel my lips tremble.

"Sky, what's wrong?" Her voice is concerned and this time I cry down the phone, hearing her tell me to take a few deep breaths and to tell her what's wrong. I finally start to calm down and I tell her everything. I tell her about my parents, my past with Lake, the deal, the contract and me now having to leave.

In the Spotlight

"I need your help with this." I sniffle.

"Fuck, Sky, no wonder you are who you are. You having been brought up like that is horrible and now you're going to go back? To them controlling you? To marry some dick who will probably be fucking other girls along the way?" I feel the tears sliding down, knowing that it's the truth.

"I signed a contract. I can't hurt Lake; she has done so much for me." I grab a tissue and blow my nose.

"Fuck, okay, I am doing this for you, even though I want to get a blunt knife and stab their black hearts." I giggle down the line.

"Thank you." I giggle again. "Thank you for helping me."

"Of course. Leave everything to me. Just tell Lake and the guys where to go, we will do the rest."

"Thank you." I'm about to hang up when she says my name.

"I'm sorry you have to go through this, you are a good person. I wish I could do more."

"I know." We say our goodbyes and hang up.

I walk to the window and look out to the beautiful scenery. At least I got to travel. At least I know I lost my virginity to Dominic; they can't take that away from me. I go back to the desk and write a quick note to him, wanting him to know how much he meant to me, and leave it on the pillow next to Lake's. I just don't know how I'm going to cope for the rest of the day.

Kym came through for me and has set up everything that I needed. I told Lake and the guys I have something I need to tell them and to show up at club Ascended. I went to the club early to prepare myself and the manager was nice enough, even though I'm sure he was paid well.

I walk to the stage to see Absolute Addiction setting up the instruments and walk towards them. I hear a scream and see Kym running to me then wrapping her arms around me.

"I can't believe you will be leaving all this." She looks around her, and I look around too, seeing everything for the last time.

"Just make sure you live everyday like it's your last, okay? Promise me you will be happy." I start to cry and she cries too, holding me once again.

"God, you have turned me into a girl." She wipes her eyes and we laugh. "We are setting everything up so, if you come with me, we'll make sure the sound system is okay." Her hand goes in mine and I can't help but smile, remembering when she kissed me. That's something I'm happy my parents will never know about.

"Sky?" I turn around and see Jensen setting up his guitar. There's concern and pity in his eyes.

"Jensen," I say quietly.

"Kym told me everything. I am so sorry but, if you let me, maybe I can help, maybe I can make them change their minds." He walks to me and grabs my hands.

"I can't, my future is set in stone." I shrug. "I'm going to marry a guy who will see me as a trophy or a possession. This is my life Jensen." I try to not cry again but he pulls me to his chest and I let a few tears fall.

"I don't want that life for you." I hold his shirt in my fist.

"Neither do I." I pull back. "Thank you for helping me with this. Are all the guys ready?" I try and change the subject. I look around the club to see people starting to file in.

"Yeah, everyone is in place. Are you sure you want to do this?" I nod my head at him.

In the Spotlight

"I have to; it is what it is. Come on, this will be your only chance to play with me." I talk in the microphone to make sure it sounds okay and I watch Jensen, Kym, Lloyd and Travis try out their instruments. They go in the back and wait till Lake and the guys show up. I stand there watching everyone sit down, getting drinks, talking and laughing and I smile, knowing that I experienced it all. I experienced a normal life.

If it wasn't for the deal I made, I would have never seen this stronger side of myself; never would have experienced whole hearted laughter, to be free, have my first kiss, my first date. To fall in love. I will cherish these memories for the rest of my life.

I hear screaming and see Lake and Dominic walk through the doors heading to the table I reserved for them. Lake is laughing as Leon and Chris follow behind them. Lake looks up to the stage and sees me and she smiles, pointing me out to the other guys. When I look at Dominic, his smile is so beautiful and I know that I am going to miss him so much.

I walk back to the microphone and hold it, gathering all my strength for what I'm about to do. I smile to my friends, to my family.

"Hello everyone. I'm not sure if you know me but my name is Sky and I want to sing a song to my family, with the help from my new friends." AA comes out and the crowd goes wild; I chuckle at the response. "Lake, Dominic, Leon and Chris, I want to thank you for welcoming me into your lives, for making me a part of your family. You have done so much for me; I will never forget it. I love you all so much." I look at Jensen and he starts to play.

Chapter 28

I hold the microphone stand in my hand as I start to sing *Power of Goodbye* by Madonna, swaying to the beat. I feel like this song has the emotion I'm feeling; the words resembling my experience of the freedom I so long craved, but knowing in the end I was always going to leave.

I hope they can read between the lines of what I'm trying to say. I look at Lake as she smiles up at me; I am trying so hard not to cry. I look at Jensen during a line of the song and his eyes are trained on me with amazement. He was a lesson I had to learn, not everything is as it seems.

I look back to the crowd and look at Dominic as I sing to him. I sing to the *what-ifs*, to the future of sharing many happy memories even if it was just friendship. I take in a deep breath and sing with every inch of my heart.

I let the music take over, knowing this will be the last time I will ever feel this euphoria of what a song, what the music, does to me; letting me be in another world. I sing the word goodbye to the family I am leaving behind; singing to the person I turned into, to the person I was happy being.

I feel the tears start to slide down my cheeks but I continue, I look at Lake and see she is looking at me with concern. I look up to the doors just as my parents walk through, looking at me like I'm a stranger, their faces emotionless, and I notice Jefferson right behind

In the *Spotlight*

them; my future husband.

Lake follows my gaze and she stands up. I know that now she knows what I'm saying. I'm saying goodbye to her. She screams my name but I ignore her and continue to enjoy this last moment of freedom. She says something to Dominic and he looks at my parents to Jefferson and then he stands, looking to me.

Lake comes running to the stage but, true to Jensen's word, he got his security team to stop anyone from coming up. Lake is crying and trying to reach me but they don't let her past. I sing to her, my voice trembling and as I sing the line, *learn to say goodbye*, she cries harder. I close my eyes and sway my body to the music, wanting to block all thoughts from my head just for this moment.

🎸★🎸

Dominic

We walk into the club, sitting at the table Sky has reserved for us and when I see her standing up on the stage; my heart thumps louder just seeing her. I want to tell her that I want more than one night; that I want her to be mine and I want to be hers.

When I see Absolute Addiction come onto the stage, I'm confused, especially when she starts singing and during one of the lines she looks at *him*; looking like she has peace with what he has done even though I still want to kick his face in. Especially with him looking at her like she is some goddess. *Well you ruined it you dick*, I think darkly.

I watch her sing, mesmerized by her voice, and when I see tears coming from her sad eyes, I know something is wrong. I can feel it. Lake turns her head and she stands, looking petrified. She starts screaming Sky's name but I sit there confused about what's happening.

"Lake, what's wrong?" I try and grab her arm.

"Our parents are here; they're going to take her away!" She is breathing hard and fast; this time I grab her arm so she is looking at me.

"They came here this morning, what's going on?" She looks at me, tears streaming down her face. Leon and Chris look back and forth, Leon trying to hold Lake's hand, trying to calm her.

"Our parents aren't nice people, Dom, they are here to get her, to take her away." I look at her, trying to digest her words, but all that echoes in my head is they are going to take Sky away, to take her away from me. "Fuck." Lake looks at her parents and I look and see how they smirk at Lake. There is some guy with them, probably the same age as me, and he is looking at Sky like she is meat. "That's who she's going to marry," Lake whispers but I hardly hear her. Before I have time to question her, she runs to the stage, trying to get to Sky, but some guys who must be security block her path and she tries to push them away.

I look up at Sky and her eyes are closed, her body swaying to the music. Her face towards the ceiling, the light bathing her, making her look like an angel. I feel my heart beating a million times a second. I can't let her go, how am I supposed to face each day not seeing her smile? Her big blue eyes looking at me with so much adoration, with so much love.

She opens her eyes and looks directly to me, singing to me. I feel like my heart is going to jump out of my chest. I move to her and her eyes follow me. She is saying goodbye to me. I feel a tear escape and when she stops, and Jensen plays the last of the strings, she mouths to me *I love you* and I almost crumble to the floor.

In the Spotlight
Sky

I mouth I love you to him, the last notes being played, then the stage goes into darkness, like how my soul feels. Jensen quickly grabs my hand and stops me from leaving.

"You don't have to do this." He looks at me and looks behind me where I'm sure my parents are there waiting for me to come to them.

"I do. Thank you Jensen, for helping me." I go on my tip toes and kiss his cheek. "Remember, don't be an ass." I smile at him and he tries to smile back but I know it's forced.

I walk to my parents who are waiting for me, with their own security people around them. Jefferson eyes me up and down and when he grins, I feel my blood go cold. My mom grabs my arm, her nails digging into my skin. I'm moved along the crowd, hearing my sister and Dominic screaming out my name. I let the tears fall, not caring that I will be punished later for showing weakness. I know I'll be punished as soon as I'm home either way.

Our family car pulls up and our driver, Clifford, opens the car door. He gives me a sad smile and I nod in acknowledgment. I go in after my mother, my dad following, then Jefferson. My arm gets pulled towards my mother as she glares at me.

"Hope you enjoyed your little vacation; now it's going to go back to how things were. I think you need a reminder of how things are supposed to be," she whispers in my ear, causing my whole body to shiver. I know I'm going to get punished as soon as we are behind closed doors.

I look out the window and see Lake and Dominic running to the car, Chris and Leon right behind them, but it's too late. The car starts pulling away. They run after us but Lake soon stops. Dominic keeps running and my heart breaks. I see the determination but he trips and falls, his head bowing in defeat.

Dominic

My lungs are burning as I see the car go around the corner and out of view and that's when it kicks in; I'm not going to see her again. I saw her mother grabbing her, I saw Sky wince in pain; it was subtle but I saw it.

How could I be so blind to not notice that there was something wrong when I saw her with them this morning? Her whole body seemed off but I just thought she was embarrassed knowing we had just made love and seeing her parent's right after. I had quickly tidied the room in case they came in.

"Come on man, let's go back to the suite and talk about this." Leon puts his hand on my shoulder and I look up to see Lake sobbing into his chest, holding onto him for dear life. I stand and we head back in silence.

I sit on the couch and look around, everything reminding me of Sky. I feel so many emotions but the one I feel the strongest is anger. I stand up and flip over the coffee table. I start throwing lamps, vases, anything I can get my hands on and when I can no longer reach anything, I fall to the floor, knowing my light is gone.

My Sky.

I feel someone's hand on my shoulder and look up to see Lake. She kneels to the floor and places my head to her stomach as she holds me. I feel her body tremble as she cries. I wrap my arms around her, wanting to be close to Sky in any way I can.

"I'm so sorry, Dominic. I made you stay away from her and I know now that I was wrong. I saw her tell you that she loved you.

In the Spotlight

I'm so sorry." She cries even harder. I should be angry with her but I can't, she did it to protect her sister. "She fell in love with you."

"I don't blame you, I understand. I just want to be on my own." I stand up and she nods, walking back to Leon who holds her.

I walk into Sky's room, images of what we did twelve hours ago flooding my mind; her body close to mine, her giving herself to me. The room still smells of her. I look around the room and my eyes land on two letters on her bed. I walk towards them slowly; they are addressed to me and Lake. I scream out to Lake and she runs in. I hand her the letter as I look at mine. I open it slowly and see her perfect handwriting.

To my Dominic,

Thank you for being there for me, looking after me along this crazy journey.

Thank you for being my hero.

I gave you my most precious gift. I want you to know

I will never regret it. It was perfect.

I love you Dominic,

I love you with all of my heart.

Please don't be sad, please enjoy the rest of your life.

Be happy.

But please keep me close to your heart.

I know you will go far; I believe in you.

Goodbye Dominic,

I will never forget you.

Yours always,

Sky

I re-read the letter over and over. She loves me, I know she does, but it's different seeing it in black and white. I sit on the edge of the bed just looking at her words. This amazing girl, who had never even experienced the simple things in life, changed me without even knowing it. I can't not have her in my life. I need to do something. I need to fight.

"Dominic." Lake sits next to me, holding her letter in her hands. "She mentioned that she made a deal, signed a contract." I look at her confused. A contract, they made her sign a contract?

"What do you mean a contract?" I ask, confused.

"They used her naivety to make her think she didn't have a choice. She was allowed to see me for five months but after that she would have to go back and follow their rules and marry the guy of their choice which is Jefferson." I tighten my fists, knowing another man is going to claim her but this time permanently.

"She is going to marry that guy from the club?" I try and keep my voice calm.

"They brought us up to be the perfect submissive future wives to a blue blooded man. I got away but they must have done a number on Sky. She is going back and I know they are going to punish her; do something to keep her in line." I look into Lake's eyes and see fear.

"What do you mean punish her?" I already know the answer before I even ask the question.

"They will hurt her, to make sure she knows her place." I shake my head; they are going to hurt my Sky. I stand up and start pacing; I can't let her stay with people who are going to use her as a punching bag.

"You said something though about a contract." I sit back next to her.

In the Spotlight

"Yeah, they made her believe she has no other choice; she thinks if she doesn't, they will sue me. She doesn't have to do this, it's like slavery, they are lying to her. We can get her back." I stand up and feel hope.

"What do we have to do?" She stands up and I see her eyes fill with strength.

"We make a plan and get our girl back." I smile and nod my head.

Chapter 29

Sky

It has been three days since I came back home and I haven't heard anything from Lake or Dominic, but I wasn't expecting to. If they did try to reach out, it's not like the messages would actually come to me. I've been locked in my room for two whole days with no food; mother saying that I gained too much weight while I was away. I've been living on water and ice cubes; my stomach cramps painfully. I was grateful when I got a slice of dry toast this morning; I was ready to pass out from starvation.

I look into the mirror; my hair has been cut back to the length it was when I first left, the purple tips now nonexistent. It's like the last five months never happened, but I know they did from the memories I will cherish until the day I die.

I'm sitting on my bed reading a book when I see our maid Zelda walk through the door, her eyes brimming with tears. I run to her, holding her. She knows what my life has been like and she wished that when I left that I stayed hidden. I missed her so much.

"I'm sorry they found you." She looks at me and I wince when she touches my arm. When I returned, Mom gave me my punishment for acting like a whore.

"Zelda, I've missed you." I sit on my bed and she sits next to me.

"I've seen you on the TV, the music video, man when you try

In the Spotlight

and live, you go for it." She chuckles at me. "That Dominic, what a hottie." I feel my cheeks blush; God I miss him so much.

"Zelda, I can't believe I'm back here. I knew I would have to but I was hoping I could have stayed with my sister. I've changed and I know I am going to be punished every day until I go back to that girl I was when I first left. And to top it off, I have to marry Jefferson," I breathe out.

"Oh Sky, I can see new strength in you, this glow; I know they are going to try and beat it out of you. I can't sit back and witness it but I will be sent back home, I can't leave you here alone." I hug her. She is the same age as me but she has some nasty people after her back where she is from. I understand if she told the police what my parents do to me, they would send her back; plus, my parents would deny every word.

"I know, I will cope." I hold her hand.

"There is some bad news though." I look at her and see sadness in her eyes. "Your engagement is being announced tonight at the party. I heard your parents talking." I close my eyes, hating how quickly this is happening. I was nervous showing some skin in front of the camera and right now I would rather do that a million times than marry a man I don't love.

"Thank you for telling me." She squeezes my hand.

"I will talk to you soon; they will be wondering where I am." I watch her leave my room.

I look around me and see my childhood bedroom. The walls, perfectly white; no posters, no photos. The furniture matching the walls, plain and boring. I already hate being back. Hate how a sordid thought pops into my head about ending my life just so I don't have to bare being in this hell.

I am wearing a white summer dress covered in black flowers that reaches my knees, my hair tied up with a few tendrils framing my face. I am in a hall full of people I don't know, celebrating my future engagement. There will be a speech from my father at some point. I am at Jefferson's side, smiling when someone comes along to introduce themselves and I politely say hello and nod at the right times.

A man with messy blonde hair approaches us and Jefferson and this man hug and laugh as they catch up. I stand by his side, looking at the floor like I've been trained to do. I look up when I feel both their eyes on me, praising me. The man, Leighton, licks his lips and I shudder.

"You really have some girl," Leighton says.

"Yeah, she really is. Sky, will you go get us a drink?" I look at Jefferson and want to say no. I know he can sense it as he grabs my wrist, clasping it until I start to feel pain. "That okay with you?" I nod my head and he releases me. I walk to the bar and order two whiskeys with no ice, since that's what I have seen Jefferson drink.

I am about to return when I am stopped by my mother and a woman who is smiling at me. "You must be the beautiful Sky; I now know why. Your eyes are mesmerizing, such a dark blue. I'm sure I can see purple in your irises." I smile politely.

"Yes we thought Sky was a fitting name when she was born," Mom says nicely, putting on her social face.

"I heard you can sing, Sky." I see Mom tense up. "I heard you were in so many plays and choirs in school." Mom relaxes, as do I. "Would you be able to sing something for us?" I start to shake my head, not wanting to ever sing again since I know it will bring pain I

In the *Spotlight*

don't want to experience.

"Of course she will. Sky would love to, won't you sweetie?" She smiles at me but her eyes are telling me to do this or else. I nod my head.

"Great, let me go introduce you." I watch the woman head to the stage and talk to the orchestra.

"You ruin this and there will be consequences," Mom spits in my ear.

"Ladies and gentlemen, Sky Emeraldson is gracious enough to sing for us tonight, let's give her a little encouragement." Everyone looks towards me and starts clapping and I head to the stage. Before I go up the steps, Jefferson holds my waist and kisses my forehead, giving everyone a show. Making it look like we are a loving couple.

"Don't you dare sing one of your disgusting rock songs," he whispers in my ear. I hate that I have to marry this man. I'm going to be punished and living under someone's thumb for the rest of my life.

I walk up the stage and head to the microphone, so many memories flooding back. I never thought I would sing again. I look out to the crowd, seeing the people in their business suits, sipping their drinks. I can't help but smile. If they ever heard me perform one of my songs, they would be horrified. I turn my head back and tell the conductor the song I'm singing and face the crowd once again.

The music starts and I look back out to the crowd and then close my eyes and start to sing *My Immortal* by Evanescence. I sing with all the pain that I'm feeling. I think of Dominic; of everything we went through. My heart aches for him; I can see his eyes smiling at me, his fingers entwining with mine.

I sing for him, I sing with my soul; like if I sing hard enough, he will be able to feel me. I never once open my eyes. I let this song be for him and me, not for these people, not for my parents, but for us. For the pain my parents have caused me. I finish the last word and open my eyes and everyone applauds, looking at me like others do when they first hear me sing.

I walk down the stairs and just like that, I'm surrounded by people; re-introducing themselves, telling me how amazing I was, how beautiful my voice is, how they want me to sing for them at their next event. My parents and Jefferson are at my side, telling them how proud they are of me, how they never wanted to exploit my talent.

I smile but I don't say a word, I feel like everything has turned into white noise, my thoughts start to go darker; I shake my head, trying not to go there. I know it would kill my sister, even though I can never see her again. I couldn't do that to her. I try to clear my thoughts when I hear music and a voice that causes my heart to skip a beat.

The people that were talking stop, everyone turning to the voice and, like in the movies, the crowd moves so I can see Dominic, singing to me. My eyes fill with tears as he sings a song from the first movie we watched together, *Copacabana*. He sings *Who Needs to Dream* by Barry Manilow.

I can't help but giggle at him; his eyes are on me and the crowd moves, knowing he is looking at me. I watch him standing there, not making a move to come to me. I watch him, feeling like it's been years since I last saw him and not just days. He looks like his Godly self; his brown hair sweeping over his eyes; beautiful eyes that look at me like I'm the only person here.

In the Spotlight

I laugh when I see Chris and Leon behind him playing their instruments and they wink at me. Dominic's voice gets stronger and I cry with love and happiness that he is here, that he is fighting for me. That's when I realize that he wants me, he really wants me. He starts to walk to me and my eyes are blurring with tears but I keep wiping them away. I want to watch every second of him.

He sings the last bit of the song in front of me, his vocals go high and he stops, grabs hold of my waist, and pulls me close to his body. He wipes the tears away with his thumbs.

"I love you, Sky. Please be mine." I laugh and wrap my arms around his neck and his lips land on mine. I kiss him so desperately, afraid if I stop he will disappear.

"I love you, Dominic, so much." I tell him and we smile at each other.

He takes my hand and starts to guide me away but my other hand gets grabbed and I look back, seeing my father holding me, stopping us.

"Who the hell do you think you are, taking my daughter?" my dad tries to say calmly and I know he wants to shout but he would never with all these people around.

"I am taking her away from your abusive hands. She is coming with me." Dominic pulls me away and stands in front of me. I see Chris and Leon stand at my side.

"I don't think so; she's about to be married," he spits out.

"Yeah, because you are forcing her. By the way, we know about the contract; you are a lying bastard, making her think she didn't have a choice." I look at Dominic and back to my dad.

"What do you mean?" I ask Dominic.

"Sky, that contract is bogus, you don't need to stay here. You are twenty-one and can do as you please. They knew they could lose you so they made you think you had no choice. They can't sue Lake; it's all lies." I look at my parents and they are glaring at Dominic.

"Is this true?" I ask them.

"We raised you; we have every right to do with you as we please," Mom seethes and I hear a few gasps around us. My parents look around and they try to cover themselves. "That's not what I meant," Mom says weakly.

"You abused your daughters to marry them off to who? The highest bidder? We are going and if you ever go near them again, I swear I will press charges." Dominic looks at them with disgust. We try to walk away again but I feel my hair being pulled. I accidently let go of Dominic's hand to stop my hair from being ripped out and I land on the ground on my hands and knees.

"I should have aborted you when I had the chance!" Mom screams at me and my eyes fill with tears and then my face is being slapped.

"Claudia!" Dad shouts at her but she ignores him.

"You are a waste of space, you *and* your sister!" I'm slapped again but then Dominic pulls her away from me and when I stand, she is acting like a crazy person. "Let go of me!" My dad looks at the people around him then walks out of the room.

Some security guards come in and take my mom away, her kicking and screaming, and she reminds me of Shelly. No wonder why I cowered away from her all those months ago. Dominic comes to my side and looks at my face.

"You need to stop crazy women from hitting you," he jokes and I giggle, shaking my head.

"What can I say, I bring out the worst in people." He smiles at

In the *Spotlight*

me and kisses my lips softly.

"I love you, Sky." I beam up at him.

"I love you too, Dominic." I go on my tip toes and kiss his lips, wrapping my arms around his neck. I look into his eyes. "Thank you for rescuing me."

"Always."

Epilogue

Since Mom confirmed what my parents had done to my sister and me, they were sent to jail for abuse. We were compensated for the money that belonged to us that our parents kept hidden. Our grandparents left us trust funds but we only knew about a small amount of it. It seems our grandparents knew what our parents were like and wanted to make sure we had a comfortable life.

Being a rock star kept my bank account full but I grew up with responsibilities so I opened a savings account. I like knowing I have something to land back on when this career does eventually finish. I became even more famous when news got out that Risen Knights lead singer was abused and contracted to marry. Fans even threatened to punish my parents.

I'm on a set to film our new music video; we are doing a cover of *Mirrors* by Natalia Kills and this time I can't wait to see Dominic's face. I am in a tight, red dress and I walk onto the set that is made to look like a bedroom. When Dominic sees me, his eyes roam my body and I give him a smirk. He is wearing an expensive suit, looking like a CEO.

I walk to him and give his lips a lick before taking a few steps back when the director says places. I walk to the door that enters to the bedroom and wait for the intro to start. I push open the door and start to sing. I walk to the middle of the room and turn my head; Dominic's eyes have gone dark. I reach behind me and pull my

In the Spotlight

zipper down, letting the dress pool around my feet, standing there in just a red lace bra and panties.

He walks to me slowly and holds my hand, turning me around and placing a blindfold around my eyes. I feel his stubble against my cheek as I continue to sing. He grabs my waist and pulls me into him as he starts nuzzling my neck. I raise my arms and feel him tie my wrists before turning me around again and pushing me onto the bed. I can feel him crawl up, hovering above me. I arch myself to feel him, then the director says cut and I groan. Dominic pulls the blindfold down and smiles at me then kisses me.

"We are continuing this later," he promises and stands.

The next scene I say the lines *sex, love, control, vanity*. The love line goes to Leon and Lake and the camera goes to them looking down at one another, showing their love through their eyes; the sex line goes to Chris who pins a girl against the wall, starting to strip her. The control goes to Dominic who has me in chains, circling me with a flogger. The vanity goes to me; I'm sitting in front of a mirror singing to myself as I place my hair in a high ponytail. The video continues to go back and forth between all of us.

─ ★ ─

The music video went to number one and our second album will be released in two weeks. We will be starting our very own tour shortly after; even going to Europe which I can't wait for. Dominic and I are at the stage of our relationship where we can't keep our hands off each other, which I don't mind at all.

Dominic and I are with Lake, Chris and Leon in a club and I have a surprise for him; I can't wait to see his face. We are laughing and having a few drinks when I tell them I am heading to the bathroom. Lake has helped me get this together so I go to the stage, sit on a stool, and grab a guitar that belongs to Dominic. I sit down in front of the mic and the light shines on me and everyone looks up. When I first started singing in front of a crowd, I would always get nervous, but now I enjoy it. I let the music take hold and that, I will never give up.

"Sorry everyone but I wanted to sing, well play a song, to someone who I love with all my heart, who is my always. Dominic this is for you." I start to strum and sing Michelle Branch's *Everywhere*.

I have practiced my ass off and I want to show Dominic that he is everywhere to me; even when I left he was always in my heart. I sing to him, my eyes only on him. His smile brightening my life. I sing and let the song once again bring me to a calm that I always feel. I strum the guitar like I have played for years.

The crowd screams when they realize who I am. Phones and cameras come out, but I don't care. The only thing I'm thinking about is him. I play straight through with no mistakes and after I'm finished, the crowd goes crazy. Luckily Lake got us a security team and they stopped the crowd from getting to us.

I walk to Dominic and he lifts me and spins me around.

"You were amazing." He beams at me.

"I had a brilliant teacher." I smile at him.

"I love you." I will never get tired from hearing those words.

"I love you, too."

"Always."

"And forever." His lips softly touch mine.

Play List

All You Wanted – Michelle Branch

Poison – Alice Cooper

Just a Little Girl – Amy Studt

In my Head – Jason Derulo

Break Even – The Script

Breath – Michelle Branch

Never Going to be the Same Again – Lori Ruso (Teen Witch)

If You Could See Me Now – The Script

Power of Goodbye - Madonna

My Immortal – Evanescence

Who Needs to Dream – Barry Manilow (Copacabana)

Mirrors – Natalia Kills

Acknowledgements

Thank you, thank you, thank you for reading In The Spotlight. The characters have been screaming at me for months to write their story and I'm glad I did.

To my gorgeous little boy Jake, my number one fan. Thank you for putting up with such a busy Mummy, I love you lots and lots like jelly tots. To the moon and back.

Daniel Martin, thank you for letting me talk to you about my ideas for this story even though you joked saying it reminded you of the little mermaid, thank you for still supporting me, you will always mean the world to me.

Elmarie Pieterse, my brain twin, my book whore, you are so patient with me as I go on and on about where I want this to go and thank you for giving me ideas to make this story better, you mean so much to me, thank you.

Hannah Clarke, my family, my mini me, you support me that much you are letting me drag you to my future book signings to help get my stories out there, thank you for believing in me.

Lauren Haley, thank you for letting me bounce off the hot scenes to you as I know you would make sure it is done right.

Bernie Ivison, thank you for supporting me and telling the world I write, you are amazing.

Caron Armstrong, thank you for reading over the story, I am thrilled that I wrote a book you really loved and felt enthusiastic about.

To my betas, you guys rock.

Paula Tarpley Genereau, thank you for reading so fast giving me input on how amazing the book was, helping boost my ego. Thank you for beta reading for me.

Autumn Bronson, you made me want to write faster as you begged for more and I'm glad I never left you disappointed, thank you for beta reading for me.

Amanda Pierre, thank you for spotting the odd details I missed and making my book be better, thank you for beta reading for me and sharing my books nonstop.

Jamie McDowell Reinhard, you saw the small details that I missed, you have a good eye, thank you for beta reading for me.

Naomi Dentith, my first ever reviewer to message me, thank you for sticking by me for the last year, thank you for beta reading for me.

Kev Smith from the band Die No More, thank you for answering my band questions and helping me find the name for my band, you rock.

Nouvelle Author Services, thank you for making sure my book is perfect and putting up with my many grammar mistakes, it has been amazing working with you.

Jen Wildner, you so rock, giving me an extra pair of eyes, seeing things we have missed, thank you for reading and going over everything. You are amazing. You are my guardian angel. Planning and organizing my blitz and parties, you are awesome.

Leigh Stone, thank you for formatting my book, you made my interior look amazing.

Again thank you to all my readers, you guys are amazeballs

Books by J.L. Ostle

The Change Series:

A Simple Change

The Hardest of Changes

Stepbrother Romance series:

Tempted part 1

Craved part 2

Standalones:

My Screwed Up Life

In The Spotlight
(A Rockstar Romance)

About the Author

J.L. Ostle was born in Antrim, Northern Ireland and was raised as an Army brat. She is now living in Carlisle England. J.L Ostle is a full-time mother looking after her cute, active four-year-old boy.

When she hasn't got her head stuck in a book or writing, she's watching movies, hanging with friends. J.L has a little obsession with Supernatural. She enjoys catching up on her TV shows Vampire Diaries, Big Bang Theory, Geordie Shore, and Grimm.

Connect with me

I enjoy messages and posts you send me, so if you have any

questions, or want to talk about any of my books, drop me a line x x

Facebook

www.facebook.com/J.L.OSTLE

Goodreads

www.goodreads.com/author/show/12682033.J_L_Ostle

Amazon

www.amazon.com/author/j.l.ostle

Made in the USA
Charleston, SC
30 July 2016